FIRE AND RAIN

OSWALD RIVERA

FIRE
AND
RAIN

FOUR WALLS EIGHT WINDOWS
NEW YORK

Published by:
Four Walls Eight Windows
PO Box 548
Village Station
New York, N.Y. 10014

First edition.
First printing October 1990.

Library of Congress Cataloging-in-Publication Data:

Rivera, Oswald, 1944–
Fire and rain/by Oswald Rivera.—1st ed.
p. cm.
ISBN: 0-941423-41-7
1. Vietnamese Conflict, 1961–1975—Fiction.   I. Title.
PS3568.18313F57   1990
813'.54—dc20   90-34078
                                                                CIP

ISBN: 0-941423-41-7

Designed by Cindy LaBreacht.
Printed in the U.S.A.

This book is partly a work of fiction. It is based on a true incident that did occur and of which the author had first hand experience: the Da Nang prison riot during the Vietnam conflict. Only the names of the participants have been changed.

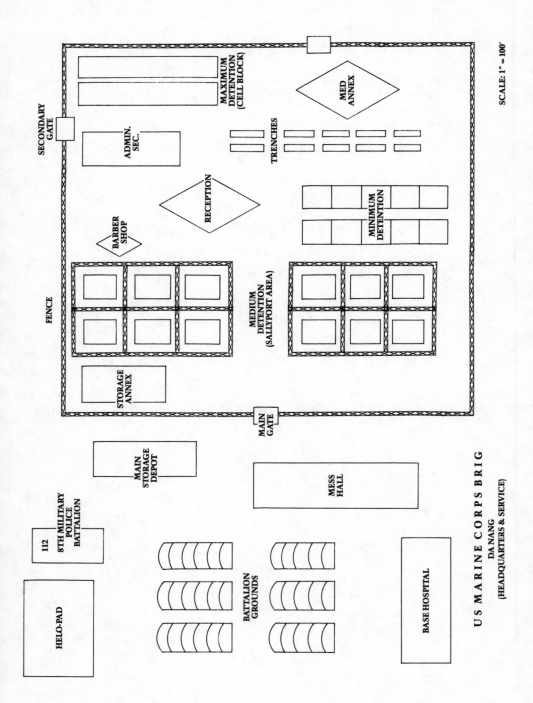

US MARINE CORPS BRIG
DA NANG
(HEADQUARTERS & SERVICE)

SCALE: 1" = 100'

PART ONE - THE JUDGMENT

We are unknown, we knowers, ourselves
to ourselves. This has its own good reason—we have never searched for ourselves so how should it come to pass that
we should ever find ourselves.

—NIETZSCHE

VANDEGRIFT COMBAT BASE
QUANG TRI PROVINCE
JULY 1ST 1969

They came for him that evening. The arresting party included Sergeant Major Lowrey of CID, Captain Seversky, the company commander, and two other men armed with .45 caliber pistols. Big, black Sergeant Collins, the third platoon guide, was at a loss for words when he was informed of the charges against Corporal Dawson. No one had suspected Dawson would be foolhardy enough to do in the gunny. Dutifully, Collins told his radioman, Private Baker, to go get Dawson. Baker gave the group a disparaging look and departed.

When Baker found him, Dawson was about to leave his foxhole and head for the company area where a movie was to be shown that night. Dawson asked Baker what the hell did Collins want now? Baker said he didn't know.

Dawson told the other three men in his foxhole he'd see them later on and reminded them to come back as soon as the movie ended. The new company exec, Lieutenant Wilson, had warned he was going to have an early check of the perimeter, and it wouldn't look good if he came around and found one man guarding a four-man hole. The three Marines said they knew about it and would be back early. Not that it made any difference to them, of that Dawson was certain. Line duty

3

at a firebase was the most boring shit around—apart from mine-sweeping on the road leading up to the Z. At least then you could razz the gunners riding atop the twin 40 half-tracks. In the rear, it was digging holes, filling sandbags and daily inspections by some peach-faced looey just out of OCS who couldn't hold his cock straight enough to pee. Shithouse duty it was called. Real Mickey Mouse. The only break was at night when guarding the perimeter, you could watch the twin 40s open up with tracer rounds that formed long beautiful red lines snaking into the hilltops surrounding the firebase. Like roman candles digging craters into mountains. The next day it would be back to the same old shit, except for the mornings when a squad would have to go out fifteen meters beyond the wire to check on the Claymore mines set up the night before. The gooks had a murderously funny habit of sneaking into the outer perimeter and turning around the mines so that they faced the grunts guarding the holes. That way, in case of attack, when the grunts activated the Claymores, assorted missiles, ball bearings and shrapnel would rain down back on the grunts within the perimeter. But the gooks hadn't moved on the firebase in a while. Six months at least. And a fatalistic complacency had set in among the men. Most hoped the gooks would attack. It would shatter routine.

No, rear duty wasn't good for the squad. Mainly because it made no difference where the hell you were in-country. There was no rear area, Dawson constantly reminded himself. He remembered the time his unit had first landed at Da Nang Airport. They had been mortared the second day and a bunch of kitchen dudes had been blown away. Sometimes he wondered if the bean burners didn't deserve it. They should have known better than to head for the mess hall during incoming. Dumb pogues.

Yeah. Stupid Duty. Though some would call it skatin' duty since it was really better than tramping in the bush, looking for some illusive NVA regiment that was already halfway up the Ho Chi Minh Trail. All in all, not a bad deal. Not skatin' exactly, but not bad.

Dawson scanned the area surrounding the foxhole, and satisfied that all was taken care of in his position, followed Baker back to the platoon CP.

Travelling up the footpath leading to the tent, Dawson asked the radioman again what it was all about. Baker glanced at him and said, "It's serious, Vic. That sergeant major from the fuzz is there and so is Captain Seversky."

Dawson frowned. "What the fuck they want?"

"Whatever it is, it don't look good," Baker said.

"Is it about the gunny?"

"I think so."

"Are they accusing me of something?"

"I don't know, man."

"Anybody else there besides the sergeant major and the cap'n?"

"Yeah, there's two other dudes I never seen before."

Dawson shook his head in resignation. "They probably come to get me."

"Vic, they don't have shit on you," Baker said suddenly. "Ain't no way they can screw you."

"Tell it to the sergeant major. He thinks I killed the gunny."

Dawson could feel the early morning sweat on the back of his neck. "Did he say anything to Collins about bringin' up charges or anything like that?"

Baker hesitated. He wanted to tell Dawson the truth, but it would make things worse. Dawson would find out soon enough anyway. "I don't know."

Dawson knew his friend was lying. Baker kept his gaze straight ahead, not looking at him. The strained silence that followed alerted Dawson. He had the anxiety of a felon about to face the judge, except that most felons knew what the judgement would be.

They entered the tent. Sergeant Major Lowrey was there, a curve of a smile on his face; Captain Seversky seemed somewhat glum, and Sergeant Collins, well, Collins had assumed that official nonpartisan pose that could only be described as grave.

Lowrey wasted no time. "Corporal Dawson, you're under arrest," he chanted.

Although Dawson was half-expecting it, the force of the blow was acute. He tried to remain as calm as possible.

"I must advise you," Lowrey continued, "that you have the right to counsel before you make any statement, and anything you say may

be held against you. As of this moment you are under legal detention. Pack up whatever gear you have and come with us."

"Don't he get to know the charges against him?" Collins called out.

Lowrey glared at Collins, who stared down at his shoes, his face a
blank mask. The sergeant major faced Dawson, placed his hands on
his hips, and cleared his throat. "You're charged with the murder of a
noncommissioned officer—to be exact: Gunnery Sergeant Yeager."

"Where's your 782 gear at?" Seversky asked Dawson.

"Down in my hole," Dawson said.

"Pick up everything except for your rifle and ammo," Seversky
commanded.

"What do I do with my battle gear?" Dawson asked.

"Forget your battle gear, we'll take care of that," Lowrey said.
"Where you're going you won't need it."

"Where am I going?"

"Don't worry about it till you get there," Lowrey said shortly. He
turned to the guard. "Make sure he picks up his trash and gets back
here real quick."

The two men with the .45s nodded, then escorted Dawson out of
the tent.

Collins watched him go. He had a sick feeling in his gut. "Can I ask
you a question, Sergeant Major?"

"Yes, Sergeant?"

"Where they takin' Dawson?"

"To Da Nang," Lowrey said.

"To H&S Casual?"

"Yes."

"Is the trial going to be held in Da Nang?"

"I don't know, that's for the regimental CO to decide."

Collins extracted a pipe from his breast pocket, then began to fill it
with tobacco. "Do you think they'll make the charges stick?"

"Yes, Sergeant, I think they'll make the charges stick." Lowrey's
voice exhibited a slight irritation. "You won't be seeing Corporal
Dawson again, that's for sure." Pointedly he added, "I'd start looking
for another squad leader."

There was nothing more to talk about and an uncomfortable
silence descended on the tent. They stood about quietly, very aware
of each other's presence. Collins lit his pipe, and puffed on it brood-

ingly. Baker went back to his radio unit, which was perched on his cot. He took out an old rag and began to dust the case. Collins walked over to the tent entrance and looked outside. Nothing seemed right. The more he thought about it the more it grated. Vaguely threatening, like the darkness out there staring back at him. He looked at his hands; the light of the Coleman lantern gave them a new texture, a fine brown. He decided to pace back to the center of the tent where the light was brightest.

Fifteen minutes later Dawson returned with the guards. He was carrying all his equipment: full pack stuffed with three days' rations, poncho and poncho liner, rubber air mattress, rain jacket, four canteens of water, three grenades, hunting knife—everything, except for his two bandoliers and rifle—and these were carried by one of the men.

Lowrey spoke to Captain Seversky. "You'll be informed when the trial is, sir. We'll probably need a statement from you—and you too, Sergeant. You might be called in as witnesses for the hearing. These matters take quite a while before they're set, so don't worry about it for now, it won't be no time soon." He turned to Dawson. "You all set, Corporal?"

Dawson nodded.

"Okay, let's go." Lowrey led the men outside.

Baker stopped wiping the radio case. He flung the rag on the ground. "Goddam-motherfuckin' crotch."

Captain Seversky looked at Baker, but didn't say a word. He turned and gazed at the lantern.

"Why they have to put him in H&S Casual—and the investigation isn't even finished yet?" Collins asked him.

Seversky shrugged. "I don't know."

Collins licked his lips, then spat to the side, feeling as helpless as the rest. "It isn't right. They should at least hold him here while the investigation's going on."

"Maybe they need bodies up at H&S Casual," Seversky said.

Baker picked up the rag from the ground, slapped it against his pants. "What's this H&S Casual?" he asked aloud.

"That's where they're takin' Dawson," Collins answered.

"Yeah, but what is it?"

Collins removed the pipe from his mouth, and looked at the pipe well, rubbing the stem with the palm of his hand. "It's grunt slang for the Brig at Da Nang. 'H&S' stands for headquarters and service, and casual . . . well, 'casual' is for the good times people have there."

The sarcastic tinge in the sergeant's voice was not lost on Baker. "Oh, I see," he said quietly.

"Poor gunny," Seversky sighed.

"Poor gunny—shit!" Collins said vehemently. "Compare to where Dawson's goin' the gunny has it made."

Seversky made no answer. He continued staring at the yellow flicker inside the Coleman lantern.

They took Dawson to the main battalion bivouac. He spent the night in one of the tents used by the headquarters people who worked in the Administration Section. The five other men in the tent were very congenial. They were all office pogues and each one assured him the paperwork would be done in no time so that he could leave for Da Nang the next morning. They didn't even put a guard on Dawson. The two men who escorted him decided to return to their own company area. He passed the night playing poker with the Admin people.

At 0630 his guard came back, and the three men left for the operations hut to start processing for the flight to Da Nang. Nothing ever works out right, even with the guarantees from the Admin pogues, and Dawson had to wait an hour before the travel orders were completed. This done, he was driven to the landing strip where they sat around several more hours. The MPs who were to take custody of Dawson had not arrived. At the crowded shack that was the flight center, amid transient personnel, seabags, packs with equipment, Dawson and his escort spent the morning hours playing cards on the floor.

Around 1400 hours the MPs showed up—two tall, ropy individuals wearing jungle utilities, camouflaged cloth caps, and carrying .38 caliber revolvers in shoulder holsters. The old guard detachment turned Dawson and the travel orders over to the new men. The MPs, glum silent types, took him outside to the flight pad. One of the MPs produced a set of handcuffs. He sparingly asked Dawson if the handcuffs would be necessary. Dawson assured him they would not be necessary; the MP put away the handcuffs.

Dawson couldn't interest the new men in a game of cards so he lay down on his pack, right there on the landing strip, and tried to nap while they waited for the shuttle flight. Forty minutes later one of the men patted him on the shoulder. A plane had landed. Dawson got up, donned his flak vest, pack and jungle hat. He joined the long line that led inside the camouflaged C-130 transport.

The flight took about three quarters of an hour. The aircraft was alive with the rattle of pipes and tubing and packed with all types of personnel: MPs, prisoners, R&R people, even Vietnamese servicemen—everybody standing up. There were so many green body bags lying about that there wasn't any room to sit down.

PART TWO - H&S CASUAL

How much youth is barred within these walls in idleness, what great strength had perished here for nought! For it must be said frankly: these are remarkable men. These are perhaps the most gifted, the strongest of all our people. But this mighty strength has perished for nought, perished unnaturally, illegally, irreparably. And who is to blame?

Yes, who is to blame?

—DOSTOEVSKI

U.S. MARINE CORPS BRIG
DA NANG
JULY 3RD

Once they reached Da Nang things began to move with a little more efficiency. The flight center, same as in Quang Tri, was congested, but there were no delays. They waited exactly fifteen minutes before they hitched a ride on a truck headed for the Brig compound.

Dawson had gone seven hours without eating, but this was of little consequence. He had missed breakfast and lunch but he couldn't eat anything even if it had been offered to him. The prospect of the Brig negated other needs he may have had. How often had he heard of the infamous Da Nang Brig? That closed compound of large squad tents and concrete structures housing cell blocks with chain-mesh windows. Some of the old timers rumored that it began in 1965 as a Maximum Detention hole for deserters, then was humanized to its present condition. A structure well-known for secrets it kept behind its fence. Until recently it was one of the last Red-Lined Brigs in the world. Someone had told him it wasn't like that anymore. The old detention center with bread and water rations was gone. The last Red-Lined Brig, where you had to walk a certain red line or be beaten, was on a Navy base in Japan somewhere. Da Nang had progressed. It wasn't even called the Brig; he had read in an old copy of *Stars and*

Stripes that the whole affair was now known as a Corrective Custody
Center. How did it get the reputation of being the toughest brig in
the Marine Corps? Don't you worry your little heart about it, Dawson
told himself, you'll soon find out. But he had survived boot camp.
Nothing could beat that.

The two MPs led him into the open back of the six-by. One of them
signaled to the driver, and the final ride began. Soon the three men
settled in the corners of the two-and-a-half ton vehicle, soaked with
sweat, surrounded by clouds of dust. One of the Ps slapped Dawson
on the knee. "Them canteens full?" he asked, pointing at the three
canteen pouches strapped to Dawson's cartridge belt.

"Yeah," Dawson said.

"Can you spare some?" the MP asked.

"Sure." Dawson removed the canteen and handed it to the MP.

The MP took a long swallow. He offered the water to his partner
who also took a drink. The man gave the canteen back to Dawson.
"Thanks."

Since the MP had drunk the prisoner's water it was incumbent
upon him to reciprocate with some conversation. "Who were you
with up in Quang Tri?"

"Two-sixteen," Dawson said automatically.

"Sixteenth Marines?" The MP whistled slowly. "The Walking
Dead." He shook his head dismally. "Even down here we know about
'em. They hit the shit more than anybody else up north. Don't blame
you for going over the hill, mac."

"I didn't go over the hill."

The MP looked at his companion. "What did you do then?"

"Nothin'."

The MP wiped his dust-flecked chin with the back of his hand.
"Yeah. That's what they all say." He gave his friend a familiar grin.

Dawson shrugged. Fuck you if you don't want to believe it. The
truck went over a bump. His body jerked to the side and his buttocks
bounced on the floor. He reached overhead and took a firm hold on
the wooden railing.

The MPs had gone back to their silence. Apparently they had
reciprocated enough for the water. The bumps eased, and Dawson
sat back to endure the ride. He brought his knees up to his chest

and folded his arms over them, then lowered his head to avoid the dust.

The truck brought them to the MP battalion grounds—a large area adjacent to a small helicopter pad.

"Okay, slick, here we are," the MP announced. Dawson flung his pack over the side and climbed down from the truck. The MP waved to the driver. "Thanks loads, friend." The vehicle roared back on the bumpy road that led to the main landing strip with its wooden barracks, and freedom. Dawson took up his pack, holding it by the pack straps. He was wearing his flak vest, and underneath, his shirt was damp.

The MP was obviously a mind reader. He watched Dawson staring at the omnipresent red ball. "Hot, ain't it?" he asked.

Dawson nodded.

"This ain't nothin'," the MP said, "wait till you been on the road detail or on the sandpile." He grinned indulgently. "This gonna seem like winter compare to them places."

Dawson took off his flak vest and held it under his arm. His shirt was totally soaked.

"They're at it again, Moe," the MP said to his companion. He pointed to the helicopter pad that was about twenty meters from where they stood.

The other MP, the silent one, looked toward the helo pad and grunted.

Dawson turned his head and caught a most unusual scene. On the helo pad a squad of twelve MPs were going through various drill movements. The rubber heels of their boots echoed loudly on the steel plates of the forty-eight foot square. One MP, most likely the squad leader, stood to one side, giving out mixed drill commands. The group did column movements, facing movements; it marched up to the edge of the square and back again to the center. Incredible, thought Dawson. Right here under the scorching sun, doing god-damn drill, as if this place were a parade ground.

"They do this often?" he asked.

"Yeah, just about every day," the MP said. "Our CO got a hair up his ass 'bout a month ago and now he wants us to do drill. Ain't that some shit? *Drill*. In-country, right under the sun."

Pity the poor MPs, their fatigues soaked through with perspiration. They went through their movements sloppily, without spirit. The squad leader mouthed his commands dully, without enthusiasm. He didn't like it any more than they did.

"Your CO's crazy," Dawson said.

"I know," the MP conceded.

They walked across the battalion grounds that were lined on both sides with Quonset huts. These were the MP quarters. It was the first time during his tour Dawson had seen such structures. Outside each half-cylindrical shack was a trench squared with rows of sandbags. Most of the huts had their doors and windows open but there was nobody inside.

They passed the Quonset area and came to a small yard facing a large, drab green shack. Outside the shack, piled up against the walls, were sandbags, packs and willy peter bags. Every item was set up neatly in a separate batch. The MPs led Dawson through an open doorway and into a storage room partitioned by a wooden counter. Behind the counter was a Spanish-looking guy, probably Mexican, sitting on a portable chair, his feet atop an old desk. He was reading a comic book.

"Hey, Rodriguez," one of the MPs called out.

The man put down his comic book, looked up. "Ah, we got new visitors." He stood and walked to the countertop. "What's happenin', Turner," he greeted the men. "This new blood?"

"Yeah. Check his shit in, will ya?"

The MPs removed their pistol shoulder holsters and gave them to the supply man.

Rodriguez surveyed Dawson. "Where you from, slick?"

"Quang Tri, Two-sixteen," Dawson said.

"No, I mean back in the world." Rodriguez said.

"Ohio," Dawson said.

Rodriguez snorted. "Ohio? Damn, you're the first dude from Ohio in this Brig." He grinned at the two MPs. "Shit, I didn't even know there was an Ohio."

"C'mon, Rodriguez," the MP cajoled, "I wanna get this dude inside the compound 'fore chowtime."

"Okay," Rodriguez sighed. He went back to the storage bins and exchanged the pistols for white cartridge belts. From another bin he picked two billy clubs and inserted them into the club loops on the belts. He returned to the countertop and handed the belts to the MPs. "Put your stuff on top of the counter," he instructed Dawson.

Dawson placed his flak vest, pack, cartridge belt and helmet on the countertop.

Rodriguez handed Dawson a small manila envelope. "Put all your valuables in here, money included. We'll give you a receipt for it."

Dawson put his wallet and wristwatch inside the envelope, and gave it back to the supply man. Rodriguez wound the string around the two buttons on the outside of the envelope. He tossed the envelope on his desk. He took out a sheet of paper and pencil, asked Dawson his name, rank and unit. After getting all the information, he placed the form under the pack. He went back to the storage bins and began picking out toilet articles for the new prisoner.

One of the MPs, the silent one, lit a cigarette. His friend tapped him on the shoulder and put out his hand. The silent MP took out the pack, snapping his wrist so that one cigarette came out about half an inch. The other man pulled out the smoke, nodding to his friend.

"Can you spare a smoke?" Dawson asked him.

The silent MP looked at his companion. The other man nodded. "Yeah, I guess he can have one, fuckit." The silent MP gave Dawson a cigarette.

"Thanks," Dawson said.

The silent MP put away the pack and said nothing.

A regular gossip hound, ain't you, Dawson thought.

The other MP handed him a book of matches. He lit the cigarette, inhaling deeply. His first smoke all day and he felt delirium.

The supply man came back to the counter. "Here you are." He gave Dawson a small green bag containing the toilet articles. "Don't lose none of this crap, Ohio, or you'll pay for it outta your own pocket." He began to sort out Dawson's equipment. "Don't worry 'bout your stuff. We'll keep it for you safe and sound until you come back to reclaim it." He looked at the talkative MP. "You can take 'im away, Turner, he's all yours."

Dawson took a final drag on his cigarette, and stripped the ash on the end. He put the half-smoked cigarette in his breast pocket.

Just as they were about to leave, Rodriguez called out, "Hey, slick, what you in for?"

Dawson turned around slowly. "Pre-meditated murder, they say."

"Was it an NCO?" Rodriguez asked.

"Yeah."

Rodriguez rested his forearms on the countertop. He shook his head sorrowfully. "Man, they gonna fuck you up."

The MP coaxed Dawson. "C'mon, we gotta go."

Rodriguez watched them go out the doorway. When he could no longer see them in the yard outside, he went to the desk and picked up the manila envelope. He frowned upon discovering there was only five dollars of military script. In his search through Dawson's wallet he came across two faded pictures of an attractive brunette with a winsome smile. There was also a Geneva Convention card, military ID, social security card and driver's license. No more money. He tossed the wallet on the desk. Dawson's wristwatch did strike his eye. It was one of those Japanese watches with a metal band and large headpiece with luminous dials. Yeah, this was much better. He put the money and wristwatch in his pocket.

The three men walked past the Quonset hut sector and proceeded into the inner compound. This sector was enclosed by a chain-link fence held up with construction stakes that bent at an angle when they reached the height of eight feet. The angular part of the stakes constituted a second layer of fence supporting an additional five strands of double-hooked barbed wire.

A guard came over and opened the gate. Like the fence, the gate was also a chain mesh affair with two sides joined by small locks attached to a knot of chain. The guard unhooked the locks, removed the chain, and they went inside. The guard, like all the personnel in the compound, carried no weapon except for a white garrison belt with a billy club attached to it. The standard uniform for the sentinels was jungle fatigues with cloth utility cap.

Dawson was in an entirely different world, as final as landing on another planet. Once the gate behind him was locked, he cringed internally. There was a unique sound to that rattling of lock and chain. He was no longer his own man. Dawson, although he would not show it, felt dread.

They led him past a row of squad tents that were unlike any he had seen before. Each tent was surrounded by a wire-mesh fence, a scaled-down version of the main compound boundary. It also had a small gate with a lock and chain. Inside the confined areas were various prisoners; they ranged from two to five men, looking out past the wire, each giving Dawson the once-over. One thing Dawson noticed instantly: the men inside the fence kept to themselves in closed groups. To one side would be two or three black prisoners and a few feet away would be an identical number of whites. Somehow this disturbed Dawson.

He passed six of the caged tents, and these were the only ones he could see. In back of them were many more which he could only glimpse briefly as he left the area known as the sallyport.

Dawson heard the familiar noise of drill and cadence. Looking to the right he saw a squad of prisoners going through maneuvers barked out by a burly, barrel-chested guard. Right-face, about -face, left-face, it was all there. Remembrances of an age long passed and called Basic Training. Twenty minutes ago he would have sworn on his mother's grave that he would never get to see any kind of drill in-country. It just wasn't done in Nam, his troop handlers at Infantry Training had told him so. Well, I'll be a monkey's uncle, Dawson thought. Everything changes once you get into Corrective Custody.

The squad of prisoners did pretty good. They marched like superb automatons. Dawson wondered if in a few days he would be among the motley group. He noticed the prisoners bore no special markings to denote their status. There were no identifying numbers or letters stencilled anywhere. They wore fatigues same as the guards except that most had on floppy-brim jungle hats which the MPs were not allowed. The prisoners' clothing was shabbier with some men sporting torn shirts and trousers. The only features that denoted the authority of the guards were the white cartridge belt and billy. He hadn't seen any MPs carrying arms inside the compound.

Then he viewed another squad marching in his direction, clearly not in drill competition. The men carried E-tools and shovels. Leading the group was a guard armed with an M14 rifle. Another guard was at the end of the line, also armed. They stopped at the gate where the lead guard handed the gatekeeper some kind of pass. The gate was opened and the squad marched out, followed by the rear guard who took up his rifle at port arms.

"Where they headed?" Dawson asked.

"Sorry, mac, can't answer no question," the MP said, "and you can't ask 'em either. You're in the sallyport now, you can't talk to no one. Don't speak unless you're spoken to."

Dawson bit his lip. Holy shit, the dragnet bit.

They led him to a fly tent that unlike the other shelters did not have a wire fence around it, although by its very nature it looked compressed and suffocating. The flaps were rolled up and inside the shelter was one man sitting on a portable chair. He was obviously a prisoner, perhaps a trustee, and at the moment he was reading *Playboy*.

In spite of the rolled flaps it was insufferably hot in the tent. The man inside didn't seem to mind it and stood up, grinning broadly. Dawson was put off. Goddamn, they all seem happy in here.

The man put the magazine in his back pocket. "Another one," he bellowed, as if welcoming a guest into his private reserve.

"Yeah, another one," groaned the MP. "Get 'im done quick, we gotta leave."

"Anything you say, *sir*," leered the prisoner. He smiled at Dawson, but with malefic intent. "Take off your hat, dude."

Dawson complied.

"My, my, you got a lotta hair. You musta been in the bush for quite a while." The prisoner picked up a manual hair clipper that lay on top of a number ten can next to the chair. "When did you go UA?"

Dawson was about to respond, but remembered the MP's edict. He stopped just in time and looked at the MP.

"That's alright, you can talk to Murphy here," the MP said. "He's one of our *model* prisoners."

"Thank you, *sir*," sniped the model prisoner.

And lo and behold, the silent MP finally spoke. "Don't get too cute, Murphy," he warned. His voice was heavy as the bass vocal in a barbershop quartet.

The model prisoner smirked. "Awright, awright, anything you say." He turned to Dawson. "You din't go UA, huh? What you in here for?"

Before Dawson could answer, the talkative MP had filled the breech. "Murphy, we got here a genuine NCO killer."

Murphy gave Dawson a pitying glance. "Oh, man, they gonna fuck ya over." The second time Dawson had heard the warning. He felt renewed fear.

"If it's one thing the CO hates," Murphy was saying, "it's an NCO killer." He spat on the floor. "What was your rank?"

"Corporal."

"Oh, wow, so you were an NCO yourself. Hmmm. Mebbe it won't go so bad for you." He shook his head at the afterthought. "Still? An NCO? Man, why couldn't you pick on a private?"

"C'mon, Murphy, get it done," the MP ordered.

"Okay, okay," Murphy said wearily. "Take a seat," he told Dawson.

Dawson automatically ran a hand through his hair.

"Don't worry, it'll grow back," Murphy consoled.

Dawson sat in the chair. Ain't no big shit, he argued, just a haircut—a fuckin' lifer haircut! Goddamn. Murphy spread a dirty green towel over his shoulders. Dawson took a deep breath. Murphy began to clip the brown hair.

Ten minutes later Dawson had acquired the most humiliating symbol of the Brig. When he touched his head it felt like coarse sandpaper. At his feet, spread out in knots, lay what had been his mane.

"Man, you look different," the MP commented.

Dawson massaged his almost bald pate. "Yeah, I can imagine."

Murphy removed the towel from Dawson's shoulders. "That's it, you can take 'im away," he told them.

"Everybody looks different without their hair," Murphy said. "Like you for instance—" he pointed at Dawson's scalp—" your head is shaped like an egg with a sorta blunt end on top. Makes ya look funny."

"That it does," the MP concurred.

"You don't hafta worry 'bout it here," Murphy said authoritatively, "there ain't no women around so there's nobody to impress."

"Let's go," the MP ordered. "So long, Murphy, and if I don't see you again it'll be too soon."

Murphy bared his spiteful grin. "Goodbye, *sir*."

They walked out the rear entrance and continued about twenty meters until they came to the Administrative Section of the compound. This was a rectangular wooden structure about the size of a small barracks wth chain-mesh windows and iron-bar doors. Dawson followed the MP through the doorway and down a long tunnel-like corridor. They passed two heavy doors with iron railings on the top portion. He didn't see any locks or chains but by the look of the construction he knew the doors were locked tight. He turned his head and noticed two men peeking through the iron railings. What's this place? he wondered. Obviously another section. Maybe they kept the recalcitrants in there. I wonder if I'll wind up here.

They reached the end of the passageway and made a right turn. After passing through an open doorway, they came to a large room aligned with two desks on each side and multiple filing cabinets everywhere. There were six people in the room and all seemed tremendously busy, working typewriters, filing papers, filling out forms. On one of the desks a cassette recorder was blaring away with country and western music. Dawson recognized the melody immediately, and the tape, *Johnny Cash at Folsom Prison.* Some of the men gave him cursory glances.

Dawson waited with the silent MP while the other man walked across the room and knocked twice on the doorway that led into another room beyond the office. Stenciled above the doorway was a sign in black lettering: COIC.

A minute later, the MP came back from the CO's office. "We gonna leave you here," he told Dawson. "These people will take care of your shit." He took out the travel orders and gave them to one of the men behind a desk. He turned to Dawson. "See you around, mac, lots o' luck."

"Thanks." Dawson watched them go out. They really ain't such bad dudes—

"Dawson!"

The man behind the desk was calling. "C'mere, Dawson," he yelled.

Dawson hustled over to the desk.

"Stand at attention," the man growled. He was a stocky, sandy-haired youth with metal-rimmed glasses. "From now on when any of the Brig personnel speak to you, you shall stand at attention. You will not speak unless spoken to, and you will address the Brig personnel, no matter what their rank, as *sir.* Is that clear?"

"Yes"—the man glared at Dawson—"sir," he added quickly.

The office man looked at Dawson's papers. "You're here as a general prisoner. That means until your trial or hearing or whatever is set, you'll be confined to the Brig, but in no special designation."

He lifted his eyes menacingly. "That is, unless you decide to make trouble." He went back to inspecting the papers. "You'll be confined to Admin Sec, that's the section reserved for general prisoners such as yourself." He put down the papers and leaned back to his chair, joining his hands on top of his chest. "I know you saw those two big doors in the corridor when you were coming over. Them doors is Admin Sec Detention. In all likelihood you'll stay in one of those detention rooms. You're lucky. Next to Minimum Detention that's about the best place to be in. It's *easy* in Admin Sec, nobody bugs you that much. But if you're a shitbird then we got the right to send you someplace you don't like, and that can mean anywhere, even the cell block." He stared into Dawson's eyes. "You don't wanna go in the cell block. Nobody does." He leaned forward and placed his arms on the desk. "Tonight we'll keep you over at Reception while straightening out the paperwork on you. Tomorrow you'll be moved to your regular section. You'll also get a briefing from Master Sergeant Lidel on how we run this place. You best listen to him if you wanna keep your nose clean." He reshuffled the papers on the desk, placing two of them upside down so they faced Dawson. "Sign these two sheets, one is your detention orders, the other is a receipt for your trash."

He held out a pen. Dawson bent down and signed the two forms. He put the pen on the desk.

"You're still at attention, mister," the Admin man snarled.

Dawson snapped back to position.

"Grear!" the man yelled.

Another office worker came to the desk. He looked at Dawson with casual interest.

"Grear, take this man to Reception. Make sure he gets up there."

"Will do," Grear said. He returned to his own desk and picked up an MP belt and billy club. He came back to Dawson. "Let's go, buddy." Grear was also a six footer of the type that had escorted Dawson all the way from Quang Tri. Goddamn giants.

Dawson turned to leave—"Dawson!"

It was the Admin man with the same bark. "You don't never leave no personnel unless you're dismissed. Y' hear? And when given permission to leave you do a facing movement—get back at attention."

Dawson snapped back to position.

The Admin man looked him up and down as if he were on a parade field. "Alright, left face. Forward harch!"

Once he passed the doorway Grear gave him a column left movement. He then marched down the long corridor and turned at the exit leading to the outside. They came to a large squad tent standing a few feet from the barber shelter. Like the barber shop, the tent had no enclosure around it, although it did have a guard outside, sitting on an empty fuel drum. He saw the two men approaching, and nodded at the MP. Grear acknowledged the guard with a wave of the hand.

Someone yelled, "Attention!" the moment the MP entered the tent. There were five men inside, each standing rigidly in position. Grear commanded them to stand at ease.

"This is Reception," he told Dawson. "You'll be here till we get your permanent quarters. That'll probably be tomorrow. You ain't allowed to go nowhere without asking permission from the guard outside, not even the head."

When the MP left, Dawson again experienced that pang of finality he had at the Brig gate. A loneliness, a terrible loneliness, and moreover, a symptom he could not define. It was the same feeling he had the first time he entered a Marine barracks, uncertain what to expect yet always aware of the fear that hounded him. That first day he had been made to stand at attention for ten hours, and he had almost passed out. So far in the Brig he hadn't been subjected to anything remotely similar to that initiation. It was comforting to know. But this was only the first day. There would be more to come. Dawson had no idea how long he was to stay in the Brig.

He found an empty cot and laid his supply bag on it. Sitting down, he searched for a cigarette before realizing they had confiscated his smokes. Not quite, he still had the butt the MP had given him in the supply room. He looked around the tent. He could see everyone in the hooch asking to share his one smoke. Fuckit. He decided to check the toilet articles he had been issued—Gillette razor box with razor, service-issued soapdish with soap bar, service issued foot powder, toothbrush, toothpaste, bar of service-issued shaving soap— shaving cream was not allowed in the Brig. Usual crap, just like boot training. The Brig is just like Basic. They break you down, take out all those contaminated ideas like disobeying orders and give you a new set of ideas so that you'll obey the next time. In boot camp they rid you of those civilian ideals and make you think military. In the Brig they make you think even more military. Does it work? he wondered.

Most of the men in the tent sat by their cots, each alone in his world. The exception were two black men who huddled in the far corner, talking and joking among themselves. Dawson watched them and, without admitting it, felt envy. Fuckin' brothers always stick together. They probably think they own the joint.

Besides the two black prisoners there were two other inmates. One was a thin youth of dark complexion with full red lips and what seemed remnants of curly brown hair on his close-cropped head. He sat on the ground, kneading some dirt in his hand. Across from him on the other side of the shelter was a short, plump individual who looked like a cook. Unlike the rest of them, who had the red and brown coloring of the Viet sun, this young man was still quite pale. His skin was almost white, like a death mask. He sat with his hands folded over his knees and his head down, staring glumly at his feet.

A good assortment of hairless oddballs, Dawson thought, and I'm one of them.

The curly haired youth looked up at Dawson. "Hey, buddy, you ain't allow to sit on the rack," he said.

Dawson was surprised and gratified to get a response from somebody in Reception. "What?"

"You ain't allow to sit on the rack," Curly repeated.

Dawson slid off the cot and sat on the ground.

Curly eyed him warily. "You got smokes?"

Dawson shook his head. "Nope. They took 'em away from me."

Curly grimaced. "Yeah, same here." He wiped streaks of dirt from the palm of his hand. "Motherfuckers. Don't even leave ya no smokes."

Dawson pushed his knees to his chest and folded his arms over them. "How long you been here?"

Curly reacted. "Where? In Reception? Two days already." He grimaced again. "They still can't figure out where t' put me." He wiped a finger under his nose. "What'cha in here for?"

"They say I killed somebody."

"Good for you," Curly said sociably. "I hope you kill more."

Dawson narrowed his eyes.

Curly pushed up his knees, rested his arms on them. Two seconds later he spread out his legs and put his hands on his lap. One second later he pulled on his earlobe. He crossed and uncrossed his legs, folded his arms on his chest.

Dawson gazed at him suspiciously. "What are *you* in here for?"

Curly smirked. "I beat up my sergeant with an E-tool." He smiled. "Almost kilt that cocksucker, too. He in the hospital now. He won't get out for a long-ass time."

"Who was you with in the bush?"

"One-seven," Curly said.

"I hear you people had beaucoup shit around Dodge City."

Curly scowled. "Yeah, them gooks did us a job up there. We lost half our platoon 'cause of our fuckin' sergeant." He made a fist. "But I got even with that bastard, I did 'im a job. A job!"

Dawson had a premonition. This dude is a kook.

Curly loosened his fist, looked at his hand intensely. "Who was you with in-country?"

"Two-sixteen."

Curly snorted. "The Walkin' Dead? Shit, you're lucky you in the Brig. Least here you're alive."

"It ain't been that bad lately. We been skatin' for a month now."

"Maybe so, but last I heard you people was wiped out over by the Laos border."

"Almost wiped out but not quite. We still got some people left."

Curly wiped a finger under his nose. "Yeah?" He kneaded his thighs with his bony hands, then folded his arms back on his chest. After about five seconds he got tired of this and put his hands on his lap. He sniffed once or twice.

Either the man is nervous or he has some sort of condition, Dawson calculated. "How long you been in the bush?"

Curly again wiped the dirt from the palm of his hand. "This my second tour. Ten monts on this one."

"You must like the coins. I couldn't see doing this shit a second time."

"I don't mind it, long as they don't fuck with me." Curly grimaced. "Back in the world they fuck with ya too much. I can't stand that garrison duty. Too much crap, all that spit and polish shit." He shook his head negatively. "Naw, they fuck with ya too much. Over here there ain't none of that inspection jive."

"You a four-year man?" Dawson asked.

Curly nodded. "Yeah, home, I'm a four-year man." He kneaded his thighs. "Fuckin' worse mistake I ever made."

Dawson agreed with that—he had made the same mistake. "How long you think you'll be here?"

"I don't know." Curly looked around. "I hear mebbe tomorrow we move out." He scratched his chin. "No big thing. If we don't sky tomorrow we'll sky the next day."

Dawson looked up at the tent roof. "I don't dig this place, it reminds me of boot camp."

"Boot camp?" Curly scoffed. "Fuck, you think that was petty? You ain't seen nothing yet, slick. Wait till ya gotta go to the head, or chow. In this joint you don't go nowhere unless your guard okays it. You can't even take a crap unless he say so." He sneered. "You think them C-rats in the bush was bad? Wait till you see the type of chow we got here. I wouldn't feed that shit to my dog."

While Curly was talking, the pale plump youth got up and walked out the tent entrance. Dawson heard him rattle off the formula. "Sir, requests permission to make a head call." Silence. Dawson and Curly strained to hear the exchange. "Go 'head," the guard snarled.

"I think that kid's sick," Curly diagnosed. "This the third time today he gone to the head. I think he got a case of the shits."

"Who is he?"

"I don't know. Think he's an air winger. He sure as hell don't look like a grunt."

Dawson turned his face in the direction of the two black prisoners in the corner. "They grunts?"

"Guess so. Never met a brother in-country who wasn't a grunt."

"What they in for?"

"Don't know, didn't ask 'em." Curly closed his eyes and dropped his head.

Dawson assumed this was the end of Curly's conversation for the afternoon. He rested his head on his forearms.

A short time later the air winger came back. He looked much relieved but no less pale. Curly lifted his head, looked at him scornfully. He motioned to Dawson and smiled. His teeth were stained yellow. Dawson, not knowing what was expected of him, shrugged.

The pale young man sat by his cot and looked at the ground stolidly.

The two black prisoners burst out laughing. Dawson found their mirth irritating. Now what the fuck could be so funny about this place? The brothers enacted the black power handshake, giggling among themselves. And oddly enough, Curly looked in their direction and smiled. Dawson watched him with interest. What the fuck is with him?

Two guards entered the tent. "Atten-HUT!" one of them bawled.

"It's chowtime, ladies," the guard said. He placed his thumbs inside his MP belt. "There's a procedure to chow here. You ain't on the outside no more." He looked about contemptuously. "We gonna march to chow, ladies. Once you get in the chow hall it's just like your basic training, if you can remember it. You march up the chow line, at attention, and you put out your plate if you wanna be served. If ya don't, nobody gonna force you to eat." He spat to the side. "It's shit anyway."

Curly smirked and nodded his head.

The guard saw him. "You got something to say, mister?

Curly looked at him innocently. "Sir?"

The guard stared him in the eyeballs. "You think you're cute, prisoner?"

"No, sir." Curly had to look up at the tall lean guard with the dark blond hair and hard features. When his eyes met the guard's glare he dropped them immediately.

"We don't like cute prisoners around here." The guard's voice was heated. "You stand at attention when a guard speaks to ya, and that means your face, too. If you're gonna smile about somepin' I'll make you smile. Is that understood?"

"Why sure, sir."

The guard looked at his partner standing quietly at the tent entrance. He took a step away from Curly, and just as quick, landed a punch in Curly's lower belly.

Dawson started. The pale air winger jumped up nervously. The two black prisoners looked at each other.

Curly's cheeks puffed up and his breath caught. He doubled over with his hands pressing his stomach. The guard eyed him impassively. "Is that understood, prisoner?"

"Yes, sir," Curly gasped. He managed to straighten up, massaging his lower belly.

"You best get back at attention, prisoner."

Curly made himself straight as a nail.

The guard tossed Curly one last glance, then paced up and down the length of the tent. "As I was saying, the chow here is shit. Ain't no use lying to you fuckers. But you gonna eat it like you was dining at the Ritz. You gonna go to the table and you ain't gonna sit down till you're told to. You ain't gonna eat till you're told to. Bear this in mind, you ain't allow to rest your elbows on the table. Even if you're an animal you gonna eat with your hands but you ain't gonna touch the table. You keep your paws on your lap when you ain't using 'em. Warrant Officer Randazzo is very particular about table manners. Fact is, like that broad, Emily Post, he insist on it." He stood next to his partner at the front of the tent. "You don't hafta worry 'bout seconds 'cause nobody goes up for seconds. The last time that happen our cook had a heart attack." The other guard guffawed. He paused and looked at him. "Well, it's the truth, ain't it?" The other guard nodded his head, suppressing his laughter.

"You obey the rules, ladies," the guard continued. "If you decide you don't wanna—" he looked at Curly—"well, we got ways of changing your mind." He glanced at his watch. "Okay, everybody form outside in one file."

They ran outside and formed into a line facing the tent. The tall blond guard looked up and down the squad. "Awright, prisoners, right face! Forward harch!"

He marched them to the main gate where he called a halt. He didn't show the gatekeeper any pass, he just stated, "Chow call for these turds." The guard nodded and opened the gate. The prisoners marched through the MP area to stop before the large wooden mess hall that looked like another storage depot. From there the prisoners were guided to the back of the mess hall, keeping a long line by the rear wall where the kitchen was located. A man leaned against the screen door that was the entrance. He held in his palm a tiny gauge which ticked off the number of men coming inside. Perhaps he reflected the quality of the mess hall, perhaps not, but his white messman's uniform was soiled with grease and mud, and reams of mucus streamed from his nose.

The prisoners had to walk through the kitchen in order to get to their tables; all along the way noxious odors of condiments mixed with male sweat invaded their nostrils. Dawson noticed scabs and open sores on some of the messmen handling the food. The steam, the heat, all collided to bring about a quaking nausea in the stomach.

The mess hall itself was divided into two sections, one for the Brig personnel and one for the prisoners. The prisoners' section was separated from the MP's messroom by a wooden partition that was eight feet high but did not touch the low-hung ceiling. There was a doorway in the partition and every so often the MP would come from the other side to get a cup of coffee from the metal keg inside the prisoners' section.

Dawson took up a paper plate, paper cup and plastic spoon from the stack table, then followed the chow line, holding out his plate while the messman ladled out measly portions of chili con carne, rice and two meat patties, no vegetables.

At the table they stood at attention holding their steaming plates until the guard gave the "ready seat" order. Once they sat down, they were allowed to stand up again and get their coffee or warm Kool-Aid from the refreshment stand.

Each man ate quietly and by the book—no elbows on the table. No one went back for seconds. The rice was caked and dried, the chili con carne had the savor of cooked sand, and the coffee was bitter. Each man in his heart agreed, any fucker who goes up for seconds gotta be outta his mind.

One of the black men at the table stood up, and was about to move.

"Prisoner, atten-HUT!" the blond guard ordered.

The black man went immobile, holding the paper cup.

The guard shouted in his ear, "Where the fuck you think you're going?"

"To get some Kool-Aid," the prisoner mumbled.

"To get some Kool-Aid, *sir*, " the guard corrected.

The black man looked straight ahead and said nothing.

"Well?" the guard demanded.

"Sir, request permission to go get some Kool-Aid." The prisoner almost choked on the words.

"Permission denied—sit down."

The prisoner clenched his jaws. His biceps trembled from his violent hold on the paper cup. The guard glared at him. The prisoner sat down.

The other black inmate showed outright antagonism in his face.

"Something wrong, turd?" the guard asked roughly.

The inmate stared at his plate.

"I asked you a question."

Both prisoners kept their faces down. One of them lifted a coffee cup to his mouth. The guard knocked it out of his hand, splashing the brown liquid on the table. The prisoner jumped up—a no-no. Another guard came from behind and pulled him back, tripping him over the wooden bench. The prisoner fell to the floor, but he was up in a fraction of a second, his face indignant.

"Get back on the bench," the blond guard ordered.

"Fuck you, motherfucker," the black man yelled.

The other guard again approached from behind and struck him in the back of the neck with his billy club. The impact made a sound like the crack of a high-powered rifle. The black man fell forward, dazed. His friend lunged at the guard who had swung the billy.

In less than ten seconds six guards had jumped the other man, wrestled him to the ground, and reduced him with swinging billies. Some prisoners from the other tables got up and began to boo and shout. Every guard in the mess hall took out his billy club and banged it on a table, ordering the men to sit down.

Dawson and Curly stood up, shouting and hooting with the rest. A guard pushed them back on the bench.

Out of nowhere appeared three additional guards standing in the entrance way. They were different, they carried rifles. The noise abated; the guards moved forward, holding their rifles at port arms, and the prisoners retreated to the safety of the benches, backing away like dogs fearful of a master's reprimand.

At Dawson's table the six guards struggled with the two black men. One prisoner had a fresh gash on his forehead, blood dribbled down his face. Reinforcements came in. Three more MPs joined the fray. Dawson and Curly stood up again. "Sit down," one of the guards yelled. "This don't concern you."

The blunt end of a billy struck Dawson in the small of his back, sending a sharp ache down to his feet. "Sit down, prisoner!" a guard roared in his ear. Dawson dropped into his seat. He looked across the table and saw Curly go through the same ritual, with one slight difference—Curly was pushed into his seat.

The pale air winger sat at the end of the table, his head down, aware of the plate and nothing else. His lips trembled.

The guards dragged the two blacks, kicking and swearing, out of the mess hall. A renewed chorus of boos and hisses followed the trail of blood and teeth left behind by the two rebels.

A new man appeared at the rear entrance. Behind him were three additional guards, also armed with rifles. He was a tall, husky type with close-cropped graying hair and a leathery face. On the collar of his loose jungle fatigues were the chevrons of a master sergeant. He carried no arms or billy club, and he spoke with the authority of the six loaded M14s stationed around the mess hall.

"Shaddap!" he hollered. "Quiet!"

The noise died down.

The master sergeant surveyed the messroom. "You prisoners calm down and eat," he demanded, casting his glance from side to side. "Let's have no more of this cheap shit. The next time we have any more crap in the mess hall I'll make sure you all get the hole for ten days." He checked his watch. "You just lost your chowtime. Guards, take 'em back to the hooches."

The guards at each table shouted their commands to get up and march out. This was done in orderly procedure, by sections, every table waiting for the order to rise, face, and leave.

The remainder of the night was spent in the quiet of Reception. Fortunately there was a topic of interest to keep up a conversation; each man wondered what fate befell the two black prisoners who no longer shared the tent.

"Them brothers had balls," Curly commended. "They prob'ly in solitary now." He spat on the ground. "We'll never get to see 'em again, that's for sure."

"Yeah, they had balls," Dawson admitted grudgingly, "but it got 'em fucked up. Who knows where the fuck they at." He added thoughtfully, "They're probably gettin' the hell beat outta 'em."

Curly lowered his head in the direction of the Coleman lantern. His face was cast in a sleepy white shade. "I don't doubt it." He rubbed the spot on his stomach where the guard punched him. "Them Ps don't cut no slack for nobody. But I swear, one day they gonna push me too far and I'm gonna fuck up their dope. Just let 'em keep fuckin' with me."

"That's crazy."

"Why?"

"You can't fight the power, man, and they got the power."

Curly was adamant. "That's true, but if they fuck with me too much they gonna be sorry. Could never stand that petty shit. That's why I did in my sergeant. Just let 'em keep fuckin' with me, I'm gonna do 'em a job. They gonna take me outta here dead."

Dawson felt an icy chill creep over his body. "Don't pay 'em no mind, man. If you start thinking too much about them dudes it's gonna get on your nerves." He made his voice firm. "I'm just going to take it as it comes. Just keeping my cool, not letting them fuckers get me all shook up." You liar, Dawson, he told himself, you're so shook up already you can't even see straight.

"They better not fuck with me." Curly's voice was flat and distant as though he were speaking through a void.

"Aaah, don't worry about it." Useless. Dawson couldn't convince himself either.

Curly looked at the pale air winger sitting alone by his cot. "Hey, what you in for?" Curly called.

The air winger lifted his head. "Huh?"

"I said: What you in for?"

Paleface had the feeble air of a suspect in the back of a police station. "UA," he mumbled.

"UA? Where you go?"

"Saigon," Paleface mumbled.

"How was it?"

"Fine," Paleface said. End of exchange. He bowed his head and went back to his meditative position, sitting with his knees up and his arms wrapped around them.

"That dude gives me the creeps," Curly confided to Dawson. "There's somepin' about 'im." Curly scratched his neck. "He makes too many head calls."

They went on like this for hours, touching on every conceivable topic concerning the Brig. In the course of the exchange Dawson found out that Curly was a Puerto Rican. Initially, Dawson had suspected Curly was Mexican. They're both just about the same, he decided.

"Yeah," Curly said proudly, "I'm spic, and glad of it. Name is Hernandez. They call me Chi-Chi. Lived in Spanish Harlem all my life before I got into this cocksuckin' crotch."

"Spanish Harlem?" Dawson asked. "There's a dude in my platoon comes from Spanish Harlem. His name is Carlos. I think he come from a hundred and something street somewhere."

"Prob'ly a Hunnert-tenth Street. That's the heart of the barrio, man. That's where it's happenin'."

"Maybe you know the dude," Dawson said. "He's a short guy with a mustache."

Chi-Chi Hernandez rubbed his chin. "Carlos? Mmm. What's his last name?"

"Perez."

"Wow, there's a million Perez's in New York. Maybe I ran across him sometime, though I can't place the name. Where you from?"

"Ohio."

"Ohio? You a farmer or somepin'?"

"No, I ain't no farmer."

"Shit, Ohio must be on the other side of the world somewhere."

Dawson grinned condescendingly. "It's quite a ways from New York."

Chi-Chi was silent for a moment or two. Being city-born and bred he couldn't conceive of anything but New York City. Ohio, the Midwest, the Heartland, these were foreign things that had come into existence only when he joined the Marines and found there were other people out there.

"Really," Chi-Chi said thoughtfully, "it makes no difference where you come from when you're in the crotch. Whether it's near or far, it's still the same old shit, you're still in the crotch—and that means you're fucked up."

Yes, fucked up. Chi-Chi now saw life cut no slack. And he knew very well this process of self-discovery began in the Brig: He did owe them the gratitude or ingratitude for that. Life cut no slack. Certainly the crotch cut no slack. Yeah, he thought, whether you're near or far, it's the same, especially in this organization.

Chi-Chi turned in his cot, forgetting the presence of Dawson, of the tent, of the out *there* that signified their world. He thought of how in boot camp, in so-called "training" every night it'd been the same torment. They would stand next to their bunks, which they affectionately called "racks," and that lousy sonofabitch DI would yell, "Platoon One Sixty-five, prepare t' mount." Since the fools didn't know any better they also would yell, "Platoon One Sixty-five prepare t' mount." The drill instructor would say, "Mount!" And they'd jump into their racks.

But the DI was never satisfied. So he would turn the screws. He'd say, "Ladies, you got two seconds to get outta them fuckin' racks— and one second is gone already." They would jump down from their racks and stand at attention on the cold floor, and the drill instructor would say, "Prepare t' mount." They would repeat the command. The motherfucker would yell: "Mount!" And they would jump in the bunks again.

But he still wasn't satisfied, just like the Ps, so he would repeat, "Ladies, you got one second to get outta them racks, and that second is *gone*." Back to jumping down again. He'd make them do knee bends and pushups until the platoon couldn't breathe. Then, when they were sweating like horses he'd smile and say, "Platoon One Sixty-five prepare t' mount." Again they would jump in their racks like greased lightning and stay in them at attention, frozen like mummies. They would hope against hope the bastard wouldn't harass them the whole night. They would pray—and that was striking since they were a bunch of non-believers anyway. The DI would turn off the lights and holler: "At ease!" They would sleep.

Chi-Chi wouldn't sleep. He never slept. Soon as the DI left, Chi-Chi would slide under his blanket and grab hold of his cock. He and his cock would play silly games. He would pull it and choke it and put a strangle-hold on it. He and his cock would have a high time.

Then it was morning, and he'd have to get up, run with the rest of them. Run to the head. Shit, shower and shave in ten minutes. The DI would come back, and he'd start all over, especially with Chi-Chi because Chi-Chi was rotten, mean, no good. At least he thought of himself that way. The DI would make him do pushups, side-straddle hops, rolls. Chi-Chi would be exercised until he couldn't move. Then they would beat him.

Finally, they had to send him to Motivation Platoon, and from Motivation to Correctional Custody Platoon, and from Correctional Custody back to Motivation. He was unique. The DI would say to him: "Hernandez, you puke, you're the most shitless, worthless worm of a recruit I've ever met. You're a pig, a turd. You don't know shit. You don't know yore left from yore right, or which way is up and which way is down. You can't march for shit. You are the worse Marine recruit I have ever seen. I'm gonna kick yore ass till you become a Marine. Hernandez, you sweet pea, get on the deck and gimme fifty pushups, and when yore done gimme fifty more for the Marine Corps." Like a fool, he would do it.

The DI wasn't finished yet, he'd yell, "What you got to say, puke?" Chi-Chi replied: "I want my mamma." The DI gave him a strange look, saying, "Yore mamma! Boy, she can't help you now. You better call for yore poppa, too—" Back he would be on the floor, doing more pushups, more bends and thrusts.

Pretty soon they got to the rifle range. There he was beaten again— he had pointed his rifle at the marksman instructor. But he qualified. Chi-Chi got a sharpshooter's badge. He was proud. Then came the big day. Graduation. They all stood at attention in front of the stands, listening to the Marine Corps hymn, and he let out a big fart. After graduation the platoon went to the snack bar. They ate hot dogs, burgers, pizzas and milk shakes—all that good junk they hadn't eaten during boot camp. There he saw his drill instructor. The old bastard was in the snack bar, just like the rest of them. Chi-Chi was so screwed up in his mind after boot training he couldn't even think for himself anymore. He stepped up to the DI and said, "Sir, Private Hernandez requests permission to go to the head." The DI glared at him and then laughed. "Don't call me 'sir'," he snarled. "I ain't yore daddy, fool. You a Marine now, motherfucker. You suppose to think for yourself. I ain't your drill instructor no more. Boot camp is over for you. Now you goin' to the Great Nam to get yore ass blown away. Get away from me, puke. Lemme drink my ice cream soda in peace."

He was a Marine. The bastard himself had said it. If he was a Marine, he was going to fuck like a Marine. That same night he sneaked into the women Marine barracks. Someone had told him the women in there were all in heat, all wanting some big cock; and he did find one near the swimming pool area. She was dying for sex. She hadn't had a man in two months. She was a graduate just like him.

Chi-Chi frowned at the recollection, for the lady was *ugly*. He was lucky it was nighttime. If he had seen her during the day he would have turned to stone. No matter. That night he forgot about five-finger Mary.

Afterward, he came back, sneaking into the squad bay after taps. The next day he was off for Infantry Training Regiment to start the whole gruesome process all over again. But then ITR was never like boot camp. It wasn't as strict. There they just taught you how to kill, and there was nothing to that. Then it turned bitter. Just when he thought he had it made, just when he figured he was through with the boot camp ritual, they threw him in the Brig. What a shaft, H&S Casual. And he was there because he believed all they told him in training. Something to confound the skeptics. He believed all the lectures about teamwork and looking out for the other guy. When he was in combat that dumb platoon sergeant of his didn't know his ass from his elbow. The idiot thought he was John Wayne. The last time they went out on a night ambush not fifty meters from their perimeter they lost three men, all because of the sergeant's stupidity. The nincompoop had forgotten to check with another squad that was going on a later ambush. The natural thing occurred. Morning came and Chi-Chi's platoon headed back to the line, and they, the ambushers, were ambushed by their own men. Grunts killing grunts. They lost the two best men in Chi-Chi's fireteam.

He couldn't take any more after that. He went after the platoon sergeant with the first thing he could find. He had no rounds left in his rifle, and it's difficult to bash somebody's head with an M16, the weapon is all plastic, so he grabbed an E-tool, a sort of modified shovel and let his sergeant have it right in the cranium. He knew it was either them, the team, or that one incompetent who would destroy them all.

For trying to be a good Marine he ended up incarcerated.

Chi-Chi could laugh at it now to a certain extent. There was nothing else he could do. He knew they were trying to break him. They were trying to break all of them, every single manjack in the Brig, and so he laughed at them.

Taps came at 2100 hours. "Lights out," boomed the guard outside the tent. Chi-Chi snuffed out the flame in the lantern. Dawson did not immediately lie down. He sat on his cot, watching the movements of Paleface the air winger. In the dark, the plump youth rose from the ground and lay on the rack, quietly. Except for the interlude when Chi-Chi had asked about the charges against him, Paleface hadn't volunteered one word all night. Quiet bastard, Dawson thought. He was beginning to agree with Chi-Chi. Dude is weird, making all those head calls and all.

Dawson took off his boots and lay on his cot, contemplating the non-light above him. Already he could hear the purring of Chi-Chi's snore. He smiled. Another kook.

He began to hear sobs, like compulsive moans. Dawson lifted his head and tried to pierce the darkness that separated him from the other man. Paleface was weeping, unashamed, with his face sunk in his cot.

Dawson lay back his head, feeling depressed. Oh, man, I gotta get out of this place. He closed his eyes and looked for the solace of sleep.

He dozed, and the night closed in on him.

At 0430 the guard shook him from his slumber. "Git up, prisoner. Reveille."

Dawson rubbed his eyes, rolled off his cot. It was as dark as when he had crashed. The guard put a match inside the Coleman lantern. Moody rays blanched the shelter's jagged forms. Chi-Chi sat up and grumbled. Paleface got up quietly, expecting the worst of a new day, and his possible end.

"You got ten minutes to wash up," the guard told them. "At 0445 we head for chow. If you miss that formation you don't eat. The head is outside, to your right. There's a water bo next to it, that's where you wash up. So let's all go outside and stand at attention like good little cunts." He pointed to the exit. "Now!"

The men formed outside in one row. They were shown to the water tank that was about ten yards from the tent, hidden by the bleak light, a rotund can on wheels with the appearance of a bloated bull.

The guard checked his luminous wristwatch. "You got five minutes to wash up, prisoners." He motioned to the water buffalo. "Go at it. Quickly!"

The prisoners trotted to the tank. Chi-Chi opened the spout at the front end and they washed their faces. It was the coldest water Dawson had ever experienced. He cupped his hands under the big rusty faucet and drank eagerly. The taste was the same as anywhere else but goddamn it was cold. Chi-Chi had his mouth wrapped around the faucet when the guard called them back.

0445. The guard took them to chow. Powdered eggs and one slice of bread, a banana for cereal, and warm Kool-Aid.

0510. Back to the hooch where they did nothing until 0630 when they were summoned outside.

The morning light had come in all its glory, bringing with it a harbinger of things to come—Master Sergeant Lidel, the Brig's second-in-command, who gave the new arrivals a briefing as to what it was all about.

Dawson recognized the NCO as the same one who had quelled the disturbance in the mess hall. Up close he appeared even more formidable. He was tanned with a deep coloring that could not hide the creases on the worn skin. Lines massed at the corners of his eyes. The Master Sergeant wore a cloth utility cap with the brim pulled very low, almost covering his brows. When he looked straight at a prisoner all the latter could see were two beady spots with a tinge of green. Enough to make any man shiver.

He's probably in his middle forties, Dawson figured—though his body didn't show it except for a hint of a pot belly below the massive chest. But this was almost lost in the huskiness. Dawson decided he had good reason to be wary of this hulk.

"I am Master Sergeant Lidel," the NCO announced. "You are all prisoners in this correction center. We run things here like on a ship, real tight. We do not allow for any bullshit. We got rules which everybody obeys. They are for your benefit. All of you are here because somewhere along the line you did not obey one of the rules. We strive to change your thinking and give you back the discipline you lost. If you prove to be a good inmate, if you obey the rules and do what you are told, then we got no problems. But if you decide you gonna be a badass and disobey the rules, then we got problems. For those of you who want to create waves we got special accommodations, and you can hang it up."

As he talked he went down the line, giving each man a glimpse of

the green pebbles leaping from under the hat brim. "There are three
sections to the Brig. Depending on your conduct and the nature of
your offense, you will get assigned to one of these sections. For the
model prisoners we got what is known as Minimum Detention. If
you keep your nose clean and do not get in any trouble you *may*
become a model prisoner." He put his massive hands on his hips and
his chin jutted out. "You got more freedom in Minimum Detention.
We do not keep you in the sallyport along with the other fuckups.
Most times a prisoner in Minimum becomes a trustee. Then you
really got it made." The green orbs bore into each man. "If you really
wanna skate this Brig I suggest you become a model prisoner and
land your worthless ass in Minimum."

Dawson kept saying to himself over and over, Minimum, Minimum.

"The next section we got is Medium. This is for the majority of the
prisoners." His voice was severe. "People, Medium *is* the Brig. Almost
all of you will wind up in Medium. Until you prove you want to
change, you will stay in Medium."

Dawson had a vicious itch on his left cheek. If he didn't scratch it
soon he was sure his eyes would water. He looked straight ahead, not
moving a limb—except for his fists which he rolled into balls with
the nails pressing in his palms.

"The last section we got is for the shitbirds, the cell block." Lidel
gave his voice a reserved earnestness. "I would advise you prisoners
not to get into the cell block. That's Maximum Detention." He
showed his teeth. "Believe me, people, you will suffer."

Dawson wrinkled his nose. The itch was unbearable.

The formal part of the briefing over. Lidel asked if there were any
questions.

There were none.

"The guard will now take you to the doc for a physical check. After
that you will be assigned to a hooch in Medium Detention. Those of
you who are waiting some paperwork will stay over in Admin Sec."

A part of Dawson's mind breathed out, that's me—Admin Sec.

"Guard, take over."

The guard gave the men a right face and marched them to the
Corpsman Tent. The physical check that followed was summary. All
the corpsman did was ask the men to bare their genitals, and then he

looked for scars or lesions. Afterward he instructed them to turn round, bend down, place their hands on their buttocks and spread their cheeks. For some reason or other, which Dawson could never discern, they always took a look-see at the rear passage. Chi-Chi stifled a giggle.

After the check-up they were marched to Admin Sec. Dawson was told by an Admin pogue that they didn't have any room for him in the Admin Sec detention hall so he was being temporarily confined to Medium Detention. Dawson asked the pogue how long it would be before he was brought up for trial. The pogue told him not to worry about it, he would be in detention as long as necessary, but issuing a rough guess, he said it usually took over six weeks for the paperwork to be done.

Dawson and Chi-Chi were picked up by the blond guard who had instigated the uproar at the mess hall the day before. They were taken to the sallyport area. The pale air winger, lucky bastard, was retained at Admin Sec.

The new prisoners marched to a squad tent with the wire fence around it. "Welcome to H&S Casual," the blond guard said. He opened the lock and pushed the gate aside. They found the inside of the tent a stifling oven. Dawson and Chi-Chi began to roll up the flaps. The guard stuck his head inside the shelter. "Nobody gave you permission to roll up that canvas, prisoners."

They jumped to attention. "Sir," Chi-Chi called out, "request permission to roll up flaps. . . sir."

The guard looked around. "Shouldn't let you do it, but you'll prob'ly suffocate in here. Okay, roll 'em up." He sat on one of the cots and removed a bent cigarette from inside his shirt pocket. After straightening it he let it dangle from his lips while he searched for a match. "As you noticed, the other prisoners ain't here right now. They's out working on the road—that hard, hard road." He lit the cigarette and inhaled languidly. "You people new here so's you skate for today." He smiled, showing two crooked front teeth. "But tomorrow you'll be workin' on the road." He contemplated his cigarette. "Believe me, workin' on the road is hard, 'cause you see, I'm gonna be there tomorrow and I'm gonna make it doubly hard on ya."

Dawson and Chi-Chi stood by uneasily.

"I don't like prisoners," the blond guard continued. "Mebbe it's because I was a jailbird myself back in the world. I know all the tricks you fuckers pull. I pulled them once." He took a leisurely puff. "Don't try to con me, ladies."

Dawson glanced at Chi-Chi and shrugged, giving out that physical statement that said, What the fuck is this asshole talking about?

Chi-Chi smirked.

"You still at attention, ladies." The guard stood up and paced over to Chi-Chi. He jabbed Chi-Chi's chest with his finger. "You're the funny boy, ain'tcha? The one who got funny with me yestidday. I don't like funny boys, you know that?"

Chi-Chi was slowly turning white.

"Answer me," the guard demanded. "D'ya know that?"

Chi-Chi nodded his head up and down like a trained seal. His eyes were large and gloomy. The guard smiled in his face. "Maybe you need another lesson—discipline, like the Top says. Huh?"

Dawson looked straight ahead, fear creeping into his mind.

"Maybe I should teach ya some manners." The guard grasped the handle of the billy hanging from his MP belt.

Another guard stuck his head inside the tent. "Hey, Miller, the Top wants ya."

"What?"

"The Top wants ya, man."

"Okay, I'll be right there." Miller was still staring at Chi-Chi.

"He wants ya right now. Dee-dee."

"Okay, I'm comin'." Miller headed for the tent exit, before he stepped outside, he turned and said, "At ease."

The men relaxed.

Dawson gave a sigh of relief. "Goddamn, what's his problem?"

"I don't know, man," Chi-Chi said bitterly. "That dude's buggin' me. Motherfucker. Just 'cuz he got the billy he thinks he's God." He pursed his lips. "Just let 'im keep fuckin' with me, just let 'im.

"Ahhh, forget it. It don't mean nothin'."

The offensive smell of the guard was alive in Chi-Chi's nostrils. "That cocksucker. I'd like to see 'im without the billy."

The other men returned from the working party late that afternoon. There were five of them, three blacks and two whites. The first ones to enter, the black prisoners, gave Dawson cursory glances and headed for their cots, where they took off their shirts and wiped themselves with them, showing the sweat gleaming on their skin. The two men who followed, the whites, were no more congenial. However, one of them, a dark-haired youth with a crooked nose that seemed to have been broken and then poorly set, approached him. "You new blood?" he asked.

Dawson looked up at the crook of the nose. "Yeah."

"You're settin' on my rack," the prisoner stated.

Dawson got up and grabbed his toilet bag. "Sorry, din't know it was your rack."

The prisoner pointed to another cot in the far corner, next to where the black men were bunking. "That rack over there is empty."

Dawson nodded, and walked over to the far corner. He sat on the cot. The three blacks eyes him cautiously. He removed his hat and arranged it on the cot, then he lay his head down.

He could hear the black prisoners talking among themselves, "Hey, man," one of them called "you got smokes?"

He turned in their direction, "No, man, I don't."

The blacks went back to their conversation. Dawson caught snatches of it. They were talking about soul music. He heard some familiar names, James Brown, Aretha, Otis. Can't they talk about anything else? He cupped his hands behind his neck. Just like brothers. Music and sex. "I owe it to myself, home," one of them was saying.

Home? Where the fuck they get that phrase from?

"You blew it, home," another one yelled. "You blew it!"

Dawson lifted his head. One of the brothers was holding out his hand. "You better give it to me, whore," he declared, "I ain't kiddin', Simms."

The other prisoner smiled. "Aw, home, I'm only jivin' you."

"I don't dig that jive."

"Okay, home, maintain. . . maintain," the other man soothed. He gave back something to his friend. Dawson couldn't see what it was.

The prisoner opened his hand and showed a dog tag chain with a crucifix and no tags. He placed the chain around his neck. The other prisoner spoke to the third black man. "Niggers will always be Holy Rollers," he quipped. The two men guffawed and gave out black power handshakes.

The prisoner handled his crucifix. "Thass awright. You all gonna burn when yore time comes."

His companions laughed uproariously.

Dawson lay back on his cot, and felt the sand in his face. I need a shave. His shirt was damp. A shower, too. Wonder how that works here? Do they have inspections? Naw, not here. Not even in this place. That'd be too much. Must think of something, do something while I'm here. Gotta learn all the connections. He recalled what the master sergeant had said. Minimum?

He lifted his head and gazed at Chi-Chi who had obtained a cot on the other side of the tent. Chi-Chi was laying on his back, silently moving his lips, like he was praying with his eyes open. Chi-Chi wasn't religious, that's for sure. Wonder what he's saying. Dawson lay his head down. A dude can go crazy in this place. Except for the three black prisoners, the other men kept to themselves. He was left very alone.

The guard, the blond one, came back and marched them to the mess hall. They enjoyed the same fare as before, chili con carne and rice. There were no incidents this time. Marching back to the tent, Dawson felt the chili fermenting in his bowels. He farted twice. Not a loud discharge, but of the silent odoriferous variety. When the guard wasn't watching, Chi-Chi turned his head and winked. Dawson grinned back at him.

Nighttime was monotonous. From 1730 to 2030 it was ostensibly free time for the prisoners. In the interim they played cards—one of the blacks had procured a deck from somewhere—talked and wrote letters. They were allowed to write one letter a night. While the black men were attentive to five card stud, Dawson and the other men engaged in a talkfest. The topic was of particular interest to him and Chi-Chi. The prisoner with the broken nose explained to them about the nemesis known throughout the sallyport area as Miller the Mole.

"I tell ya," Crooked-Nose said in his sibilant voice, "that Miller the Mole is the one t' watch. You'd be wise to stay away from him. That bastard is billy-happy."

Chi-Chi rubbed his stomach. "I know."

"That ain't nothing, man," Crooked-Nose said. "When I came here I got this because of that motherfucker." He pointed to the twisted lump of cartilage planted on his face.

"He do that?" Dawson asked.

"That's right." There was a gleam in Crooked-Nose's eyes, like the pride exhibited by a Prussian Junker showing off a dueling scar. He touched the bridge of the misshapen snout. "Caught me right there with a billy."

"What didja do?" Chi-Chi asked.

"I punched 'im. He got me pissed, pushed me all over the place, and I hit 'im." He massaged his nose, grinning behind his hand. "The fucker got a coupla friends and took me up to the cell block. They weren't suppose to leave no marks either, but that Miller the Mole goofed. I was in sick bay for two days."

Dawson stared at the lump above the mouth. "Din't the people in sick bay say nothing?"

Crooked-Nose smirked. "Fuck no, man. All they do up there is patch you up and send you back here." He jabbed his finger at his nose. "You know what they said about this? An *accident*. That's right, an accident. I fell outta a six-by and broke my nose. That was it. Man, over here nobody gives a shit about you. They could kill ya an' get away with it." He bit the fingernail on his pinky, and spit it out. "It's that Miller the Mole you gotta watch, though. He like one of them psycho people. He got it in for everybody. Fucker like him shouldn't even be a damn MP. He should be in here, with us."

"Does he come around often?" Chi-Chi asked.

Crooked-Nose snorted. "Does he come around often? Shit, he the guard for this hooch. Every hooch has like a keeper, y'know? Well, Miller the Mole is our keeper. Keeper of the zoo. He take us to chow, cut off the lights, wake us up, all that crap."

Dawson gazed around the tent while Crooked-Nose rambled. The tent was like any other shelter in I Corps or further north. The men rapping, joking; two lanterns flickering a golden hue above tight-set features. The place did not seem like a Brig. He had not imagined it to be like this. He had expected rows of cells, iron bars, machine gun posts; the popular conception manufactured by the cinema. If it wasn't for the fence outside, no one could guess this shelter consti-tuted part of Medium Detention.

"That Miller the Mole, he sick, man," Crooked-Nose was saying.

Dawson came back to the topic. "Why they call him the 'Mole'?"

"'Cause he a sneaky sonofabitch. Motherfucker always sneaking up on ya like some gook. When you least expect it he'll be there behind you. One time that fucker sneaked up on some dudes who were taking a break behind the sandpile. He caught 'em shootin' the shit, told the Top about it and had 'em thrown in the cell block. That's how he got the name. I tell ya, in here, that's the bitch to stay away from."

Chi-Chi wiped a finger under his nose. "Sometimes it's hard to do."

"I know. The fucker likes to fuck with all the new dudes. Don't worry if he fuckin' with you now, that's usual. He do that with all the new people. It's his kicks." Crooked Nose looked at Dawson. "Every new man gets a taste of the Mole. You will too, buddy, in due time."

"That's what I'm afraid of," Dawson admitted. "I wouldn't mind having it out with him if it was a fair fight, but that fucker has all the power on his side."

"He ain't got the power, he got Lidel, and that's enough."

"He bad, too?" Chi-Chi asked.

"He don't fuck with ya 'cause he don't need to," Crooked Nose said. "He's the second in command of Casual. If he wanna fuck you up all he gotta do is give an order and it's done."

Dawson scratched his armpits. "What about the CO? Don't he ever show?"

"The CO?" Crooked-Nose sneered. "Hell, you don't ever see him around. He's always too busy, doing I don't know what. I been here four months and I seen 'im just two times. He some sort of a warrant officer. You don't hafta worry 'bout him. He only come around when they have an inspection."

Chi-Chi was alerted, so was Dawson, but Chi-Chi was faster in his response. "Inspection?"

"You don't hafta worry 'bout it. Ain't no big shit. The CO just comes in the hooch and looks around once or twice. He just want to see the place clean, that's all. Most of the time he don't even stay in the tent for two minutes. Just comes in, takes one look and says, 'Carry on.' The whole show is real stupid."

"How often they got these inspections?"

"Oh, whenever the CO or Top get a case of the ass."

The conversation flitted back and forth, from Miller the Mole to the CO to Medium Detention. A depressing chain that left a rancid flavor on the tongue. Eventually Dawson got bored with it. Throughout the discussion he caught glimpses of the three blacks relishing the card game. They were the unknown ingredient. Wrong. The known ingredient. Startingly, it touched him. The tent was *not* like any hooch in the war zone. It was a squad room back in the world, a Quonset hut, or a barracks. He could feel it but not describe it. He was not on a fire support base at the rim of the DMZ. This was the world, the one he had left behind. The old components were here. They could never be brought out in the field. The element of self-preservation negated that instinct. Here in the Brig the real danger subsided, and old grievances flared. The realm of garrison duty and all it contained, the invisible line that was always there, tacitly acknowledged yet never in the open. *They* stood on their side and *we* stood on ours. A time-worn equation: them and us. Two years in the Corps, basic training, ITR, staging, Nam, and he had never really considered it before. He had noticed it, certainly, but never deeply enough to realize the extent of the separation—until now. In the rear areas there was a nonexistent durable barrier that no one ever trespassed unless he was an outcast from his peer group; the whites, the blacks, the spics, and within the spics an agglomerate of Mexicans, 'Ricans, Cubans, etc. There were certain instances—he had seen it at Camp Lejeune and Okinawa—of a further grouping, a tenuous union of 'Ricans and blacks, but this was a loose offshoot applicable only when there wasn't a sizable grouping of either one. He thought of the clique back in his old platoon where everyone was lumped together for mutual protection. How long would that little circle last in the outside world? He need not ask. Had it been a regular post anywhere else, his field companions would have never united. Everybody sticks with his own because he feels more comfortable. Combat distorted this basic relationship in some way. Or was it that the basic relationship was always there and a lack of combat distorted it? We cooperate with outlanders out of the necessity to survive. But what *was* the basic relationship?

Dawson dropped out of the talk that ran between Chi-Chi, Crooked-Nose and the other white man in the tent. Oh, oh. Where did Chi-Chi belong in all this. A white 'Rican? Halfbreed. Able to communicate with both groups but never belong to either? Or had he made his choice already?

He sat up and untied his boots. Ah, fuckit, the niggers got their own thing and we got ours. He removed his socks and massaged his feet.

For some reason he felt depressed.

JULY 5TH

Heat. Relentless, intense. Dawson had melted under some rays, but never like this. He swung the pickax one more time, heard the thud of metal against rock, cursed under his breath and wiped his mouth. He looked at the dust smears on the back of his hand. Ridiculous. The whole jive, ridiculous. He wiped the sweat from his forehead, shaking his hand so that trickles of perspiration fell on the ground and mingled with scarred rock strata. Another swing of the pickax, more crumpled rocks. The pick handle was stiff in his palms, and he felt the pinch of the wood hardening the skin into blisters sensitive to friction. He swung the handle and the wood slid through his grip. His hands were too moist to grasp the pick extension properly. He wiped his hands on his trousers, and looked directly at the sunlight. A jarring brilliance; red spotty crystals covered his eyes. He squinted, and his eye sockets burned. Someone had conned him. He had been led to believe the worst sun possible, the most overbearing of all, was in the northernmost tip of the DMZ. Countless operations under that fiery egg had convinced him of it. You couldn't beat the Quang Tri sun or the mountain heat. Them hills had it all over the jungles and paddies further south. Bullshit. The worst sun ever was here on top of him. Da Nang was not all jungles and paddies. It was also dry land like in the north, and the heat was something.

49

He scratched his chin on his naked shoulder. Maybe not. Maybe the fact that he was lugging a pickax and standing barechested with no helmet or cover changed things. Dawson would have gladly traded the pickax for a pack and rifle. "Roasting," he muttered. Another swing of the pickax. Rest, for a couple of seconds while the man wasn't watching. He lifted the pick over his head, letting it fall on its own weight. The metal point dug in the ground. He pulled back the handle, wrenching the ax tip and breaking apart a globule of earth.

The earth was different here, he noticed. It didn't have the red overlay of the terrain up north. Up there the ground was a second cousin to Georgia clay. The terrain in the Brig was more natural, more of the kind associated with the sparse land, brown, heavy and solid. The type of ground that would be conducive to growth if anybody put it to use. In the rain it would turn muddy and viscid, but unlike its northern counterpart, it could sustain vegetation. A big difference.

He straightened his back and scanned the mountain ranges around him. More level, and massive green, covered with a huge canopy, not bare and desolate like the hills in the Z. I could never hack the bush over here, he thought. All them paddies. Place is perfect for booby traps. Nah, never hack it here.

"You waitin' for the job to do itself?" the blond guard needled.

Dawson eyed Miller the Mole standing on the road a few feet above him. Miller was formally arrayed with M14 rifle, cartridge belt with canteen, and four magazine pouches. He also wore military suspender straps that held up the cartridge belt, although it didn't seem very effective. Miller's belt sagged to his thighs.

Dawson was contemptuous. Just like a chickenshit MP. Don't even know how to adjust GI belt suspenders. The thought appeased him.

"You been takin' too many breaks lately, turd," Miller said. "How about swingin' that pick." He spat to where Dawson stood. The spittle landed an inch from Dawson's boot. Dawson lifted the ax over his head, letting it fall on its own weight.

Miller took off his cap and wiped his forehead with his sleeves. He hitched up his cartridge belt.

Dawson looked over his shoulder and saw Miller walk back to the other side of the road. He took one last swing, and left the pickax sticking in the ground. He put his hands on his lower back and stretched out. It was like a piece of elastic. A subtle pain had crimped his lumbar region, traveling up the flexible shaft that joined the neck.

"Here we are, slick," the voice behind him said. "You got dirt for us?"

He turned and caught the full features of Chi-Chi. "It's about time you come. There's beaucoup dirt here."

Chi-Chi held a bundle of sandbags under his right arm. Crooked-Nose stood behind him, holding an E-tool with the digging part folded back like a shovel. "Actually, we din't wanna come," Chi-Chi joked, "but our good host Miller the Mole insisted we come and assist you in pilin' up this dirt."

"You musta busted heavy with the pick," Crooked-Nose said. "You got yourself a lotta dirt there."

Dawson rested his palms on the end of the pick handle. "It wasn't my doing. I came here with the intention of takin' it light but that fuckin' Miller the Mole been on my back all morning."

Chi-Chi put down the bundle of sandbags, sat on them. "I know, man. That fucker been bustin' our asses too. Right now he's ridin' the brothers." He spat between his feet. "I think he take turns—that flaky cocksucker."

The flaky cocksucker appeared at the top of the quarry. "How about gettin' some work done, ladies?" Miller exhorted. "It ain't gonna do itself. You, with the curly hair, get off your ass and start bustin'."

Chi-Chi got up sluggishly. "Bastard," he whispered.

Slowly they began filling sandbags, Chi-Chi holding the bags open while Crooked-Nose filled them. Dawson went back to his pickax.

Miller watched them for a few minutes. He knew they would start talking again and he waited so he could catch them. Miller had a mission. For some obscure reason he enjoyed catching men red-handed when they infringed on some trite rule of corrective custody. It was part of the pride he had in himself and his job.

The men below him worked quietly. Ah, maybe next time. Reasoning he wouldn't have much luck with this group, he strode across the road and looked into the other quarry that was an excavation running ten feet down alongside the road. The three black prisoners were together in the hollow, also filling sandbags. They seemed quiet enough, each man going about his own work. They were probably cursing him under their breath. He smiled to himself. An odd feeling of power swept over him. To know they hated and feared him. He had the thrill of a GI who goes into a village with a loaded rifle on full automatic in order to question the inhabitants.

One of the black men giggled. To Miller it sounded obscene. "What's so funny down there?" he asked.

The men looked up. In the sunlight their brawny flesh gleamed like smooth oil. "Ain't nothin' happenin'," one of them said.

"Don't give me that shit, I heard one of you turds laughing. I wanna know why."

The men stood their ground, silently.

Miller hitched his cartridge belt higher on his waist. The fuckin' suspender straps are too low, he thought. The belt was pinching his ass. He scowled at the men. "Git back to work. I don't want to see no shootin' the shit." He reached behind his back and took out his canteen. It was the old type made of metal with a chain top. The canteen cork bounced on the metal surface, making a sharp, clinging sound. He took in a small amount of water, rinsed his mouth, and spewed it out. Another gulp, which he swallowed. He was aware that the prisoners in the quarry were ogling him. Spitefully, he took another drink, and wiped his mouth with the back of his hand. One of the prisoners licked his lips.

A smile played on Miller's face.

He put away the canteen, then walked to the other side of the road. The whites were working diligently, or appeared to be. They sneaked a couple of glances at him. Miller looked down and said nothing. He lifted his head toward the sun. Instant blindness. He lowered his eyes, rubbed them vigorously. The blur diminished. Fuckin' heat. He was thirsty again. Damn, I just drank. He doffed his cap and wiped his forehead. Stains of sweat splotched the sleeves of his fatigue shirt. He put on his cap, unslung his rifle and held it in his hand, at his side. His right shoulder ached. M14s can be shitty. He held up the rifle, ran his hand along the wooden stock. Good weapon, but heavy for this climate. We should be carrying 16s. Brig always gets leftover shit. Old equipment, old guns, old canteens. He thumbed the bayonet stud at the barrel of the rifle. Fuckit, a 14 can kill a man just as good as a 16.

The cartridge belt began to slide down his hips. He groaned. Fuckin' suspenders is shitty. The four magazine pouches nipped his thighs. Irritating. He put the rifle on the ground, unhooked his cartridge belt. He adjusted the suspender belt hooks so that when he put on the cartridge belt it was high on his waist. The suspenders pinched his shoulders but that was better than having the belt hanging on his belly. He picked up his rifle and walked back to his side of the road.

In the quarry the black prisoners were sitting down and talking. He caught them in the middle of one of their black power handshakes. "Get up!" he ordered. The men jumped to their feet. "What the fuck do you think this shit is? Pick up them E-tools and get crackin' or I'll have you in the cell block."

Two of the men picked up their tools. A third, the one who had been filling sandbags, remained still, looking up at Miller.

The Mole pointed a finger at the prisoner. "You, nigger, take that E-tool and fill them bags."

It was a calculated insult, and not one he regretted.

The prisoner did not move immediately. He stared at Miller for perhaps another second. His friends likewise stopped what they were doing.

"C'mon, you, get back to work. I don't want no shit from you people.'"

You people made his previous jibe sound worse.

Miller unslung his rifle and aimed it at them. "You goin' back to work?"

One of the prisoners put a hand on the shoulder of the man Miller had insulted. He whispered something in the man's ear. The man looked back at Miller. If a glance could kill . . . The man took up a pickax and began to batter the ground. The others resumed filling sandbags.

Miller lowered the rifle. Freakin' niggers. If I was back home I'd kill that black bastard. He slung the M14 on his shoulder and went back to the other side of the road.

Dawson and his crew had ceased their labor. They were listening to Miller's bellowing. When Miller had called out "nigger," Chi-Chi put a finger to his lips and whispered, "Lissen." They heard as much as could be expected across ten feet of road that began about eight feet from where they stood. Miller's voice was loud but garbled. He was ordering the men back to work. They heard no more. Chi-Chi cupped his ear.

Dawson was curious. "What's happening?"

Chi-Chi put up his hand. "Shush." He listened intently. "He's comin' back."

They picked up their tools.

Miller appeared on top of the road. They could feel his glare on them. Dawson lifted his ax handle, letting the pick fall. He swung the pick repeatedly, not looking up at the Mole. The other men filled the sandbags cautiously.

An electric mule cart came up the road; it screeched to a dusty stop. Another armed guard dismounted from the platform of the vehicle. He walked up to Miller. "'Bout time you got here," Miller greeted.

The other guard slung his rifle, barrel facing down and stock hanging parallel to his shoulder. "Couldn't help it, man. Top had another inspection."

"Inspection?"

"Yeah, on our equipment."

Miller grunted. "Glad I missed it." He watched the mule cart drive off in the direction of the flatlands that constituted the Brig. The road they were on was an extension of a main highway running through the Da Nang complex. Like all the tributaries it was flat, unpaved ground. It was also the last lap of a route that ended in the wilderness area used as a firing range for heavy base artillery. The road sector where the prisoners worked was split into two clefts on each side of the diminishing roadway. After a few meters the clefts leveled off into a minor range that led to the mountainous area ringing the base.

"I'm glad you're back," Miller said. "It's a bitch tryin' to keep an eye on these turds. They're workin' both sides of the road and I can't scope both groups at the same time. So tell you what, why don'tcha go over at that side and keep an eye on the brothers while I watch these dudes."

"Okay, don't make no dif'rence to me. I'll guard the niggers."

Miller smiled thinly. "Yeah, you do that." He looked down at the quarry where Dawson and his co-workers were laboring. "You people bustin' heavy down there?" he chortled.

The men looked up, and continued filling sandbags.

He smiled to himself.

After a while he got the itch. "Hey, Gault, how them niggers doin' on your side?"

The other guard glanced at him from across the road. "Dudes over here doin' their work, man."

Miller scanned the sand quarry as he spoke. "Yeah, them brothers do alright with the pick and shovel. Them good boys, alright. I think they's better than these people down here."

Dawson swung his pick and let it fall on the ground. He listened dully to the exchange between Miller and the other guard.

"Always did say niggers was better bustin' with the back," Miller said. "Don't you think so, Gault?"

The other guard was wary of the turn the conversation was taking. More so, now that the blacks were sending hostile glances his way. There was something unclean about a conversation like this, especially when *they* were watching. It was different in the safety of the hooches or on guard detail at night, but when you began deriding a man right there where it was obvious to all . . . the guard was uneasy. "Yeah, I guess they work alright," he said, feeling their eyes on him.

"Yeah, a good nigger is hard to find," Miller said in his indulgent tone. "I like blackies who do good work. Makes me feel better." He grinned at the other guard. "If I was you, Gault, I'd give them niggers a break, seein' as how they's workin' so hard." Again he looked down at his side of the road. The men labored in silence, but it was tension-filled. "Yeah, I'd give them niggers a break."

One of the black men in the quarry threw down the pickax and cursed audibly. The guard saw him, and thought of unslinging his rifle. He was wise enough to realize that would make things worse. The prisoner glared at him. Another man put a hand on the prisoner's shoulder and drew him back. He said something which the guard could not hear. The black man jerked his shoulder, removing his friend's grasp. The other man faced him, seeking to calm down his companion.

"A good nigger is worth his weight in gold," Miller remarked. "Everybody should have one . . ."

The guard was becoming concerned. The man who dropped the pickax was looking at him with hatred contorting his face.

"It's nice to keep a nigger busy, you don't hafta worry 'bout 'em then . . ."

The guard walked across the road. "C'mon, Miller, quit it." He referred to the quarry. "I got brothers down there."

"I know," Miller said, undisturbed.

"You know what the Top said about things like that."

"I know." Miller gave a comforting grin. "I'm only talkin', that's all."

"It ain't good talkin' like that with the brothers around."

Miller shrugged. "Fuck 'em. They don't like it, they don't hafta eat it."

"You know what the Top said—"

"I know what the Top said. Look, Gault, if they don't like it—tough." Miller looked down at his side of the quarry. "The niggers workin'?"

"Yeah, they workin'."

"How do you know? You're here, you ain't watchin' 'em."

The guard was exasperated. "Man, I know they're workin', okay? Just lay off the race talk."

"I don't believe they're workin' at all," Miller contended. "'Fact, I'm gonna check myself." Before the guard could reply, Miller had walked across the road and started on the black prisoners. "You suppose to be workin', ladies."

The prisoners looked up. They stood with their work tools in hand but there was no movement.

"This ain't a goddamn rest camp, ladies. How 'bout shakin' yore ass?"

The prisoners did not move.

Miller unslung his rifle. "You niggers gonna work or do I hafta blow you away?"

The other guard put a hand on Miller's arm. "C'mon, Miller."

Miller moved his arm away, his eyes set on the three men ten feet below him. "I'm warnin' you, ladies, let's use them E-tools. I don't want no trouble from none of my niggers."

The man with the pickax stepped forward. Miller raised his rifle to his shoulder. With his thumb he pressed the safety catch in front of the trigger guard.

"Hey, whatcha doin'—"

"Stay outta this, Gault." Miller had the silhouette of the prisoner centered in the peephole of the gun sight.

The prisoner halted, and stepped back.

"You going back to work, nigger," Miller called out from the side of his mouth. His cheek pressed against the rifle stock, and he waited.

The prisoner looked down, loosened the grip on the pickax. "The bitch," he muttered sullenly.

Miller concentrated on the sight oval, wrapping his finger round the trigger. "I'm giving you five seconds to get back to work, nigger."

On the other side of the road, Chi-Chi said, "I think he threatenin' him with a gun."

"Who?" Dawson asked.

"The nigger—I mean, the brother."

Crooked-Nose looked up at the side grading of the highway. "If he dings a brother that's gonna be bad. You got quite a few brothers in the Brig."

Back on the road, Miller had changed his stance, and the rifle barrel was still aimed directly at the black man's head. His pulse was pounding . . . Stand at the ready . . . Hold left arm under the rifle in the most comfortable and balanced position . . . Grip small of stock, holding right elbow in line with the shoulder . . .

The black man retreated. He resumed working the ground with the pick. His friends relaxed.

Miller lowered the rifle. His pulse slowed. He was both relieved and disappointed. He had no idea what his reaction would have been had the prisoner called his bluff. He strode over to his side of the road. The other guard turned away. The prospect of looking down at the quarry was repugnant to him.

Down in the quarry, the black captives felt debased. The man with the pickax swung it savagely, tearing the ground at his feet, trying to stifle the sob of anger in his chest. His friends said nothing. They shared a silent loathing for the guard's brutality.

On the other side, Dawson stared at Miller standing above him.

"You got somethin', turd?" Miller threatened.

Dawson dropped his gaze. He took up the pickax and attacked the earth.

While he shoveled dirt into a sandbag, Crooked-Nose sneaked a glance at Miller. "That fucker should be in the psycho ward," he whispered.

That night the blacks were quieter than usual. Their side of the tent became a separate cubbyhole reserved for themselves. No loud rap but serious downhome talk of the humiliation. The only way they could see it. No one was ever happy with the Brig, but the blacks had found special cause for disenchantment.

If the whites lived a thousand years they would never know the feel of this shame. This was a specific hurt which the blacks sought to smother with their pride; and this sensitivity that set them apart could fabricate any number of imagined wrongs. It could work both ways, and they could get by with things their white counterparts never dreamed of, in civilian life or the military. But when the affront was tangible, when it was obvious, nothing could nullify it. A cancer that fed upon itself in hushed statements in the corner of the tent.

Dawson slept closest to them but he could not hear their talk, or lack of it. He could sense a peculiar brand of antipathy slide by his cot. He watched the blacks with interest, a strange uneasiness growing inside him and he became dispirited. He had always nurtured that unique suspicion of Negroes that every Caucasian has. But at least he had made himself look beyond that suspicion, or so he thought. He endeavored to treat the black men in his squad with the same reserve he dealt any stranger, black or white. It was neither wise nor practical to ignite the kindling as Miller had done. Some taboos you obeyed assiduously, whether you hated niggers or not. Dawson knew he wasn't too fond of them to begin with, but still, some things weren't done.

Two of the black men started a card game, and the third, the one who had been menaced by Miller, rested in his cot. Dawson watched him light up a cigarette, a regular extra-long filter nail, the type billed as a silly millimeter longer. He was taken with the idea of how they managed to sneak regular cigarettes into the Brig. The only smokes allowed, when they did allow them, were C-ration brands that tasted like wet socks. The blacks had a connection somewhere.

And he was depressed again. What good would the connection do him? He reminded himself he was outside their circle.

He saw the man take two smokes and pass the cigarette to his friends who puffed on it once or twice as though they were sharing a J. He noticed the other men in the tent casting sidelong glances at the blacks. Lesson number one: wealth is measured by the tobacco in one's pocket. His hand went inside his shirt. The half-smoked cigarette the MP had given him was soggy, and grains of tobacco rolled on his fingers. He had to smoke the butt or he'd have nothing left.

The black prisoner noticed Dawson's ogling. He returned the look, and Dawson dropped his head. A few seconds later he took out the half-smoked cigarette.

But he had no match.

Just then the black man produced a book of matches from under his hat which lay on the cot. "Hey," he called.

Dawson looked up.

The prisoner tossed him the matches. They fell on the floor, next to Dawson's feet. He picked them up, lit the mini-cigarette, and was about to fling back the matches, but decided not to. Instead he stood up, walked over to the black man and handed him the book. "Thanks," he said.

The prisoner nodded, and watched Dawson go back to his side.

The next day they found themselves in the sandpile. If the road detail was tedious, the sandpile was noxious. The pile was not one main heap. It was three accumulations of dirt that had been dug out on the western end of the base. The earth at one time was to have been utilized for the construction of a bunker complex. The plans never congealed, the engineering units were reassigned elsewhere, and the excavated dirt was left standing in three hillocks. Sandbag emplacements still had to be built and, by a pact promoted between the Brig solons and the base commander, the Brig inmates were chosen to venture into the lot and fill the needed sandbags to cover the various positions. There was a surplus of cheap labor in the Brig and what better way to meet the increasing sandbag demand? The Brig *was* sandbags, there was no way getting around it. An inmate came to know sandbags intimately.

Taking a cue from the road works, the sandpile was a relatively flat area about the size of a small baseball diamond. It was barren except for a few holes that had been dug by the frequent testing of C4 chemical explosives. The three earthen heaps stood twelve feet high and were spaced about eight yards apart. To fill the required number of sandbags the detail was set into teams of two men working at the foot of the piles. One man would dig out the earth and shovel it into the sandbag held open by his partner; the partner would tie the bag and place it in a batch. Once all the sandbags were filled, the men loaded them up on a two-and-a-half ton truck. The schedule called for one hundred and fifty bags to be completed daily. It was an eight hour process with one break for lunch at the nearby battalion mess hall. The group of men selected for the detail was assigned an escort of ten guards, all armed.

On the surface, the order for a hundred and fifty sandbags per day sounded reasonable. All the men had to do was bust heavy with the back. Identical procedure to the road party. But not quite, because the sandpile was bad news. First of all, the men were not dealing with sand but with hard dirt intermixed with rock particles that the Brig CO insisted had to be ground into sediment before they were poured in the bags. And the guards checked the sandbags after they were done, actually feeling the burlap surface, and if there were any rocks they tore open the bag and spilt the earth back on the ground. Another bag had to be filled again. If any rocks were felt once more, the same procedure, the bag was ripped open. It was a benighted, wasted effort which the prisoners resented.

Filling a sandbag was no easy task. The deal began with the prisoner digging into the base of the pile and pulling out a spadeful of earth. The principle of gravity came into play and the earth began to slide down as the prisoner advanced his shovel. In a short time he was wading in dirt. With combat boots it wasn't too bad, you couldn't feel the grinding in the leather; but as the day progressed and the sun became stronger, all the dirt seemed to fall on the men. There was no wind, and two hours after the men had begun they were caked all over. Dawson was reminded of the dusty rides on the convoys up north. Each man was covered in a coat that darkened his face in a poor imitation of a coal miner's grimy mark. They had removed their shirts and the veneer extended to their arms and shoulders. The dirt formed a glove over their hands, going up to the elbow; rings of dirt leafed around the neck and brown layers settled across their chest and stomach. And the black prisoners came out looking like copper-painted African warriors. The earth itched and teased the skin intolerably.

Dawson sneezed into his hand, and wiped the mucus on his trousers. After rubbing clean his fingers of any dust, he picked his nose. The fingers came out smeared with brown, no mucus, just dust. He spat to the side, disgusted. Placing the spade between his legs, he put his hands on the small of his back and pushed inward, straightening his upper body.

Chi-Chi was sitting in a pool of earth covering his legs halfway. A half-filled sandbag was spread between his thighs. He was holding the front portion of the bag open, waiting for the rest of the earth to be poured inside. "C'mon, man, fill up the mother," he said. "Ya still got 'bout fifty more t' go."

Dawson wiped his hands to dry up the sweat. "Cut me some slack, will ya? You another P or somethin'?"

"C'mon, fill 'er up. I don't dig holdin' up this bag."

"You ain't holding it up," Dawson said. "You just keeping it open."

"It's the same thing."

"You wanna switch jobs?"

No settlement with Chi-Chi. "Fuck no, I ain't gonna handle no E-tool. Think I'm crazy? That's hard work."

Dawson picked up the E-tool and frowned. "I know, that's why I'm doing it. I still don't know why I tossed you for it."

"Now, you know we chose the thing fair and square. We used the guard's coin to choose, remember?"

Dawson dug the spade into the earth. "I'll be damned if I'll do it again." He dug up a spadeful and poured it in the bag. "Pro'bly a double-headed coin."

"We chose fair and square," Chi-Chi reminded him.

"Yeah," Dawson grunted.

Miller passed by, cradling the rifle in his right arm. "Cut the crap, ladies." He went off in the direction of the next sandpile.

Chi-Chi scanned Miller's back. "That fucker is a bummer."

"A what?"

"Like a bad trip, dig?"

Dawson didn't know what Chi-Chi was talking about. "Oh, sure." He ladled another spadeful into the bag.

Chi-Chi wrinkled his brow in displeasure. "They's all bummers here, every single one of 'em."

"Who?"

"Everybody. All the fuckin' Ps."

"Just found that out?" Dawson asked with a sardonic tone.

"Naw, I din't just find that out, I've known it all along. If I had my way there be no fuckin' H&S Casual. You know what I'd do if I was in charge of this setup?"

"No, what would ya do?"

"I'd close this joint and send everybody home—guards, Ps, prisoners—everybody. I'd say, 'Fuckit, anybody wanna sky home can do it. If you wanna make your bird—git! And then I'd extend that proclamation to all the troopies in the field, even Army." Chi-Chi grinned enthusiastically. "Wouldn't that be somethin'? Everybody slidin' home and leavin' the Brig empty?"

"That's cool," Dawson said, "but if you take all the dudes outta the bush who gonna fight the war?"

"That's it, man. There'd be nobody to fight the war, so there'd be no need to fight one, dig?"

"Oh," Dawson said, not comprehending at all. "But what happens after everybody sky?"

"Nothing. That's it, nothing. We all go back home and fuck."

"Oh."

"Wouldn't you rather fuck than be here?" Chi-Chi asked.

"Yeah, I'd imagine."

"There." Chi-Chi nodded with conviction. "I should be a goddamn politician."

Dawson lifted a spadeful of earth. "Yeah, Chi-Chi, maybe you should be." He lowered the E-tool and rested. "What's your platform gonna be, a free fuck for everybody?"

"The bummer comin' back," Chi-Chi alerted him.

Dawson looked over his shoulder. Miller was coming their way. He stopped in front of the sandpile. "Man, you people are the most talkative dudes. I swear, can't you take a friendly warning?"

"We ain't doin' nothin', Miller," Chi-Chi said.

"That's right, you ain't doin' nothin'. And how 'bout standing up when I talk to ya, turd."

Chi-Chi sighed and got to his feet.

"That goes for you, too, turd," Miller told Dawson.

Dawson shrugged and slouched to something that resembled the pose of attention. He looked at the sky while Miller spoke.

Miller's voice was surprisingly mild. "Now, you people know you ain't suppose to gab while you're workin'."

Chi-Chi opened his mouth to protest.

"Stow it, Curly. I know you people was shootin' the shit," Miller grinned sociably. "That's a no-no. Ain't no no-nos allowed in this place. Admit it, you was gabbin'."

No answer.

About ten feet away, on the same sandpile, two black prisoners were also filling sandbags. They had ceased their work and were awaiting the outcome of this latest development.

"Sir, request permission to speak," Chi-Chi petitioned.

"Of course, prisoner, by all means, do speak." Miller sounded like a headmaster chastising some errant schoolboys.

"We wasn't talking," Chi-Chi said.

Miller showed his toothy grin. "Now, now, ladies, we know we're lying, don't we? Yes, we do." He picked up the E-tool that stood next to Dawson's foot, and looked at it admiringly. "Can't allow a no-no, ladies." And just as simple as you please, Miller went over to where they had piled the tent sandbags and commenced to rip each one apart with the digging end of the E-tool. He wielded the spade expertly, creating a foot-long gash on each bag that spurted sand like the stuffing out of a rag doll. In a minute every bag was ripped and sagging.

Dawson took a step forward but Chi-Chi gripped his arm and held him back.

Miller tossed the E-tool back on the ground. "Now I'm sure we won't talk no more. Will we, ladies?"

Dawson found Miller's grin obnoxious. "Miller, you mother—"

"There you go again, talkin' out of turn, without asking no permission, either." Miller took a leisurely step toward Dawson, but he wasn't grinning anymore. "Don't you heed no rules, turd?"

Dawson kept his eyes leveled on Miller. He looked past the blue of the irises and into the pit.

"Gault!" Miller called out.

Another guard came over. "What's up, Miller?"

"Cover me," Miller said. "I think we got a problem of discipline here."

"Aw, c'mon, Miller," the guard said.

"No, Gault, really. We got one of those disciplinary actions."

"Aw, Miller, they gotta get these bags done today."

"They will." Miller looked rigidly at Dawson. "Won't you, turd?"

Dawson stared back, regretting a little his boldness.

"What's your name?" Miller asked.

Negative.

"I asked ya your name, turd," Miller repeated.

The old sensation, as if Gunnery Sergeant Yeager were there. "Dawson," he replied, but it was a defiant retort, like an openhanded slap.

Miller's next request was cutting. "Dawson, you was talking, turd. I want an apology from you. I want you to say, 'Pfc Miller, I'm sorry I was talking, *sir*. I won't do it again.' Say it!"

Dawson tightened inside. Every nerve trembled, and his neck muscles were strained tight.

"I'm waitin', turd." Miller's voice was cold as the granite on a tomb.

Dawson felt every eye in the sandpile on him. He wasn't concerned with his anger, only the agitation in his heart.

Miller raised the rifle to his hip. With his thumb he pushed forward the safety catch. "I'm waitin' for an apology, prisoner."

Dawson's mind was racing. He wouldn't shoot me here, he *couldn't*. Would he? He remembered Crooked-Nose. *That fucker should be in the psycho ward.* He felt his legs go weak.

Miller took a step back, giving himself more room with the rifle pointed at Dawson's stomach.

The guard in back of them grasped the sling of his rifle, looking at Miller with the profoundest consternation. Miller had gone to the point where he couldn't back out if the prisoner called his hand.

The prisoner did not call his hand.

"I apologize," Dawson said weakly.

Miller shook his head. "Uh-uh. You suppose to say, '*Sir*, I'm sorry for talking. I apologize, sir."

Dawson forced it out. "Sir . . . I'm sorry for talking . . . I apologize, sir."

Miller nodded appreciatively. His Nordic face regained the luster it had suspended momentarily. "That's very good, Dawson. I accept your apology. Now pick up that E-tool and get to work."

With the greatest effort of his life Dawson limply took up the spade. He looked down, avoiding the other men, trying to forget what he would always remember.

Miller tired of the game. "Okay, you men," he told all of them and no one in particular, "let's git back to work."

Chi-Chi sat down on the earthen cushion and held up a new sandbag.

The black men ten feet from him were not as quick. One of them muttered, "Bitch."

Miller walked around the dirt pile until he was facing them. "You men on the same kick as Dawson over here?"

The two blacks continued filling sandbags, totally disregarding the new intrusion.

Miller began all over again. "You men talkin'?"

No reply. One of the men did look up for a second or so; he went back to his shoveling.

The same pattern. "I asked ya a question," Miller said. "Were you men talkin'?"

The prisoner with the E-tool dug it in the earth and very slowly raised his hand to scratch his sweaty chest. The other man was sitting down holding the sandbag. He tittered.

"What's so funny?" Miller demanded to know.

Chi-Chi and Dawson slowed their labor and watched the action.

The man who was sitting had a tacit response. He spat into the opened sandbag.

Miller's features became heavy. He attacked the only way he could. "You niggers think you're smart, huh?"

He noted killer glances coming his way, and it delighted him. The opposition of the two men encouraged Miller to push the issue a little further, a little deeper. An odious grin formed on his face. He looked at the sandbags the blacks had piled up. Substantially less than Dawson and his partner had produced, about seven bags maybe. Seven or one, did it make a difference? Miller believed what mattered was the symbolic gesture. "Those bags look like they're full of rocks," he said, rubbing his chin. He looked over his shoulder. "Don't they look like they're full of rocks, Gault?"

The other guard scuffed his boot in the dirt. He did not answer.

Miller stood before the sandbags, surveying them like a surgeon deciding the correct angle of an incision. He extended his palm to the prisoner. "Lemme see your E-tool, turd. I wanna check it." He cast a sly grin at the other guard. "I wanna see if it's in workin' condition."

The prisoner observed how Miller stared at the sandbags. He wasn't about to let the MP scatter his efforts. Wasted energy? No, man, that don't get it. On GP alone, he couldn't let him do it.

"You want the E-tool, you come and get it," the prisoner said.

Miller unslung his rifle, aimed it at the inmate.

The prisoner held the E-tool menacingly, grasping the neck of the shovel and the bottom of the handle. His body was bent slightly forward at the hips in a blatant defensive position.

Miller held his rifle steady. "If you don't put down that E-tool, nigger, I'm gonna put a bullet hole right through your belly."

The prisoner saw Miller's hand grasping the stock of the rifle, the finger on the trigger. When rankled, even a prisoner was capable of unusual courage. "You kill me, dude, 'cause that's the only way you gonna get this E-tool," he declared.

Dawson lowered his shovel, anxiously awaiting the outcome. He could not believe the other man had actually challenged Miller's firepower. And when he saw Miller hesitate, that was incredible.

Miller's sweaty paws began to stain the fine varnished coating on the wooden handguard. His tongue protruded like a small dart from the corner of his mouth. In that fraction of a second he seemed like an aerialist uncertain of his balance. He looked at the other guard, who did not move from his square foot of ground; he gazed at the prisoner, thinking that once you pointed a rifle at a man he'd back down. What's with this nigger anyway? The prospect of killing the man appealed to him. The thought of being relieved of his sinecure as MP did not.

Dawson rubbed his hands on his thighs. He could picture the black man lying on the ground with a bullet hole in his stomach. The first time during that afternoon when he wouldn't feel the sting of the sun on his back.

Miller put down the rifle, forcing his voice to be crisp. "Gault, this prisoner is threatening us. We gonna have to remove the E-tool from him."

The other guard unslung his rifle. The bolt went forward as he cocked it.

The two guards approached the prisoner, rifles aimed dead at him. The black man picked up a spadeful of earth and hurled it at the guards. He did this two more times and then swung the shovel like a baseball bat, keeping the guards away from him.

Miller brushed the dirt from his shirt, and spat out some dust. "Why you motherfuckin' nigger."

Dawson saw the expression on Miller's face. The MP was going to shoot the prisoner. The knowledge leaped at him. Oh, God, he's gonna zap 'im.

"What's going on here?"

Everyone turned his head to see Master Sergeant Lidel standing behind them. He didn't look too pleased.

Miller lowered his rifle. "Top, this prisoner threatenin' me and Gault with an E-tool."

"He's doing what?"

Miller rushed his words. He was going to get the impudent nigger one way or another. "He says he gonna brain anybody who come near him, Top."

Lidel stared at the prisoner. "Put down that E-tool."

The prisoner tightened his hold on the shovel. "I will if they stay away from me. I don't wanna fuck with nobody but if they fuck with me I'll kill 'em."

No inmate ever menaced Lidel or one of his guards. He looked at the prisoner as if he were seeing a madman. "You gonna do what?" His eyes widened. He called for two more guards and they came running. "Take this prisoner back to the compound."

The four guards closed in on the prisoner. He swung the E-tool, barely missing them, driving them back. The guards approached him again. The cutting edge of the spade whipped the air. The men backed away.

"If you don't drop that E-tool we gonna hafta shoot you," Lidel warned. "You best put it down."

The prisoner pointed the shovel at Miller. "If he stay away from me I will."

"Miller, get outta here," Lidel ordered.

Miller gripped his rifle, then shifted his weight from one foot to the other. He looked down, he looked up, he looked sideways. He was riled.

"Go on, Miller, leave. Go to the next sandpile and stand guard."

Miller slung his rifle and walked away. The expression on his face was acidic.

Dawson exhaled.

Lidel extended his hand toward the prisoner. "C'mon, son, gimme that E-tool. It ain't gonna help you to get in trouble."

The prisoner opened and closed his grip on the handle of the shovel. He looked at his friend and, strangely enough, at Dawson. He was undecided.

Lidel's tone was low key. "C'mon, son, hand it over. I promise ya won't get the hole. We'll go back to the CO and get this straightened out."

The prisoner stood in his defensive position, his eyes set on Lidel.

"You're only making it worse. Hand over that E-tool and I swear no harm will come to you."

The prisoner gazed at the other men. But he was alone. The others dropped their eyes. The E-tool was moist and heavy, his hands very wet. He lowered the spade. Lidel walked up to him and took the shovel, gently removing it from the prisoner's grasp. He placed a hand on the prisoner's naked shoulder as if he were going to guide him away from the sandpile—and just as sudden, with his free hand, he rammed a fist into the prisoner's lower stomach. The man doubled over, groaning for air. Lidel brought down his fist on the prisoner's neck.

The other black man lunged at Lidel. A guard tackled him, shoving a rifle butt into the prisoner's groin.

"Nobody ever threatens me with an E-tool," Lidel said. He called to the guards. "Pick him up."

Two guards lifted the black man by the arms, forcing him to stand upright. Lidel got in position in front of him, and struck him again in the same exact spot. The prisoner's legs warped and he went down. The guards forced him up.

Lidel stepped back, placing his hands on his waist. "Take him back to the compound." He glanced at the other man. "Take his friend, too."

The other man jumped to his feet, dazed, but still full of fight. Two MPs pounced on the prisoner and grappled him to the ground. Between the two of them they subdued the rebel and dragged him away along with his friend who stumbled weakly, held up by a guard on each side. The man coughed and sounded as if he had difficulty breathing.

"The rest of you men get back to work," Lidel ordered.

Dawson picked up the E-tool, gripping it fiercely. He gazed very evenly at Lidel. Chi-Chi tugged at his trousers. "C'mon, man."

Dawson watched the guards pushing the two prisoners into the back of a jeep. The realization was intolerable. *He* had backed down before Miller's threat. The black man hadn't. Dawson couldn't even get by on his pride anymore; his fear had neutralized him.

That night, inside the tent, Dawson lay on his cot, his hands behind his head and stared at the opaque glimmer of light from the Coleman lantern. He reflected on that fear that had been with him all along and that had manifested itself that same afternoon. Yes, it had always been there, lurking, secretive. But when had it begun? In boot camp. In combat?

He didn't have far to look. He could be honest with himself, now. Only once before had he felt it so palpably, that fear, and that had been with Yeager. He could taste it that one time. He could feel something looming that one time. They could all feel something coming. All except Yeager. It was bad enough they were choppered right into an ambush by mistake—Yeager wanted them to go out there and kick butt as if they were made of steel or something. There they were, pinned down by RPGs and that fucker wanted them to charge! He was crazy, and so was the company CO, the battalion CO, the regimental CO, the division commander—all of them, going all the way up to the guy commanding all the troopies in the field. They were all mad. They all followed orders. Yeager was like that, he always followed orders, even if it meant suicide. There was no stopping Gunnery Sergeant Yeager. When he was given an assignment that was it, and he completed his mission no matter how many men he lost. The man was a fool. Worse, he was a dedicated fool, and those you had to watch. Even now, so long after, it surprised Dawson the platoon went as far as it did with Sergeant Yeager. Anyone with any horse sense would have blown away the mother the minute he got up in the middle of the ambush and started yelling for them to move out. That was the first time Dawson thought he was going to get it. He remembered his teeth chattered with fear. They were in the first chopper to land and the gooks opened up with everything they had— mortars, AKs, you name it. As usual, S2 intelligence had had them land in a zone that was already registered by the NVA.

The pilot in his chopper got it right in the face, just as they came in. Dawson's stomach churned at the sight. The pilot's head looked like a melon that had been split in two. All there was to it was a black hole with veins and canals and all the blood mixed with the stuff inside. He ran out.

They all ran out of the chopper expecting to get killed. There were .50 caliber machine guns popping at them from everywhere. They were decimated right where they landed.

Despite that, they were lucky, that once. The chopper that came in after theirs, the one carrying second platoon, stopped an RPG round just as it touched ground. The helicopter folded like a cardboard box. The whole thing cracked in half and started burning. The explosion came later.

Dawson could remember saying only one word as he watched all those flames and the men screaming inside, and that was: "Wow."

He recalled how some men tried to get out. None of them had a chance. Almost the whole platoon burned alive. Then Dawson's landing party attracted enemy fire.

Early on Dawson had had a premonition something was going to happen. Before the operation, right during the platoon briefing he had specifically asked the lieutenant about the possibility of them landing in an ambush. It had occurred to him once before and that had been up toward the Da Krong River by the Laos border. This time they were to set down right in the middle of the Ashau Valley. Actually, they landed on a ridgeline bordering the Ashau toward the western end of the valley. According to S2 the ridgeline had been prepared by recon units for the landing. What they forgot to tell the company was that the NVA owned the whole place, recon units or no recon units. It was the sloppiest operation he had ever been on. Regiment did not soften up the place with artillery the way they were supposed to, or even pepper the area with machine gun fire from gunships, which was standard procedure when a hasty landing zone was prepared. They were sitting ducks. In the middle of it all, just as they ran for cover trying to avoid the treeline where the NVA was hidden and firing away, Yeager got up and shouted, "Follow me!"

The peach-faced lieutenant, just out of OCS and not to be outdone, decided to get up and charge the treeline, yelling for them to follow *him*.

Neither grasped a basic point: when a grunt in the bush gets in an ambush and he's got cover, he will *stay* in that protective cover and wait for the gunships to come and do their work. Unless, of course, you are caught in an ambush with no cover and nowhere to go, and *then* you charge toward the enemy fire. At least that way you catch them as much by surprise as they caught you. But there had to be two heroes in their platoon—the lieutenant and Gunny Yeager. The looey he could understand, the youth had never been in combat and was probably so shook up he couldn't think of anything but running ahead. It was a common occurrence. Sometimes a man who had never faced fire just froze, and sometimes—even though he was just as terrified—he would run forward without thinking. So their CO ran forward while the rest of the platoon, their company sergeant included, yelled at him to take cover. Dawson's squad was the point element for the whole sweep and they didn't take to the idea of getting wiped out before they even fired a shot. They hollered and yelled, and the looey kept running ahead, leaving them behind, hugging the ground—and he caught three AK rounds in the chest, one slug in the neck and God knows how many bullets in his stomach. Afterward there was an argument as to whether his stomach was ripped open by AK or SKS slugs. No matter. He died.

The lieutenant had been running right alongside Yeager, and Yeager, when he saw the lieutenant go down, bleeding out of every hole in his body, was engulfed in nameless terror. Dawson did not know how Yeager survived; no one in the platoon knew how he did it, but it was a miracle. The gunnery sergeant stopped in his tracks, looked around like a scared rabbit while the bullets whizzed all around him, and screamed. It was a terrifying cry. Like something heard from a dying man, or a beast. The reaction was pathetic and horrible. Yeager dropped to the ground and stayed there. He was fortunate to drop behind a small clump of brush so that the machine gunner on the other side of the treeline lost his target. Bullets raked all about the piece of shrub Yeager was hiding behind but they didn't hit him once.

When the platoon heard him scream they thought he had been wounded badly. Dawson concluded that Yeager must have been shot in the groin. Every man was as shaken as the gunnery sergeant. And he screamed everytime the North Vietnamese opened fire.

By this time the rest of the helicopters had landed in the LZ, but the other platoons coming in were caught in the same bind. Everybody was getting hit, and hard. The company CO was wounded in the shoulder; the company executive officer caught a bullet in the right eye. The other NCOs were in more or less the same boat so there was nobody around to take charge. Most of the platoon leaders were too busy trying to get their men behind cover to care about Dawson's squad pinned out front. And Dawson's squad was good, one of the best. Every one of them had been in combat before and knew what to expect. They were veterans and they looked after each other because their collective skins depended on it. They were tight. Dawson, in retrospect, could now say they loved each other. They couldn't help but love one another when they fought side by side and marched together, shared Js and C-rats and arguments and smokes and tiger piss beer together. There was something there; it was inexplicable. Dawson could have hated some of them, might have considered one or two of them the stupidest mothers on earth, but if a man belonged in his squad, and moreover, if he was a member of Dawson's fireteam, Dawson went to bat for him, because Dawson knew the man would do the same. Back home Dawson might have been a cop and the man a mugger, but in the bush they were brothers. That's the only way it could be. To become a good killer, a good grunt, you first had to learn to love the people right there beside you.

Yeager could never understand that. He was a lifer and the only thing he knew was the Corps, and *discipline*. But even so, he was a member of the company. And they could hear him screaming.

Two of Dawson's men decided to go out and try to drag Yeager back while the rest of them provided suppressive fire. Dawson realized it was a stupid idea. He was against it at first, because they didn't have much cover anyway, but he okayed it as squad leader. Yeager and his screams were grating on him, too.

He ordered his machine gunner to give covering fire while his people retrieved Yeager. It was heavy going, even though his two men stripped off their packs so they could move faster.

The two Marines crawled their way to the gunnery sergeant, and they found him without a scratch. They dragged him back. All the while Yeager was jabbering about going ahead. The two troopers had a hard time keeping Yeager under control.

Just as they were about to reach safety, both men were hit. An RPG round landed not far from them, and one fellow had a piece of shrapnel imbedded in his head. He died instantly. The other man, whose name was Jasper, and who had only two weeks for his tour to end, had his buttocks peppered with shrapnel. As for Yeager, a bullet grazed his left arm, but the way he carried on anyone would have thought he'd been mortally wounded. Yet scared as he was Yeager decided to get up and make a run for it. Jasper called after him to come back and stay put, it was safer on the ground. But Yeager kept on running, desperately trying to reach the platoon area.

Most of the platoon had found cover in a stretch of high elephant grass to the right side of the landing zone. That was the only real protection they had except for some bomb craters, and the craters were being blasted regularly. Luckily, they managed to lose themselves in the high grass. The NVA didn't have any targets in the open anymore, although they kept lobbing rocket-propelled grenades and mortars, and the elephant grass began to scatter up all around the Marines. The rest of the choppers had left as quickly as they came. Dawson knew they were totally alone. He couldn't bring himself to blame the chopper pilots, considering the resistance they had encountered.

Yeager made it back to them. Jasper did not. Another RPG round landed in the same spot and he was blown apart.

When Yeager got to the platoon he calmed down a bit. Dawson knew Yeager was embarrassed and ashamed. To counteract it, Yeager immediately set about running the show. At this time the men had nothing against the sergeant. A lot of people lost their nerve in combat, that was the name of the game. The first time Dawson had stumbled into a firefight he couldn't even fire his weapon until the platoon sergeant rushed over and cuffed him on the head and Dawson was so afraid of the noncom that he started firing back at the enemy.

Anyway, Dawson considered that Yeager had done something stupid, not cowardly. He was the first to land and he decided to charge, and not until he came to his senses and realized that he was out there in the open all by himself did he freeze. It happened to all of them, even in-country veterans, and the gunnery sergeant had two tours already under his belt. But the gunny was stubborn. He *had* to have things his way. He snapped at the radioman to see if they could get any artillery support. The LZ where they landed was about eight kilometers from a firebase that had been constructed only a week before.

Yeager began to shout orders on the radio, spouting off coordinates and degrees. Yeager called in for 155s. Dawson would have preferred A6 attack planes. Those jets could wreak havoc.

Yeager asked for the 155 shells to land right on top of them. He had called for a fire mission on his own men.

Later on, just before he had his retribution, Dawson fantasized bitterly how the North Vietnamese in the treeline must have laughing watching Marine artillery killing other Marines.

Dawson lost his whole squad. The platoon lost twenty-seven men. Among the survivors were the platoon sergeant and one of the corpsmen. Yeager also survived the slaughter.

Finally someone from another platoon had enough sense to call in the correct coordinates and the treeline started to get hit. Also, they hollered for air support and a couple of A6s did come to their aid. Not long after that the medevacs came in and they were all flown to Charlie Med, dead and wounded alike. The surgeons at the field hospital couldn't believe it. A theory sprang up as to how the company had stumbled upon an NVA regiment. The truth was too stark; it was so hard to imagine that someone had erred so disastrously.

The company commander remained at Charlie Med for a week recuperating from his wound. The XO and the platoon lieutenant had been killed so the only people who could verify what Yeager did was Dawson, the radioman and two others who'd been with them in the high grass. The two men eventually died of their wounds. The radioman was shot in the right leg just as he was boarding a medevac and he didn't return from Charlie Med until a week later. The platoon sergeant, another potential witness, was nowhere to be found.

When Dawson came back to Quang Tri he spilled the beans to his first sergeant, and the top couldn't believe it, either. Yeager denied the whole episode.

Dawson went to the battalion CO about it, and the CO questioned Yeager. The gunnery sergeant contended that he had been wounded in the arm while tending to his men and couldn't recall a thing. All the people at the radio shack could remember was that someone had called in for arty support using the right code designation: two-one and two-two, and had ordered 155 H and E.

The battalion colonel bought Yeager's story, and so did the rest of the brass. Dawson correctly assumed they didn't want any scandal in their command. He also assumed that only he could set things right. He felt, he *knew* he owed it to his squad. He owed it to himself; if he didn't set it right he could never face himself again. It would be as if he had become a part of the scheme, as if he had shared in Yeager's crime. That was what it was, a crime. Yeager had terminated something that Dawson loved. Dawson couldn't forgive the sergeant for this. Possibly he could've overlooked the idiotic charge on the treeline, the turning back, the selfishness, the hardheadedness, even the mistake with the arty. All that he could stomach, but not the killing of the feeling inside.

Four days later Dawson sidled into Yeager's tent. Dawson had been assigned the late night watch on the perimeter. He took a chance leaving his foxhole, but the two other men with him were asleep, and he knew there wasn't going to be any line check that night. He had planned it to the letter. He could've taken the easy way out and just flipped a grenade into the gunny's hooch, but he didn't want that. True, frags left no fingerprints, but Yeager shared his tent with the company first sergeant and another man. Dawson only wanted Yeager, not anyone else's blood on his hands.

While Yeager slept, Dawson stabbed the gunnery sergeant three times in the chest. He did it skillfully, and with a minimum of noise.

Later, the one thing he recalled vividly was the quick slide of the blade to the left of the sternum, right where he imagined the heart would be. Three quick punches, right in the chest, but muffled, since he had wrapped the knife handle and hilt around his right hand with a light towel, the type you carried into the bush around your neck to soak up the sweat and lessen the pressure of the packstraps on your shoulders. He had also bound a towel on his left hand so that it was like a glove, the better to stifle Yeager's mouth and nose. Yeager had lurched upward with the first thrust of the knife, almost as if a spring had been implanted in his back. Dawson had had to bear down with the toweled hand, pushing the sergeant back into the cot. But there was no other sound. Just the muted punches. No snap of blade hitting bone, nor the rush of blood which he had expected. With the second lunge, Dawson felt the stickiness of the hilt bound to the edge of his hand. It was viscous, as the blood seeped into the towel. There was no chance of severing an artery. Dawson knew exactly where to strike. Instead, with the final lunge into the heart, he felt a slight resistance on the blade as the knife tore through muscle. This time, Yeager was still. No more movement. The knife slid out from the chest. It had taken less than sixty seconds.

He crawled out of the tent, and once free, he ran. He didn't know how or where but he ran until his legs gave out, and then he faced the horrendous truth that in destroying Yeager, in destroying the evil of Yeager, Dawson had destroyed something in himself.

Running back to the perimeter Dawson dropped his hunting knife, and didn't realize it till the following morning when it was too late. He went back to the area, he retraced his steps but couldn't find the knife.

CID found the knife for him, and he was brought up on charges. It wasn't hard for them to put two and two together and come up with him as the prime suspect. Dawson readily admitted to the killing and he wasn't sorry, either. He had settled accounts.

JULY 10TH

A week had elapsed since he came to H&S Casual. A week to get the hang of it, take in all the angles. A week in which to realize there weren't any angles, not in the usual sense. He wasn't a corporal in a duty station back home. The privilege of rank didn't matter simply because he had no rank. He was a prisoner, not even worthy of the complimentary title of Marine. In terms of regular duty the motives were gone. But the Brig did have its caste ladder same as on the outside. The Brig, like any mass organization, was elaborately societal, with all the idiosyncrasies of the corporation. Dawson had been in the service long enough to know that any organization, whether based on the profit motive, philanthropy or fear, had its minor dispensations. There were always certain undefined niches that any employee could attain provided he knew the ropes. In the Marine Corps they called it skating, to the Army it was known as goldbricking. The civilian corporations called it driftwood, and labor organizations termed it featherbedding. Every entity provided for it. Dawson figured the Brig was no different. He had already seen one example of an inmate who had garnered a compensatory niche, Murphy the Brig barber. That man didn't know a thing about barbering. What was there to know? The Brig had only one style—straight baldy, which wasn't difficult to do with an electric clipper. There were others—the trustees who worked the laundry detail; the prisoners assigned special duty with the Admin pogues; the inmates working the supply shed.

From the first day, when he saw those two prisoners dragged from the mess hall, he knew Medium Detention was not for him. Not that he was afraid, just that he sought the best accommodation. Medium Detention did not provide it; its environment was hostile. Added to it was the aggravation of the sandpile. In that one week of confinement he had seen four confrontations between guards and prisoners—all of it at the sandpile. There was an element in the heat and the dust of the place that was conducive to flare-ups, he reasoned. And every collision involved a guard and a black prisoner. Every time, from what he had seen, the guard incited the provocation. This made for a phenomenal paranoia among the blacks. The feeling was that there was a wholesale campaign to decimate them. Even Dawson felt it. He shrugged it off. When half the sentinels were poor Southern whites, what could you expect? Only it wasn't that simple. There were underlying causes to be sure, and one of them, Dawson was convinced, was the prevailing spirit of black militancy; it worsened the situation. Black pride demanded they never bow to the power of the billy or the cell block. The guards took this as a threat to their authority. This being the case, the MPs responded accordingly. Dawson suspected that one day the whole thing would explode right there in Medium Detention. That was one day he wanted to avoid.

Where could he go? Admin Sec would be nice. A trusteeship would be better. Problems. A trusteeship took too long. The trustees were usually inmates who were confined indefinitely. Most inmates spent too short a time in the Brig to either brown nose their captors or be considered trustworthy. Dawson had neither the time nor the stomach for that type of dealing.

Dawson had a theory: the world was run by the Scheme. If a person sought a prize he invariably wrangled his way to it by hook or crook, mostly crook. Everybody was an advocate of the gimmick. On the other hand, that was precisely why a good percentage of the people who tried to gain something for nothing never got anywhere. They were so adept at subterfuge that it was the only way they could function. Dawson believed in another method. Everyone was so involved in the con that no one tried the direct approach. This method, because of its novelty, had always worked for him.

Following this deduction, Dawson went to the supply shed and told Lance Corporal Rodriguez, the man in charge, that he wanted to work in the supply room. Rodriguez, was impressed by Dawson's point-blank approach. When he was asked why he wanted to work in supply, Dawson simply told him he wanted to avoid the back-breaking turmoil of the sandpile. Rodriguez decided Dawson was either incredibly naïve or else the smartest operator in the Brig.

Dawson was assigned as a helper to the supply detail.

Nothing good ever lasts. That was another of Dawson's theories, and one which he had forgotten momentarily. In his new position he was fairly certain that within a few weeks he would get a trusteeship. His new boss, Rodriguez, had implied as much. Every privileged hire in the Brig had to be legitimized. Dawson was happy. He didn't give a continental about what the other prisoners thought or said about him. He had availed for himself the least burdensome path.

Oddly, Chi-Chi approved of what he had done. "Man, I woulda done the same if I'd had the luck," Chi-Chi told him. "Shit, anything is better than that fuckin' sun out there. Don't pay no mind to these other dudes around here, man. If they talk about how you got the cushy gig it's because they's pissed they couldn't get it first."

In his new position Dawson did well. The work wasn't difficult. Tedious, of course. All day he sorted out the equipment in the supply bins. The task involved no physical effort, with the atmosphere a lot cooler than that which prevailed on the outside details. Once in a while a load of C-rations would come into the supply shed for stacking. Dawson, along with the two other prisoners who worked the depot, would smuggle as many cans and C-ration cigarettes as he could. While the three new replacements in the tent vied for the favors of their guards, Dawson and Chi-Chi were eating C-rats at night and smoking every day.

Three days after he had been working in the supply room, Dawson received a surprise that warmed his heart. Following in his footsteps, with the same exact strategy, Chi-Chi had gotten himself assigned to the detail. The depot was already filled with its quota of helpers; this made it more fascinating as to how Chi-Chi had managed to break into the coveted realm. Between the sorting and counting of old canteens and cartridge belts, Chi-Chi explained to Dawson how he had convinced Rodriguez to take on another man. Very simple: Chi-Chi had appealed to the basic chauvinism of any Puerto Rican. It was his ace in the hole. Being a kinsman himself, Rodriguez just couldn't deny a fellow compatriot the chance to take it light. Invoking everything from memories of the *barrio*, Hunts Point Palace, *cuchifritos*, *merengues*, and Johnny Colon's *Bugaloo Blues*, Chi-Chi drilled into the man mercilessly. Rodriguez was being snowed and he knew it, but in spite of it, this kid was blood. Chi-Chi fed on it: "Man, there ain't no other blood but us two, and 'Ricans gotta stick together. It make no dif'rence that you an MP and I'm a prisoner. If we don't watch out for each other, who will?" Rodriguez laughed his head off, calling Chi-Chi the biggest brown-nosed bastard he ever met, but being a good-natured individual, what the hell. The supply room took on a new addition.

Dawson grinned at Chi-Chi. "You bullshitting motherfucker, you mean the guy actually bought all that crap you handed him?"

Chi-Chi smiled roguishly. "I'm here, ain't I?" He looked around, making sure Rodriguez wasn't in the room. "Man, spics is all the same. They got this real heavy sense of unity, dig? Just like the brothers. Any 'Rican, I don't care who he is—may be my worst enemy, but the minute I start rappin' to 'im 'bout our blood and all that shit, that dude will help me get anythin'. I seen it happen so many times. Two 'Ricans hate each other, but the minute a cop threatens one of them, they's the best of friends together against the fuzz. That supply P Rodriguez knew I was bullshittin' him, but he a 'Rican and so am I. He can't deny that."

"Ethnic awareness," Dawson said.

"Whut?"

"It's a phrase I read in a book somewhere."

Chi-Chi picked up a handful of cartridge belts from the floor, tossed them in a bin. "You read a lot, don't 'cha?"

Dawson counted the belts and posted the amount on his supply sheet. "Just Marvel Comics."

"I serious, you sound like you're smart. Sometimes you use them big words and stuff. You go t' college?"

Dawson leaned his back on the edge of the bin. "No, I din't go to college, and I ain't so smart. If I was, I wouldn't be here."

Chi-Chi spat on the wooden floor. "Guess you can say that about all of us."

"Yeah, guess you can."

A moment of silence stretched between them. Dawson stared at the floor, the clipboard in his hand. Chi-Chi stretched, groaned. "Man, this job gets boring after a while."

Dawson smirked. "You wanna go back to the sandpile?"

"Fuck no, man." Chi-Chi winked. "Being a brownie is better."

Dawson grinned. "Chi-Chi, you're a man after my own heart." He hung the pencil on his ear. "C'mon, let's start on the canteens."

They went across the room to a pile of canteens scattered about in a far corner. Chi-Chi picked out an empty supply bin on the half section covering the wall. "We can put 'em here."

"Okay," Dawson handed the clipboard to Chi-Chi . "Here, you mark 'em down. I'll do the counting this time."

"Fair 'nuff," Chi-Chi said. "By the way, where's our honcho?"

Dawson squatted on his haunches and examined some plastic canteens. "He down in the laundry having his game."

"Game of what?"

"Game of chance."

"What does that mean?"

Dawson stood up and tossed one canteen into the bin. "That means, my dear friend Cheech, that every morning our supply honcho, after he checks us in, goes over to the laundry tent and has a running poker game with the Ps from Admin. They keep it up till chowtime when Rodriguez comes back. Then he checks to make sure we're still here, and he skys back to the game. The game usually ends about four in the afternoon, whereupon our supply honcho comes back, goes into the back storage room, and sleeps—when he ain't reading a comic book, that is."

Chi-Chi was amazed. "Man, what a life. Does he know there's a war goin' on?"

"Dunno, I seriously doubt it."

"Talk about skatin'," Chi-Chi said soberly.

"In a way it's good," Dawson observed. "He's never in the storage room. We do the work anyway we please—as long as it gets done. He don't fuck with us at all."

"That don't sound too bad. I think I'm gonna dig this place." Chi-Chi looked around expansively. "Yes, sir, I can feel I'm gonna dig this place."

Dawson pointed to the canteen pile. "We better get this done if we wanna stay here."

"By all means," Chi-Chi said.

Dawson sat next to the canteen batch and began to sort out the ones that were usable. He examined one canteen with a large dent on the flat side. It looked like a compressed rubber ball. "You think this is usable?"

Chi-Chi took the canteen in hand. "I don't see no holes. Don't think it got no leaks." He threw the canteen in the bin. "Fuckit, it's usable." He marked it down on the clipboard.

Dawson snorted. "If I was in the bush and they gave me a canteen like that I'd shoot the supply sergeant."

"Fuckit," Chi-Chi said. "They wanna use that equipment, let 'em use it. We don't hafta worry 'bout the bush no more."

Dawson smiled sadly. That was right, they were in detention now. The freedom of the field was no longer theirs. "Yeah, I guess we don't."

"What's your count?"

Dawson crossed his legs Indian style, and counted the assortment of canteens. "We got ten usables and twenty-nine unusables."

Chi-Chi jotted the figure on the pad. "Heavy. Now we can put 'em away." He lowered the clipboard. "What we gotta do after this?"

"Nuthin'. Just take it light and wait till Rodriguez gets back."

"Mmm. That don't sound too bad."

"Right on." Dawson stood up and helped Chi-Chi load the canteens on the bin. They were done in four minutes. "Now all we do is sit and wait."

"*That* sounds groovy."

They sat with their backs to the wall, smoking contentedly.

"You hungry?" Dawson asked.

"Sure," Chi-Chi said, "You got some grit?"

"If you don't mind C-rats we got a whole bunch."

Chi-Chi didn't quarrel. "Slick, I'd love me some C-rats."

Dawson got up and went over to the countertop. He knelt behind it, searching the hollow interior facing the storage room. He brought back three ration cartons.

"Hey, where you get them from?" Chi-Chi asked.

"Once in a while we get a shipment of emergency rats. We stack 'em in the back storage room. In between, we liberate a few."

Chi-Chi smacked his lips. "Man, this place is together."

"It is, Cheech, it is." Dawson checked the carton. "What you want, spaghetti, beef slices, or beans and franks?"

"Gimme the beans and dicks."

"There you are," Dawson said. "You got an opener?"

"Yeah, I got one." Chi-Chi removed the various cans from his carton, picking up a dessert tin. "Goddamn, pound cake. Wow, never thought I'd see that again. I love pound cake."

"So do I," Dawson hinted. "It's my favorite dessert. Why don't 'cha give me half? I'll give you half my fruitcake."

"Yuk. You can keep your fruitcake, I hate it." Chi-Chi winked. "But I'll give you half my pound cake. Us spics got good hearts."

"With Irish food," Dawson added. He held up a small tin. "Look at that? See what it says? Finney Peanut Butter. Good brand name."

Chi-Chi was unimpressed. "It sucks. The best peanut butter I ever tasted in C-rats was Gillis Peanut Butter."

"Gillis? Never had much of that in Quang Tri."

"That's 'cause you people up north still using World War Two C-rats. Down south we gettin' the new stuff, just produced."

Dawson was curious. "Let's see." He read the label on the carton. "Individual Combat Meal . . . here it is—1950."

"1950?!" Chi-Chi was astonished. "Is that the date on that?"

"That's what she says." Dawson threw away the carton. "So you people gettin' new stuff, huh?"

"Man, 1950." Chi-Chi looked at his meal can. "This from Korea!"

"Chi-Chi, the only ones who get new stuff is Army. Marines always get the leftovers."

"No argument there, bro'."

Dawson looked at Chi-Chi, felt a weird spasm. Bro'? he thought. He had heard the phrase so often among 'Ricans, blacks and their fellows. It was the most common exchange between brothers in his former platoon. Not knowing why, he felt a comforting warmth. Bro'?

Chi-Chi unwrapped a plastic spoon, dug it into the beans and franks. "Man, this is living. After that crap at the mess hall this is like a feast."

Dawson chewed his beef slices. "There's beaucoup more of this shit in the storage room, so dig in."

Chi-Chi put down his can. "Somebody coming."

"I don't hear no one."

Chi-Chi held up his hand. "Lissen."

Footsteps were dragging on the small yard outside the supply room. The footsteps grew louder.

"Damn, Rodriguez come back early today," Dawson guessed.

Chi-Chi started to get up. "Looks like the party's over."

Dawson held his arm. "Don't worry 'bout it. Ol' Rodriguez won't say nuthin' so long as the work's done."

"What about the C-rats we eating?"

"He don't care about that. All that dude cares about is poker and getting the work done on time."

Chi-Chi rested his back on the wall, picked up the meal can. "Okay slick, if you say so."

"You don't hafta worry about Rodriguez," Dawson assured him.

They didn't have to worry about Rodriguez, but they did have to worry about Miller who entered the supply room, lifted the countertop, went to the storage area and came to a halt in front of Dawson and Chi-Chi, who stood up immediately. Miller had found the pot of gold at the end of the rainbow. Two turds, standing there, food smears on their faces, cigarette butts strewn at their feet. Miller felt a chill and then a thrill. He had caught them without redress.

"What the fuck do you turds think you are doing?" he brayed. "What is this? A fuckin' banquet? Is it the Marine Corps ball or something? You turds suppose t' be workin', goddamnit. Where's Rodriguez?"

Dawson stood at attention, staring straight ahead. "Sir, request permission—"

"Speak, motherfucker!"

"Sir, I don't know where Lance Corporal Rodriguez is at, sir."

"What you suppose to be doing here?"

"We're sorting the storage equipment, sir."

Miller stood with his legs apart, arms akimbo. "Why ain't 'cha doing it?"

"We did it already, sir."

Smart alecks, Miller thought. "Who gave you permission to have a banquet?"

"Sir, we're not—"

"Shaddup! Where you steal them C-rats from?"

"Sir, we didn't steal no C—"

"Shaddup! Where you steal the cigarettes from?"

"Sir, we didn't steal no cig—"

"Shaddup! Who gave you permission to take a break?"

Chi-Chi and Dawson looked at each other.

"Who gave you permission to look at each other?"

Chi-Chi and Dawson did not look at each other.

"You fuckers are too smart for your own good. You thought you could beat the system, you thought you could beat me. Well, you can't ladies. The minute I found out you was in supply I knew what you was up to. I don't know how you got in supply, but I'm gonna make sure you're back in the sandpile—tomorrow! I don't like smart alecks who think they can break the rules and get away with it."

"We ain't breaking no rules," Chi-Chi blurted.

"Shaddup! What the fuck you call this mess?" Miller waved at the tins and cartons on the floor. "Since when do prisoners get to do what they please, eat what they please?" He poked a finger in Dawson's chest. "You don't eat shit less we tell you. You fuckers stole C-rats—and on Brig time. Ladies, you are fucked. We gonna wait till Rodriguez come back, then you babes is gonna see the Top. He'll love ya when he hears this."

The weight was upon them. The rations in their stomachs turned rancid.

Miller stepped back and gazed at the storage bins. The varied equipment was stored neatly, very military looking. "This what you people did?"

Chi-Chi and Dawson stared straight ahead.

"It looks shitty to me." The old grin came to Miller's face. "Step aside, ladies. I'm gonna show you how to fix this place."

Chi-Chi and Dawson remained still.

"I said, step aside, ladies," Miller gripped the handle of the billy attached to his belt. "You ladies wanna get in more trouble than you're in now?"

Dawson took a deep breath, held it.

"Step aside, turds. I ain't gonna tell you again." The grin had departed from Miller's face.

The men moved to the side of the storage bin.

Miller's grin returned. "That's better. I like obedient prisoners. For a minute I thought you people was gonna be like the niggers."

Dawson felt his gorge rising; he strained to keep it down. Standing beside him, Chi-Chi was grinding his teeth.

Miller went into his tantrum. He rampaged through the top bins that were level with his height, tossing out all the equipment. Canteens, cartridge belts, billies, holsters, blankets, hard hats, all the supply he could grab went clanging, bouncing, clattering to the floor. He did not stop with the bins. Invigorated by his outburst, he ran to the side of the storage panel and pulled down the whole half section covering the wall. The metal bin assembly crashed on the floor, raising a firmament of dust above the room.

Miller spoke to the prisoners. "See that? Now you gonna fix that. And ya gonna do it before Rodriguez gets here. You best be done in ten minutes and be outside, standing at attention, waitin' for me and Rodriguez." He ambled over to the countertop. "You better start on it now, ladies. You got nine minutes." He raised the countertop and walked out.

Dawson smacked his fist into his palm. "That fucker! That no-good-rotten-motherfucker."

Chi-Chi took in the mess in front of them. "That no good Anglo fucker. Goddamn, look at that. He done fucked up everythin' we did."

Dawson choked. "Ohhh . . ."

"What're we gonna do, man?"

"I don't know," Dawson said angrily. "That flaky cocksucker . . ."

"He gave us ten minutes to fix it up, man. What we gonna do?"

Dawson surveyed the litter sprawled under the weight of the storage rack. The salt on the wound. "C'mon," he said, taking hold of one end of the overturned bin assembly.

Chi-Chi reluctantly grabbed an edge on the other side. They

heaved, lifting the rack back in place against the wall. Working very rapidly, sloppily, they tossed the equipment into the bins.

Chi-Chi dusted his hands. "That's that."

"Not quite." Dawson thumbed at the countertop. "Now comes the bad part. We gotta go meet our host—remember?"

Chi-Chi's lips contorted. "Shit. We did our work."

"I know, but we gotta go out and meet 'im. And at attention, too."

"Man, someday I'm gonna meet that mother on the outside, and when I do—talk about a job."

"Until that time come we gotta do what he says." Dawson reminded.

Chi-Chi rubbed his hands nervously. "Let's get it over with."

Walking out the doorway, Dawson stumbled over something and fell on his face. Miller removed his foot from the entrance way, that silly-ass grin all over his face. "My, my, Dawson, I think you fell."

Dawson turned on his side and looked up at the Mole. He didn't know whether to get up and rush Miller or stay safely on the ground.

"You should look where you're goin', Dawson," Miller said. "Never know when you might stumble over something."

Chi-Chi came over and gave Dawson a hand.

"Let 'im get up by himself," Miller said huskily. "He got two hands, he ain't no invalid."

Dawson got up, wiped his trousers, avoiding Miller's eyes.

"Rodriguez ain't shown yet," Miller said, "but that's awright, I got my friends here to take ya back." He was referring to the two MPs standing behind him, very quiet, very determined looking. Two big men, same as Miller, waiting for a chance to pounce on the prisoners. Dawson noticed they carried billy clubs in their hands.

Miller got in front of Chi-Chi . "D'ya like them C-rats?"

Chi-Chi was silent.

"I asked ya a question."

"Sir, request permission—"

"Speak."

"Yes sir, I like them C-rats."

"I'm glad. We gonna make sure you get more when we get back." Miller gazed at Dawson, and back to Chi-Chi . "I'm glad you people came out of the supply room on time. For a minute I thought you wasn't gonna come out." Miller's eyes gleamed. "I was hoping you wouldn't. But you did, which is good for me. I don't like hard asses. I want my boys to be good." He patted Chi-Chi's cheek. "You a good boy, right? You ain't gonna give us trouble. Not like no nigger, right?"

Dawson stared at his feet. Could he ever shake off the clinging shame?

Miller put an arm around Chi-Chi's shoulder. "Y'know, Curley, I believe you're the type of turd who don't want no trouble with nobody, who do what he's told, right?"

Chi-Chi was employing an almost superhuman will in repressing his anger. He wanted to tear into that grin, see the teeth roll out in scabs of blood smeared on his fists. On the other hand he was afraid of retaliation. The classic state of impotence.

Miller took out his billy club. He let it drop to the ground. The hollow thud of wood on dirt was a counterpoint to Chi-Chi's sterile rage. "Pick it up," Miller told Chi-Chi.

The prisoner bent down, picked up the billy. Miller put out his hand, looking very pleased.

The prisoner handed the billy club to the guard. Miller was satisfied, but not relieved. He slipped the billy into his cartridge belt loop. "You gotta learn you can't get away with nothin' here, Curly. You hafta be taught that this ain't no rest camp. You and your friend think you know the answers. You don't. *I* know the answers, that's what you gotta learn."

Miller picked his nose while he was talking. Very deliberately he dug out a piece of mucus, rolled it in his fingers, and smeared it on Chi-Chi's fatigue shirt, right above the breast pocket. "You gonna be a good boy, turd?"

The cord was broken. Chi-Chi could take a lot, he had been worked over by experts in the past—some actions were unbearable. He made himself stand straight although his legs were quivering. "Go fuck yourself," he said.

"What did you say?"

"You heard me, bitch."

Miller slapped Chi-Chi. Dawson rushed forward and struck Miller on the side of the face, toppling him backward. Chi-Chi jumped on top of Miller, pummeling him on the head and neck. The two guards rushed Dawson; he swung at them but his blows fell on the hard

plate of their shoulders. One of them came from the side and gave
Dawson a roundhouse punch that caught him straight on the jaw,
sent him reeling. Dawson was out of the fight.

Chi-Chi stayed on top of Miller, clutching the latter's neck in a
stranglehold. The two guards came to Miller's rescue, grappling Chi-
Chi around the neck and shoulders. He wouldn't let go. Miller gasped.
One of the guards struck Chi-Chi on the back of the head with a billy.
He had to strike him two more times before Chi-Chi let go of Miller's
neck. The prisoner fell back, blood pouring from his head.

Miller stood up, rubbing his neck with both hands, breathing
heavily. "That fuckin' spic." He strained. "I'll make sure he never gets
outta here alive."

"What we gonna do with 'em?" one of the guards asked.

Miller massaged his throat. "We gonna take 'em to the Top and
then after he see 'em we gonna take 'em to the cell block where *I'm*
gonna see 'em." His hard breathing had not eased. "Pick 'em up."

Chi-Chi stirred, moaned softly. Miller took a step and kicked him
in the stomach. Chi-Chi groveled on the ground, saliva dribbling on
his chin. The two guards picked him up, holding his sagging body
between them

Dawson rolled on his back. The glitter of sunlight flooded his eyes.
He blinked twice before he could focus on Miller's boot coming
down on him. He turned his face. The rubber sole of the boot struck
him on the side of the head, below the cheekbone.

They took him down a long corridor with five rows of cells on each
side. The blocks of cells were solid concrete construction, huge
bunkers that had been joined together side by side. Overhead, covering the cells, was a wire-mesh ceiling with a partial covering of
camouflage canvas. Gaping holes in various parts of the material
allowed strips of sunlight to peep through the roof enclosure. The
guard opened the door to one of the cells and tossed him inside. He
landed on the concrete floor, his forehead striking the pavement.

"What's this?" He heard a strange voice.

"You got company," another voice said behind him.

"This is solitary," the first voice said. "What he doin' in my cell?"

"Don't ask no question." It was definitely the voice of a guard. "Till
we find some other room for him, he'll stay here with you."

"This is a fine Brig," the voice said. "A man can't stay in his own solitary."

"Shut your trap," the guard commanded. "We'll be back to check up on you later."

Dawson heard the door slammed shut, then receding footsteps. He rolled on his back, lifted his head. It was dark inside, like a pup tent at night. A shaft of light fell through a small barred window at the top of the door. The ray had to strain through minute squares of wire mesh that overlay the steel bars. Dawson rubbed his face, feeling the broken skin near the eye. Two sturdy hands grabbed his shoulders, shaking him vigorously.

"Dawson," the voice called. "Hey, Dawson." The voice was sluggish, phlegmatic.

He removed his hand from his eye. Someone hovered over him.

The prisoner slapped his face gently. "How'd ya get here?"

He pushed the hand away, made an effort to sit up. The prisoner cradled his back and helped him rise. Dawson sat up with his head drooping on his chest. His arms and shoulders ached; the skin on the side of his face was burning. He touched his upper lip and discovered his nose was bleeding.

"Good lord, man, they did you a job," the prisoner said.

Dawson giggled.

"Hey, you awright?"

He raised his head, focused on the man in front of him. There was a dark spot in the middle of his eyes. The spot dimmed, began to evaporate. Through a residual haze he saw a steep face set apart by cuts and contusions that had hardened and curled on the skin. Beyond the tight flesh and protuberant lumps he recognized a face he had not expected to see again. "Zimmerman? Zim, is that you?"

The lump of flesh smiled, showing bare gums with six missing front teeth. "How you doin', Vic. Never thought I'd see you here."

Dawson twisted his swollen mouth enough to form a grin. "Zim, you old bastard."

"Come on, let me get you to the rack." Zimmerman helped Dawson to his feet and guided him to the hard wooden bunk on the corner of the cell. Dawson lay down on a spare board that had neither blanket nor mattress. "Goddamn, how'd ya get here?" Zimmerman asked.

Dawson wiped his nose. "It's a long story." His words were thick.
"Who worked you over?"

"The Mole," Dawson coughed.

Zimmerman removed his fatigue shirt, rolled it in his hand, and
began to wipe the blood from Dawson's cheek and mouth. "I'm
familiar with the individual. You must've goofed something bad for
him to give you this working over. Usually when they do work you
over they don't touch the face—Lidel's orders."

"I punched him," Dawson said.

Zimmerman whistled softly. "That is bad. Nobody gets away with
throwing hands with a P. What made you do it?"

"He pushed me."

"He pushed you? That's nothin'. Wait till you been in the cell block
a few days." Zimmerman touched the sensitive spot above Dawson's
left eye. Dawson winced. "That hurt?" Zimmerman asked.

Dawson nodded.

"You're lucky he din't get your eye, you'd be blind right now. What
he hit you with, a billy?"

"His boot," Dawson said.

Zimmerman peered at the wound. "He fucked up your face. We
gonna have to get some water to clean out the cuts. Can't do that
now, have to wait till chowtime. They'll bring us some water then."
He forced a loose smile. "Welcome to the club."

Dawson massaged his scraped cheek. "My pleasure to be here."

"How'd you get here anyway?"

"They got me on a murder charge."

"Murder? Who?"

"The gunny," Dawson said.

"The gunny? You mean Yeager?"

"Yeah."

"Did you kill 'im?"

Dawson didn't answer.

Zimmerman shook his head. "Dawson, you in a mess. Fuckit, we
both in a mess." Abruptly, he asked, "How's the people back in the
platoon?"

"Alright, I guess. We was out in the bush for about three days the
last time. A lotta people got hit."

"Who's left?"

"Oh, me, Smokey Collins, Doc Silva, Baker the radioman, and maybe three other dudes who got back from Charlie Med."

"You people musta hit the shit real bad."

"We did."

"Where was it—in the Z?"

"Nope. The Ashau."

Zimmerman frowned. "Sheesh. That's the worse place to get hit. Did our baby-faced looey make it through?"

"He was the first one to get hit."

"It figures," Zimmerman said without feeling.

"Yeah."

"Is Jackson still around?"

"Naw, he got greased."

"How about Jasper?"

Dawson nodded. "He got it, too."

"And Lopez, the machine gunner?"

"Same. He got greased."

"*Damn!* Ain't there nobody left?"

Dawson shrugged. "Like I said, just me, Smokey and a few others."

"What about Korn, the platoon sergeant?"

"I don't know about him. I didn't see him after the op, though I think he survived."

"What a fuckin' waste," Zimmerman said bitterly. "All those good people." It's so unfair, he thought. But then when he tried to recall their faces he could only recollect vague features, like shadows of the men he had known. Somehow this angered him. What a fuckin' waste. He sighed.

"Remember how Lopez and Jackson useta blow Js all the time?" he reminisced.

Dawson recalled quite vividly. "Yeah. They were good heads."

"True," Zimmerman agreed in a low, sad voice. "They were all good heads." What a fuckin' waste, he kept on thinking. "Has the platoon got a new CO yet?"

"No. I don't think so. When I was there Smokey was still platoon honcho, and scuttlebutt was we wouldn't get a new officer until another op was set."

Zimmerman scratched his chin, letting his fingers scrape the stubble. "The third platoon, Kilo Company, the worse bunch of fuckups there ever was, and the best platoon up north. They must be the only platoon in I Corps with an NCO for a platoon commander right now, and a good one at that."

Dawson sat up on the wooden board. He placed a hand on the small of his back.

"Were you in charge of the squad after I left?" Zimmerman asked.

"Yeah." Dawson made an effort to stretch his arms. A pain shot through his side and under his armpits. He lowered his arms slowly.

"I figured you'd take over the squad. You were the only one who could handle it."

"That had nothin' to do with it. I was the only one with the rank."

Zimmerman grinned at him. "Haven't changed much, have you? You're still the most contrary sonofabitch I ever met."

Dawson grinned back. "Fuck you, Sergeant."

"If I wasn't in such a good mood I'd have you written up."

"Sure." Dawson placed his hands behind his neck and pressed down. "So this is the cell block." He extended a hand and touched the concrete wall. "I thought it'd be different."

"This is only our guestroom accommodations," Zimmerman said. "You ain't seen none of the other suites."

"I thought this was suppose to be solitary."

Zimmerman tickled the lean flesh under his chin. "It was for me till you got here. I figure the place is so crowded now they putting two men in a cell. It's actually suppose to be a one man cell—that's the whole purpose of solitary." He sneered. "You know the crotch, they work fuckin' backwards."

"Amen," Dawson said.

"Fuckin' backwards," Zimmerman repeated.

"How long you been here, Zim?"

"About a week, maybe two. Can't tell while I'm here."

"We heard you got caught, but I never thought you'd be in Maximum."

"Where else can they put me? I tried to bust out of this joint the first day I was here."

"Shit, where was you gonna go?"

"I don't know, as long as it wasn't here. I just wanted to get out."

"Were you plannin' to go back to Saigon?" Dawson asked.

Zimmerman looked at Dawson suspiciously. "How'd you know that?"

"Back in Quang Tri we found out you got caught in Saigon. So I figure that's the only place you could go."

"Yeah, that's where I was headed," Zimmerman admitted. "Didn't even get past the base area."

"Why'd you try to escape?"

Zimmerman looked at his calloused palms. "Man, I have to get away, that's all there is to it, I gotta sky."

"I figure it's gonna be difficult bustin' outta here."

"It is," Zimmerman asserted. "But nothin' ever stopped me, not the crotch, not nothin'."

"I know," Dawson smiled.

"How long you gonna be here?"

Dawson rubbed his upper lip, feeling a tender bruise on the right side. His fingers were absorbed with the tickling sensation. "I don't know, they din't tell me."

Zimmerman rested his jaw in his palm. "Hmmm, hittin' a P. Let's see—they might keep ya here for three days, maybe more."

"What they do to you here?"

"Most of the time just let you rot in a cell. It really ain't too bad, just that sometimes you can go looney not having anybody else around. You're here all by your lonesome and then they put that camouflage cover out there, and you don't know whether it's day or night. A couple of weeks of that can get to anybody."

"Anybody ever crack up?"

"Yeah, there's been two while I been here. But they were real hard cases. One of them stabbed a P. They kept him in solitary for a month. When they let him out the poor fucker was as batty as a fruitcake. He couldn't even talk right. All he did was scream something about incoming." Zimmerman shook his head sadly. "Poor fucker. They had to take him to the base hospital to see a shrink. He's probably in the funny farm by now."

"How many times you been in the cell block?"

"Four times counting this trip."

"What was the longest you stayed in here?"

"About a week."

"Doesn't it bug you?"

Zimmerman smirked. "This place? Shit, man, I got a system. If you got a system nothing can break you down." Zimmerman's torpid eyes glistened with new fervor as he explained it all. "Remember back in the bush I always told you that? If you got a system nothing can fuck you up."

Dawson nodded.

"It's the same here. The only thing that kept my nose alive back in the field was that I took no unnecessary chances. I always knew when to back out whether it was in the bush or anything else. Here my system is the same, I don't take no unnecessary chances. In this case with my mind."

"I don't get it," Dawson said.

"Simple. Everytime I get in the cell block I do nothin' but PT."

"PT?"

"Yeah, calisthenics. I make it a point to exercise myself as much as possible. I go through my whole boot camp training all over again."

Dawson was puzzled. "You mean, just PT? Kneebends? Pushups? shit like that?"

"Exactly. It helps, friend. When you're in the hold all by yourself with no one around and you start thinkin' all sorta things, I tell you, it helps."

"Doing PT?"

"That's right, doing PT. Of course, everybody has to find their own thing, but for me, PT is it."

"You're crazy."

"Maybe so but I haven't cracked up yet."

"I figure you was crazy to begin with," Dawson said. "Maybe that's why solitary don't affect you."

"You think what you want, funny face, but wait till you're in here for a few days, *by yourself*, you'll know what I mean."

Dawson looked at the dark stained walls. Except for the beam sifting through the barred hole there was no other light. Even as they talked all he could see was the hazy outline of Zimmerman's dumpy features. When Zimmerman spoke, the teeth on the sides of his mouth shone pale white, tusk-like in the dark.

"On second thought, I think I can understand why somebody would go bug-fuck in this place."

"If you're not prepared for it, it's a pisser. There's a poor asshole across the street who's finding that out."

"Who's that?" Dawson asked.

"Right in the cell facing this one, on the other side. That's one dude who's been on full solitary for a week now."

"Full solitary? What does that mean?"

Zimmerman gestured toward the barred window. "See that? That's the only light that you'll get in this hole. This is just cell-block confinement. In full solitary they put a camouflage canvas cover on those bars so that no light can come in. This place gets dark as a rattrap. And that's what it is. Five days with no light, it can get to you." Zimmerman pointed to the doorway. "I know it's getting to him. Every time they bring him chow he just rants and raves. He don't even talk normal no more."

Dawson got up and stumbled to the door. He peered out the wiremesh hole. Through the mesh he could see a trapdoor just like the one to his cell. He calculated the other cell was about seven feet away, facing his door. On the top half of the trapdoor, where the barred hole was situated, a piece of green and brown camouflage canvas had been draped. The canvas was two feet square, much larger than the barred window. It was nailed to the door so that it completely covered the hole.

"You ever been in full solitary?" Dawson asked.

"Yeah, for the first three days I was in here. That was right after I tried to bust out. Only time I ever got the full treatment. It wasn't too bad, just three days. That's when I perfected my system. Only way I could've survived the thing."

Dawson stared at the door to the other cell. "How long they gonna keep 'im in there?"

"I don't know," Zimmerman said. "He been there a week. If they haven't let him out by now I guess they intend to keep him there beaucoup long."

"Who is he?"

"A brother."

"What he in for?"

"Who knows. Maybe he beat up a guard like you did."

"What makes you say that?"

"From what I hear, the only offense that get you in full solitary is either trying to bust out or fighting with a guard."

"If that's so, how come I'm not getting his treatment?"

Zimmerman smiled, his teeth—what remained of them—gleaming in a corner of the bunk. "You ain't a nigger."

Dawson lowered his eyes, looked at the faint outline of his feet. "So we get special treatment, huh?"

"It seems that way."

"The brothers always get their own special treatment?"

"From what I've seen, most of the time they do."

Dawson turned his back on the door. His head blocked the light shooting through the bars. "Real democratic place, ain't it?"

Zimmerman sat on the wooden board, leaned his back on the concrete wall. He observed Dawson through a full minute of silence. "I know what you're thinking, Vic. This place may be shitty but like us they got a system, and the niggers are the ones who hate that system the most. Ninety percent of the trouble here is between the blacks and the guards. Probably, except for us and a couple of other white dudes, the cell block is full of brothers. They create trouble and the guards are out to get them."

"Whites create trouble too," Dawson said. "You're here."

"I know, but with me, *and you*—whether you admit it or not—it isn't as personal. Sure, we hate the Ps, but we know, even when they make us eat shit, they're doing something worse to a brother in the other cell. No matter how bad they treat us, that brother is getting worse because that's the way it is, and we accept it."

"How about the brothers—they accept it?"

"Nope. It makes no difference whether they do or not. There isn't much they can do about it."

Dawson rubbed his right arm tenderly. The aches were beginning to subside. "It stinks, system or not. When you signal out somebody for special treatment it creates more trouble."

Zimmerman brought his feet up from the bunk. He leaned the back of his head against the wall. "Maybe there might be some trouble. I don't think so, though. The way things stand, what can the brothers do about it? What can anybody do about it? Ps got the guns and we don't. Simple. All we can do is obey and not give in too much."

"You'll never give in, will ya, ya lousy bastard," Dawson said affectionately.

Zimmerman's tusks shone in the near-darkness. "You know me, Dawson, I'll never give in."

"I know," Dawson said. "We missed you, fucker."

"I miss the platoon. We had some times, din't we?"

"Yes, that we did. Man, when I was in the bush I just wanted to get away from that platoon. Now I wish I was back there with 'em."

"Dreamer," Zimmerman sniffed.

"You feel the same way, bastard, and don't deny it."

"Yeah, you're right. I'd give my right nut to sky outta this place. Even try bustin' out again."

"I don't think you could do it with all the security they got here," Dawson said.

"Maybe not. But all I know is I have to give it another try."

"Why?"

"*Why?*—why the fuck not? You think I like it here?"

"No, man, of course not, but how long you suppose to be here?"

"I don't know," Zimmerman said. "Maybe a month, maybe less. This is mostly a transient center. They keep you here long enough for the paperwork to be done and then they ship you out to a prison back in the world."

"If that's so, your stay here is gonna be short anyway, so why you wanna bust out?"

"'Cause I don't wanta go to no prison back in the world."

"How much time you got to do?" Dawson asked.

"They gave me five years confinement and a UD."

"Damn! I thought they shoot deserters in wartime."

"No, they don't. They just put 'em away in some cell."

"That's a bit hard, ain't it? five years?"

"The colonel was out to get me," Zimmerman said. "That no good sonofabitch."

"Did he make the recommendation?"

Zimmerman scratched his armpit. "Yeah, he made the recommendation. That cocksucking, motherfucker told them to throw the book at me. He asked for no leniency, no mercy, no nothin'. I think he would've recommended the death penalty if he could've gotten away with it."

"I don't get it," Dawson said. "The colonel ain't the one who makes up the court."

"Man, don't be dumb. That fucker's the CO. He got the pull to tell that military court they can do anythin'. He told 'em right off he wanted me hung. He got his wish."

"Where was your trial held?"

"Here, Da Nang."

"If your trial was here, how could a regimental commander from up north tell these people what to do? Isn't that kinda farfetched?"

"Not really, Corporal. There's a new invention known as communications, and when a colonel wants to eat a general's mind all he does is call up and tell him about how we gotta make an example of this troopie who brought disgrace on the command. The general says, 'Will do, friend.' And there ain't nothin' that troopie or his defense counsel can do about it. Next thing you know, the dude is sent up the river for five long years." Zimmerman grunted. "I know one thing, by God, I'm not going to serve five years in no jail."

"Isn't there any way you can fight it?"

"How? They got me."

"I thought courts had that thing about appeals and stuff."

"*Sure*, I'm going to appeal while I'm serving five years in the slammer. No, ma'am, not this kid."

"If you bust out, where you gonna go?"

"Back to Saigon," answered Zimmerman.

"You gonna stay there the rest of your life?"

"Maybe. I'm not goin' back to America to serve five years. I'd rather do it in the bush."

"Zim, think about it seriously. How you gonna bust outta here?"

"I'll find a way. It's like my system, there's always a way of getting around anything, even captivity."

"So old Zim is planning the great escape."

"That's right."

"When you do get out how about sending me a postcard."

"You really think I'm kidding, don't you?" Zimmerman asked earnestly.

"Nope, I think you're very serious—that's what worries me. I never heard of nobody breakin' outta the Brig and livin' to tell about it."

"That's 'cause the Brig ain't never come up against the likes of Walter J. Zimmerman, ex-Marine."

Dawson smiled condescendingly. "I wish you luck, Zim. I really do."

"Luck has nothing to do with it, my boy. God helps those who help themselves, remember that. You can quote me if you want to, later on."

Dawson shook his head submissively. "Zim, you'll never change, that's why it's so good seeing you again."

"Every man lives his life as he sees it," Zimmerman said philosophically. Although Dawson couldn't figure out if the remark was meant to be serious.

Dawson walked over to the board and sat down beside his cellmate. Shortly he asked, "Zim, why you go UA?"

Zimmerman closed his eyes in the dark. He kept his feet up on the board, his forearms hanging over his knees. "Was wondering when you were gonna ask me that."

Again Dawson saw the faint glimmer of the cusps on the side of the mouth. "Does it bug you?"

"Yes and no," Zimmerman said. "I'm just surprised that it wasn't the first thing you asked me."

"Why?"

"It's natural. When any dude goes over the hill that's the first thing they ask, 'Why did he do it?'"

"Okay, why did you do it?"

Zimmerman smiled, keeping his eyes closed. The upper gums with the missing teeth resembled a rectangular box with white pointed ends. He spoke, and the white tips moved up and down. "Many reasons, son. Perhaps a shackjob in Saigon? Maybe I got horny? Or maybe I just got tired? Many reasons."

A long pause followed. Dawson sensed that a part of Zimmerman had receded into an internal gap, and a part of the dialogue was left pending, if not dead. He decided not to pursue the topic further.

After a decent interval, the talk went on, concerned with other fronts: Maximum Detention, the old platoon, another headlong discussion about the Brig. It was during this latter phase that they heard the noise. Footsteps and clanking of keys, opening of doors.

Zimmerman cut off the conversation. "Lissen, I think they're takin' him out."

"Who?"

"The brother." Zimmerman got off the bunkboard, walked over to the barred window. He motioned to Dawson. "C'mere, we might get to see the dude."

Dawson walked over to the lookout hole. "What's happenin'?"

"It looks like they're gonna do some work on the brother," Zimmerman said.

Dawson focused through the wire screen that made everything in the outside corridor appear in an opaque haze, like smoke reflected in a mirror. There were two men out there. Guards—big, stout types, both standing by the opened trapdoor. Cutting through the haze came the prisoner, stumbling his way to the edge. He was a burly black man. Dawson thought he saw a defiant grin on the man's face. Immediate recognition. The prisoner was the same individual who had been taken away during the disturbance in the mess hall. Two men had been dragged from the mess hall that day. Where was the other one? Dawson edged his face closer to the wire, his nose pressed against the net overlay.

The two guards said something hostile in loud, incoherent voices. The prisoner grinned. One of the guards slapped him. The prisoner kept on grinning. He stuck out his tongue at the guard. The guards yelled in his ear. The prisoner, grinning, fingered his nostrils, extracted a piece of mucus which Dawson could not see in the obscurity of the screen, and popped the particle in his mouth. One of the guards turned his head, spat to the side in disgust. The prisoner remained in place, leaning against the edge of the trapdoor, half of his body engulfed by darkness, the other half covered by the light outside. He stuck his head back in the cell, with only the right side of his fatigues in the corridor. He brought his head back into the light, still grinning. The guards grasped his arms, forced him away from the door, and marched him up the corridor. Dawson lost sight of them.

The cell door was left open. Inside was a bottomless void, the outer shaft to a tunnel. One of the guards came back, closed the door. The canvas cover on the barred hole had not been removed.

Dawson arched his neck to the side, trying to keep the guard in view. "Where they takin' him?"

Zimmerman went back to the rack. "I don't know. Maybe they gonna work him over, or maybe they figure he flipped his lid. In that case he goes to the base hospital."

"You think he's flipped?"

Zimmerman resumed his sitting position on the bunkboard. "Could be. He was eating his own snots. But then maybe he did it just to rile the guards. To convince them people you're cuckoo you gotta do beaucoup crazy shit." He chuckled. "The last fucker that went crazy in here wacked his meat right in front of the CO. That was something else."

"Damn, he *musta* been nuts."

"I guess he was, but the CO wasn't convinced. After the Ps beat the hell out of him they took him back to the CO and that fucker did the same exact thing. He took out his pecker and started playing with himself, right there in front of the honcho. By this time both the CO and Top were convinced this dude had to be crazy. So they sent him to the hospital, psycho ward."

Dawson took his seat beside Zimmerman. "I reckon that's the only way anyone can sky outta here, by going crazy or convincing them that you're crazy."

"Or by busting out," Zimmerman added.

"Dream on, sweet prince."

"Ain't no dream. No, ma'am, I'm skying out of this place, sooner or later."

"Sure," Dawson said lightly.

The cell door opened, a wedge of light invaded the sanctum. Both men stood up. A guard entered the cell. "Awright, we come to separate you two lovebirds. Got us another empty cell, so we going back to the way it's suppose to be. Which one of you pukes is Dawson?"

Dawson stepped forward. He was certain that the cell across the corridor would be his new home.

"Come with me, Dawson," the guard ordered.

Dawson turned, waved at Zimmerman still hiding in the angle of the corner. "See you around, Zim."

"You ain't suppose to speak, prisoner," the guard grunted. "Let's go."

He was taken to another cell, but not, as he had anticipated, the same cell where the black prisoner had been. The new dwelling was two doors away from Zimmerman's hole. At least he and Zimmerman were in the same cell-block row. This gave him comfort.

His spirit ebbed the instant he entered the cell. Dawson thought he loved solitude. But this aloneness was not of his choosing. Inside the pillbox was a terrible uncertainty, and he didn't know how to cope.

He had always wanted to be by himself, in peace. Back in school with the same dull teachers, the high school cliques, the meaningless studies, the fawning ritual of heavy necking that brought him closer to no one. He had felt fuller satisfaction behind the wheel of his 1968 Volkswagen—painted bright red and purchased out of his own savings via numerous part-time jobs. Driving up on the long weekends to Clinton County. Moments of full pleasure, those long rides from Cedar Rapids. It never lasted. He could not attain the isolation he needed. After high school had come one semester of state college with the same meaningless studies that he thought he had left behind. After dropping out from that enterprise—he found frats and house plans detestable—came a series of dead end jobs of short duration that neither offered nor promised the completeness he sought. "I should have been a farmer," he told himself. Shucking corn, tilling the land. The Great American myth. He had fallen for it. Just him and the land, alone with each other.

Now, at age twenty, and ten months into his first war, he had what he craved. No people, no studies. Four dank walls.

Two hours after being inside his new body, a great anxiety befell him. Just like in the stories, the walls seemed to be closing in on him. Then the darkness inside the cell became thicker and he actually saw the light from the wire-mesh window diminish. He moved and sat by the door, watching the spear of light that shot out from the hole and sprayed the far corner of the room. Then he found he had trouble breathing. At first it was a low sign, his chest tightened. Afterwards, every breath was insufficient to relieve the pressure. The more air he sucked in, the less oxygen he processed. He took in so much air he began to hyperventilate. His head became light, his lungs expanded. He breathed like a man on the point of exhaustion.

He clapped a hand over his mouth and nose. The breathing stopped for a few seconds. Slowly, he counted to ten, then removed his hand. The heartbeat had stopped. What! He turned his head at an angle and listened to the languid sounds from inside his chest. The faint thump grew louder, but not much louder. A regular fixed beat. He sat up on the cold floor, forced his muscles to relax. He counted once more to ten. He listened again; the breathing had slowed.

His mind wandered. He covered the first five years of his life in two minutes, approximately; the second five years in one minute or so, and the next ten years in a score of seconds. He realized, half-disappointed, for a young man of twenty he hadn't done much. He was back in the garage, reworking the grooves on the valves of the VW. He made love again, actually two times; once with his female cousin, age seventeen, and once with his last steady girl in the senior class at Madison High. He didn't consider the coed who was studying political science at Ohio State University, nor the receptionist at the real estate agency he had worked for; and there was one prostitute that summer he had worked as a waiter at an exclusive resort. The last three couplings didn't matter much. They had been shitty.

He concentrated on the most personal object in his reverie, the automobile. He stripped it down, tore it apart, built it up again. Every screw, nut and bolt, from the carb to the distributor cap, he inspected, repaired and cleaned. His fingers became stained with grease . . . He adjusted the butterfly valve so that he could get the proper acceleration with a minimum of push. The disc brakes were tightened so the old Volks could stop on a dime. He waxed and polished it till the chrome surface gleamed. Then he decorated the bug with decals, and dabbed the inside with fresh smelling pine scent. His passion was unrestrained—he painted a fair likeness of a nippled breast on the knob of the stick shift.

By the time the guard brought his meal, he had given the car a complete overhaul five times.

The door opened, the light crossed his path. Considerably less light than before. He reasoned it was getting toward sunset. The guard stepped into the cell, placing the meal in the middle of the floor. Dawson watched him carefully. The guard left the prisoner as quickly as possible. The door closed, the light vanished.

Dawson picked up the paper plate. Should of guessed it. Even here. Chili con carne and rice. He frowned. He sat by the barred hole, catching as much of the waning daylight as possible. By this time a small reflection peeped through the window. He ate very little.

A short time later the cell was completely sealed. No light anywhere. The wire mesh over the bars had turned to the color of a strainer smeared with dark paint. Night had come. Yet he couldn't sleep in a coffin. His anxiety heightened. In between the lures of cars, motorbikes and places he had been, he had to fight to keep from weeping.

Finally he fell asleep.

Much later they came for him.

"How do you like the cell block?" questioned Master Sergeant Lidel, arching his thick eyebrows that protruded from an outgrowth of flesh stretched on his forehead.

Dawson stood uncomfortably, constantly shifting his weight from one foot to the other. For some reason his legs ached.

"Keep still," the guard behind him warned. He felt the blunt end of a billy touch his back. His feet pressed flat on the ground. He stood straight as a board.

"That's alright." Lidel addressed the guard. "I think this man is beginning to understand our rules." He looked at Dawson. "Ain't that right, prisoner?"

Dawson knew the angles by now. His lips were sealed tight.

Lidel smiled. "See, the prisoner's beginning to learn. He don't even talk out of line no more." He leaned forward, joining his hands on top of his desk. "You're smart, prisoner, but I don't think you've learned the full lesson yet. You're just beginning to learn. You know what the lesson is?" He leaned back in his chair, joining his hands behind his neck. "Obedience, that's the lesson. It includes one rule we don't allow no one to break—attacking the Brig personnel. You broke that rule, prisoner, that's why you're in the cell block. We can't have no rebels in this compound. You're here to relearn the lesson that you forgot. For some it takes longer to relearn this lesson. That's where Maximum Detention comes in. But if you're going to fight us then the whole purpose of relearning is defeated. We can't allow that."

Lidel piped on abstractedly, as though he was reading from a text in his mind. He did not look at Dawson, he was looking beyond the prisoner, concentrating on the prepared notes he had repeated count-less times.

"We're going to teach you that lesson, prisoner. Because you have shown an unwillingness to relearn, we are going to change your viewpoint. We are going to make you want to learn. When you leave the cell block you'll want to obey. Naturally, this will make you a better Marine. This is exactly the result we want, to make you a better Marine.

"Partial solitary is only the beginning of your retraining. We're gonna be easy on you, prisoner. We're not giving you full solitary, not just yet. You've had a taste of Maximum Detention, just a taste. You're gonna get more of it in the next few days. Three days in the cell block is nothing. You're going back until you relearn obedience."

The master sergeant's face was expressionless, a blank mask. In his gaze was not the slightest curiosity about the prisoner. The stare was cold, scientific, nothing more.

Dawson stared back at him.

Lidel spoke to the guard standing behind Dawson. "Pfc, do you think this prisoner will learn his lesson?"

"No, sir," said Miller. "This man is a hard ass, Top. He don't wanna learn."

"I think you may be wrong, Pfc," Lidel said to Miller. "I think this prisoner may be willing to learn." He looked directly at Dawson. "Are you willing to learn your lesson, prisoner?"

No answer was forthcoming.

Miller jabbed the blunt end of the billy into Dawson's back.

"Yes, sir," Dawson lied.

"That's very good, but I don't believe you," Lidel said. "Let's see if a few more days in solitary can change that." He waved to Miller. "Take 'im away."

Miller touched Dawson's arm with the billy. "Come on, turd, let's go."

Dawson gave a last look at Lidel, silently cursing him to never-ending perdition. He made a smartly placed about face and marched out. Another guard was waiting for them outside the NCO's office. Dawson got in between the two men and took a few steps forward when he heard the voice of Lidel, "Miller."

The three men halted. "Wait here," Miller said. He went back into the office. The master sergeant was still sitting behind his desk. "Give him the full treatment," Lidel instructed.

Miller grinned. Escorting Dawson back to his cell, the MP whistled to himself.

Dawson was thrown inside. He got up and went back to the door as soon as it closed. He peeked out the hole for five minutes. No one passed by. He had noticed traceries of sun seeping through the canvas top roof of the cell block. The sunlight was hot and very bright. Must be about noon, he figured. Anytime now the guard would bring his meal. He could taste the chili con carne again. Bread and water rations would be better than the slop.

He meal was brought on time. Miller came into the cell, placed the food on the floor. Dawson got up from his bunk—the man was gone and the door locked before he could reach the food.

He held up the plate, took a familiar whiff. It wasn't a familiar odor. The dankness of watery chili and boiled rice wasn't there. A fetid smell arched up his nostrils. He peered closely at the food. It had the coloring and texture of the slop, only the plate felt heavier. He smelt it again. The scent was stronger. Two quick steps to the door. He held the plate up to the light. The brownish lumpy mash was indeed familiar. Feces!

His first impulse was to hurl the plate against the wall, or on the floor. He trembled and did neither. The sickened reaction was that strong. He leaned his head against the wire mesh, and groaned. This time the need to weep was severe. He closed his eyes, fighting it. The scent of the waste made him aware he was still holding the plate. The desire to weep was replaced by the need to vomit. He kept his mouth shut, forcing down the fluid. The nausea was intense.

He went to the corner and put down the plate, lowering it to the floor with a revulsion stronger than he had ever felt. He felt as though he had been forced to pick up the rotting body of a dead rodent.

The feces was hidden in the corner, but he had to endure its presence more than ever. He rolled in the wooden bunk, unable to stop his disgust.

The feeling, rather, ill feeling, lasted until the guard returned.

Usually the guard visited the cell twice for meals, and once during the morning, when Dawson emptied the number ten can that served as his toilet into a large wheeled barrel on the outside corridor. This day was special. Dawson was awarded a further visit by none other than the man who had brought his "food" some time before. Sometimes there could be great amusement in seeing how the prisoners reacted to the jest. That was the beauty of the Treatment, it was intimidating as well as degrading.

Miller opened the trapdoor, grinning, relishing the little added humiliation he had inflicted.

The plate was hurled from a corner of the cell. Miller didn't duck fast enough. The excrement plopped right on his chest, covering his shirt in rolls of shit. He stood paralyzed, trying to scream. He could only gag. Automatically he touched himself. The waste spread to his fingers and hands. A stench of decay met his nostrils. He moved his tongue but nothing came out.

Dawson stood in the corner, laughing. The light of the doorway caught the greater part of his face, full, triumphant.

Miller turned to the two guards standing outside the door. "GET HIM!" he shrieked. "GET HIM!"

The guards rushed inside, pushing Miller out of the way. They pounced on Dawson, striking his head and body with their fists. He tried to swing back; his arm was caught by one of the assailants and held down. The other guard rammed a fist into Dawson's testicles. A painful shockwave rolled over him. He cried out, going down on his knees, cupping his groin in his hands. Another blow slammed on the back of his head. His vision blurred. A welter of fists catalogued his face and neck. He cringed on the floor, rolling himself into a ball with his hands covering his head. A boot drove into his exposed thigh. He screamed. This brought on a gust of kicks on his back and sides.

Miller stood in the doorway, with the waste dripping from his hands. The excrement intensified a mindless hatred.

"Don't touch his face," he yelled. "Get 'im in the body."

The guards forced Dawson to stand on wobbly legs. They began to punch his stomach. One blow fell short, landing in his vital area once more. Dawson moaned.

Miller stripped off his shirt, tossing it in the corridor. He took out a handkerchief, wiped the scum from his hands and t-shirt. "Take his shirt off," he commanded.

They forced Dawson into a kneeling position, and while one guard held Dawson's arms behind his back, the other grabbed his shirt-sleeves, pulling the shirt from his body. They raised Dawson up again and resumed their boxing practice on his stomach. His knees collapsed, and he sagged, gasping for breath. His mouth and nose swelled with blood.

Miller finished wiping himself with Dawson's shirt. He threw the garment aside. "Take off his boots," he ordered.

The man who was working on Dawson stopped for a moment. "What?"

"Take off his boots," Miller repeated.

"What for?"

"Don't argue, take 'em off."

The guards pushed Dawson to the floor. One of them took a hold of Dawson's legs. There was still some fight left in the prisoner. He kicked out. The Ps responded accordingly: one guard kicked him in the stomach. Dawson sprawled on the floor. They managed to hold his legs long enough to untie the laces and remove his boots.

Miller took the boots, removing the laces. He tossed the boots in a corner. "Hold him tight," he said.

The guards pinned Dawson to the ground, face down, while Miller bound Dawson's hands behind his back with the bootlaces.

"Take off his socks," Miller ordered.

Four strong hands stripped the socks from Dawson's feet.

Miller tied the socks in a knot. "Hold him tight," he repeated. He went over to the wooden bedboard and, stooping down, dipped the socks in the paint can that served as the latrine. The material was saturated, and Miller's fingers grew sticky. He forced his hand to stay inside the can until the socks were completely soaked.

He walked back to Dawson. "Now hold 'im *real* tight."

Dawson heaved against his captors. The guards held him down.

"Open his mouth wide," Miller commanded.

Dawson resisted, and clenched his mouth. One guard pinched his nose, then gripped his jaw and forced it open. Miller stuffed the socks into Dawson's mouth.

He gagged, the spittle, urine and waste blocking his tongue. He couldn't spit out the filth. A guard pulled back Dawson's head, and Miller forced the woolen socks deeper into the orifice.

Dawson couldn't breathe. Everytime he tried to throw up, more of the scum would drip down his throat. He was choking.

JULY 16TH

Three days later Dawson was let out of the cell block. All of it had been partial solitary; he didn't get the canvas cover. In part, this was a let-down. He had been spared Zimmerman's vision of the fully enclosed sarcophagus with only his mind to contend with. His disappointment was surmounted by an overwhelming sense of relief. A few times while in incubation, he had toyed with the fantasy of full solitary. If the canvas covering were placed over the wire-mesh hole, he had vowed not to crack—like every prisoner before him had vowed. Sometimes he would get up from his board and see the light from the hole filtering into the cell, and this would give him pause to recharge his hope that he wouldn't bend. He awaited full solitary with the same fascinated fright of a man who sits in a dentist's chair. This wasn't any kind of a triumph. Secretly, he was glad the final test had been averted. Like a man who never faces the actual contest, he was left with the unresolved question of will.

He was taken back to Medium Detention by Miller the Mole and two other guards. Going down the corridor, no one said a word. The release from solitary was downright glum. For Dawson it was the benign end to a bad trip. For Miller, Dawson's release was part of the

111

job. Master Sergeant Lidel calculated that six days in the hole was enough to make Dawson receptive again. Miller, if he had had his way, would have kept Dawson in solitary for the rest of his natural life. A mess of shit on his shirt wasn't that easily forgotten. Since Lidel ran the show, there wasn't much he could do about it. He didn't take it as a personal defeat, but it was no victory either.

Dawson could sense Miller's disappointment. He was unusually quiet when Dawson was let out. In fact, Miller did nothing but stand aside while the guards took Dawson out of the cell, gave him a minute or two to adjust to the light, then walked him back to his old tent.

Chi-Chi was already there, having been let out the day before. Sitting on his cot in the far corner, both men relived their days in Maximum. Looking at it in the afterlight, like all hardships that cannot be endured, their ordeal in the cell block took on ludicrous dimensions.

"You threw the shit on him?" Chi-Chi asked with awed amusement. "Wow, that musta been something else."

"It was for me," Dawson said. "Look—" he showed the healing cuts on his cheek, and the fatty tip of his nose turned in at a slight angle. The corner of his right eye was still swollen, his lips were puffed.

"Damn, they worked you over somethin' bad," Chi-Chi said. "Did they hit you with billies?"

"Just in the back of the head. They used hands on my face and body." Dawson took pride in his beatings. The stature of H&S Casual showed on his face.

"How many times you get beat?"

"Four times," Dawson lied.

"How was it—they beat you everyday?"

"Naw, just after the first day when I threw the shit at the Mole. They beat me twice that time. They beat me twice again the next day."

"Man, I'm sure glad I didn't get no shit in my meal," Chi-Chi said.

Dawson noticed Chi-Chi's clear features. "They didn't touch you at all, did they?"

"No, not really. I only got a few lovetaps when they took me to the cell, but that was nothing, just a punch here and there. Inside the cell they din't do nothin'. I did get special rations, though. I don't know whether that was worse."

"What's special rations'?"

Chi-Chi wiped a finger under his nose. "That's somethin' special they dreamed up for me, though I'm told a few dudes get it. Actually, it ain't shit. All they do, insteada feed you the regular slop, they cut it down some. Since bread and water rations ain't allowed by regimental order, they give you this special ration bit."

"Yeah, but what is it?"

"It's a cuttin' down of your regular chow. In my case all they served me was some vegetables on a plate. Like for every meal I usually got some carrot sticks and a few lettuce leaves, plus the regular water."

"How come you got this deal?"

"I really don't know." Chi-Chi scratched his hairless top. "I figure Miller had somethin' to do with it. You can only get special rations by okay of the CO, so I guess Miller just rap to the man, and there I was. Old Miller, he got somepin against me, man. I can feel it."

Dawson snorted. "Yeah, old Miller got something against everybody."

"Dude's crazy, man," Chi-Chi said. "When that cat with the crooked nose told me that, I thought he was jiving. But he right, that Miller the Mole is a psycho. He gotta be—the way he does things."

Dawson smiled to himself. He wondered if Chi-Chi really knew what a 'psycho' was. "I don't know. Maybe Miller ain't crazy, maybe he just likes doin' his job."

'No, man, you can't convince me of that. That fucker gotta be unstable. I bet when he was a kid he dug tearin' the wings off butterflies and stuff like that."

"I wouldn't doubt it."

"Use to know a fucker like him back in the world. Dude was just like Miller. His kick was to get a cat, then hang him from a tree and set fire to his tail." Chi-Chi chuckled. "Sometimes it was so funny. The cat be shriekin' and screamin' and that dude he'd be standin' there just laughin' his balls off. That fucker was really outtasight. Crazy as they come."

"I use to know a guy like that," Dawson said. "It's the ten percent. They're everywhere."

"And we got one in the Brig," Chi-Chi concluded.

"Perhaps. One thing I do know, I don't wanna tangle with Miller again. Maybe on the outside, but not in here. I don't want my nose to get more bent up than it is."

"Sometimes you can't help but tangle with somebody. What happens if Miller start pickin' on you again?"

"Dunno," Dawson said. "If I fight him I'll get screwed and if I don't I'll get screwed just the same. I guess it's one of those unsolvable predicaments."

"I don't care what kind of predicament it is," Chi-Chi claimed. "If that fucker jives with me I'll fight him anyway I can."

"And be back in the cell block, pro'bly in full solitary."

"You gotta stand up for your rights, man," Chi-Chi said with sincerity. "If you don't they'll fuck ya over."

"They doin' that now."

"Maybe, but there's a difference. They may fuck all over me but they ain't broken me down. At least I got that. Now, if I was to break down and give in to them completely then it wouldn't make no difference, but since I ain't broke yet, and I don't intend to, it don't matter how much they fuck with me. They can get me to crawl in the dirt and maybe eat shit, but they can't take what I got here away from me." Chi-Chi tapped his breast.

Dawson nodded. How could he counter an argument like that? "You're right. I just hope they don't fuck with us no more, that's all."

"You're a dreamer, friend. They gonna keep fuckin' with us. That's the only thing they can do. That's the only thing they know how to do."

"Nowhere to run, nowhere to hide," Dawson quoted.

"What's that?"

"I was just thinking of the time I was in Khe Sanh. Every morning Hanoi Hannah use to play us that song, *Nowhere to run, Nowhere to Hide* by Martha and the Vandellas. Could say our situation is the same."

Chi-Chi sighed. "That is true, we is nowhere."

Dawson smiled. He felt better already. It was good to be back among the living. "Got a smoke you can spare?"

"No, man, I don't," Chi-Chi said sadly. "Miller took every butt I had."

"Same here." Dawson looked at the other three men scattered about the tent, and thought of asking them for cigarettes. No, man, ridiculous. He recalled how miserly he had been whenever he carried smokes.

All the faces in the tent, except for Chi-Chi, were unfamiliar. "Where's the dude with the crooked nose?" he asked.

He was transferred stateside."

"When?"

"While we was in the cell block," Chi-Chi said. "His papers came through and they just whisked him away."

"What was he in for?"

"Going UA."

Dawson sighed. "I wonder when we'll leave,"

"I hope it's soon, man."

Soon, Dawson thought. Soon when? Soon how? The old depression settled in. He had tried to work the angles, instead the angles had worked him. He wondered if he could regain his old post in supply. A pipedream, he concluded. Once a man was branded by the cell block he would never get anywhere. Not even his former mentor Rodriguez could help him out. He consigned himself to a bleak future—Medium Detention and the sandpile. Chi-Chi and him, together, the fuckups. Nowhere to run, nowhere to hide.

The next day Zimmerman came to their hooch. When he saw Dawson, there was a sanguine smile on his face, even though he was standing at attention next to the guard who had brought him in. The guard looked his way and asked pointedly, "What's so funny, prisoner?"

"Sir, request permission—"

"I don't want no fuckin' song," the guard said. "Just tell me why you smilin'."

"I got an itch, sir", Zimmerman smiled.

"Well, tell that itch to go away and take that grin off your face. You make me nervous."

"Yes, sir." Zimmerman winked at Dawson.

Dawson grinned back at him.

"This your new home," the guard told Zimmerman. "Let's hope this time you can stay in for at least a day before you end up in Maximum again."

Zimmerman stuck out his tongue at the guard. Luckily, the guard had his back turned.

After the guard had gone, the men relaxed. Dawson went up to Zimmerman. "How the fuck you get here?" he asked affectionately.

"I don't know," Zimmerman said. "Dumb guard just put me in here."

Dawson clasped Zimmerman's shoulder. "I thought you were a permanent member of the cell block."

"I thought so too until they let me out. It seems my three weeks of solitary was enough for them."

"Where you ever in Medium before?"

Zimmerman looked around the tent. "Yeah, but it wasn't this tent. I thought I was going back to my old hooch."

"Well, you're here now and I'm glad." Dawson took Zimmerman's arm. "C'mon, let's squat in my rack."

"Thinkin' about racks, I need one myself," Zimmerman said.

Dawson counted the available cots in the tent. "You're in trouble. There's only four racks here and they're all taken."

"Shit, they would have to put me in a hooch that's got no racks. After sleeping on that board I was looking forward to a nice comfy rack."

"You can sleep on the floor," Dawson suggested.

Zimmerman kicked some dirt on the ground. "Welcome to the bush, Zimmerman."

Dawson guided him to the corner. Chi-Chi was sitting down, eyeing the new man with distant interest.

"Zim, this here is Chi-Chi Hernandez. He another cell block veteran."

Zimmerman shook hands with Chi-Chi. "Howdy. Any man from the cell block it's my pleasure to know."

"Same here, friend," Chi-Chi said. "How long was you there?"

Zimmerman laid his toilet kit on the cot. "Three weeks."

Chi-Chi was impressed. "That's quite a stretch."

"It's nothing. There's one dude up there who been in for two months already. I think that's the record."

"Damn, what he do?" Chi-Chi asked.

"He made the supreme mistake—he took a swing at Top Lidel."

"That *is* a supreme mistake," Chi-Chi agreed.

Zimmerman sat down. "Who's got a smoke?" he asked offhand.

"You outta luck again, Zim," Dawson said. "We ain't got nothin'."

"Damn, not even C-rat butts?"

"Not even that," Chi-Chi lamented.

"How about those other dudes, they got smokes?"

"Maybe they do," Chi-Chi said, "but it ain't policy to ask anybody for a smoke unless you know the dude like your brother. You can ask 'em but they all gonna tell you they ain't got smokes even if they do."

Zimmerman gained a quick understanding. "So that's the way we live here, everybody for himself."

"That's the way it is unless you is tight with somebody."

"Don't worry, Zim," Dawson chimed hopefully, "we'll find a way of gettin' smokes sooner or later, maybe even grass."

"Guess you have to live with your environment," Zimmerman said.

Chi-Chi grunted. "Fuckit. There's only a few people in this world you can count on, 'specially in a place like this." He gestured at the four other men in the tent. "See them dudes, they're all flakes, all of 'em. All they want is to kiss ass for the Ps so they can cop some free smokes. Me and Dawson here, we know that when we get our smokes or anythin' else it ain't by ass kissin', it's by brain power. We know how to operate. That's the big difference in this Brig, there's the ass-kissers and there's the operators."

"Never kissed ass in my whole life," Zimmerman said. "Just can't see shit like that."

"There it is, friend. No matter what, a dude has to keep his dignity." Chi-Chi was very big on dignity. It was the one concept that could justify his resistance to anything.

Zimmerman agreed, although this talk of dignity and ass-kissing was way over his head since all he cared about for now was getting one measly cigarette. He hadn't had a smoke in almost four weeks, but since he had agreed to Chi-Chi's polemics there wasn't much he could do about it. So much for that.

Later, Dawson asked him, "Is that brother in the cell block still in full solitary?"

"Yeah, he still is," he answered. "Though I don't think he'll last much longer."

"What makes you think so?"

"Man, if you would've seen him yesterday when they brought him back from another workout—he looked just about done in. They're doing that brother a job. I tell you, I was looking out the hole, and you know you can't see too well with all that wire, but even so that dude still look bad. I think they busted his nose. He's a mess."

"Who's this?" Chi-Chi inquired.

"Remember that brother who had the run-in with Miller in the mess hall?" Dawson asked Chi-Chi.

"Which one?"

"You know, the one who had the cup of coffee and Miller slapped it outta his hand."

Chi-Chi recalled vaguely. "Yeah, I remember."

"Well, he's the one we're talking about. He's been in full solitary now for close to two weeks."

"More like three weeks," Zimmerman corrected.

"You mean he's the one they doin' all this shit to?" Chi-Chi asked.

"Un-huh."

"But that dude din't even hit one of the guards," Chi-Chi said. "All he did was complain about the chow, and they hit *him*."

"Yup, but he gettin' the treatment."

"There was two brothers taken away during that fight, what happened to the other one?"

Dawson shrugged. "I don't know. When I was in the cell block I only saw one brother."

"Maybe they killed the other one and dumped his body in the river," Zimmerman said.

"What river?" Dawson asked him.

"I don't know, any river around here, or anyplace for that matter. Maybe they worked him over so hard he died."

"You know, you got a point," Chi-Chi said. "Knowing Miller, I wouldn't be surprised if that mother killed somebody and then stashed the bod. Fucker like him is liable to do anything."

Dawson came out the opposite pole. "That's hard to believe. Even a nut like Miller wouldn't take a chance on killing a prisoner. There'd be such an investigation . . ."

"But's that's it," Chi-Chi cut in. "If nobody finds a bod, who's to know? Right? Miller could waste any of us, and as long as there's no corpse, he could get away with it."

"But what about the people that's waiting for us back home—and I don't mean our relatives—I mean the prisons most of these dudes hafta go back to. Remember, we're all transients here. If a man has to serve time in the world, how they gonna explain his disappearance when he never left the Brig? No, man, I just can't buy that about anybody getting killed in here and nobody finding out. The only way they could get away with it is by claiming it was an accident, and even then they'd still have an investigation."

"Man," Chi-Chi said in his prophetic voice, "never underestimate what these motherfuckers in here are capable of doing. They're like God, Jim. We're shit, and these dudes stick together. All kinds of fuzz stick together. I wouldn't put nothin' past 'em."

Dawson wasn't convinced. "I don't know. It seems to me if anybody got zapped in here, especially a brother, there'd be such a stink that people on the outside would hear about it."

"We'll have a chance to find out pretty soon," Zimmerman warned.

"Huh?"

"We're going to find out pretty soon," he repeated.

"How'd you figure?" Dawson asked.

"I got this feeling in me. When I saw them bring back that brother, he looked almost dead. That poor fucker couldn't even walk. I figure, if they keep working on him the way they're doing, and keep up that full solitary at the same time, that dude is gonna die."

Dawson felt a sudden chill. "How do you know he gonna die?"

"Like I said, I have a feeling."

"Feelings don't tell nothing sometimes," Chi-Chi stated.

"Maybe," Zimmerman said. "But figure it this way, how much beating can a body take? How much isolation in a rattrap can anybody take? You figure the brother's stubborn as hell and he won't give in, but he's no superman. If he doesn't break, he'll die. If they keep it up I give him less than a week."

Dawson nodded. Indisputable logic. "What do they want from him anyway?"

"Maybe an apology," Zimmerman said, "or maybe they just want to see him crawl. Who knows? Whatever it is, he won't do it."

"That brother has heart," Chi-Chi commended.

"At the rate he's going he won't have it for long."

Dawson bit his lower lip. "I hope you're wrong, Zim."

"So do I. I hate to see anybody get greased in the cell block, even a brother." Zimmerman looked at his hands, his voice becoming suddenly tender. "Who knows, maybe I won't be around to see it. It don't mean nothing when you're gone, does it? Maybe if I bust out in time I might miss the flood that's coming."

"You're still dreaming, eh?" Dawson asked.

"It's no dream, duke. I'm getting out one way or the other."

Chi-Chi broke in. "Hey, you planning to bust out?"

"That's right," Zimmerman said without reservations.

Chi-Chi looked at Dawson, giving the glance that said, What's with him? "Hey, man, you shouldn't joke like that," he said to Zimmerman.

"I'm not."

Chi-Chi looked at Dawson again, back to Zimmerman. "You wanna bust outta *here?*"

"That's what I said."

"Lissen, if you're serious about this thing you shouldn't tell anybody," Chi-Chi cautioned. "There's beaucoup stoolies in this place."

"I don't care if they find out about it," Zimmerman said, unperturbed. "I don't give a damn if the guards find out. I'd tell the CO himself if he asked me. See, it's inevitable. I'm leavin' this joint. They could put a twenty-four hour guard on me, it'd still mean nothing. I'm getting out. I made up my mind and that's that."

"Zimmerman here is a firm believer in positive thinking," Dawson told Chi-Chi.

"You laugh, fool," Zimmerman said. "When I'm outside that wire you'll see who's laughing then."

"You really serious about this?" Chi-Chi said.

"Fuck, yeah. I wouldn't have said it if I wasn't."

Chi-Chi shook his head. "Man, I wish you luck." I wish you a whole lotta luck, you poor dreamin' fuck, he said inside.

"Luck has nothing to do with it."

"Why you wanna get out?"

"I don't want to stay in."

"Where you gonna go?"

"Saigon."

"You really serious about this," Chi-Chi said again, not wholly believing it.

"Of course, I'm serious."

Chi-Chi looked at Dawson.

Dawson shrugged. I can't understand it either, he said with the gesture.

Chi-Chi, mistakenly, was trying to figure out this new guest in the tent. His error. No one ever figured out Zimmerman. "How much time you think you gonna be in this dump?"

"Maybe a coupla weeks more," Zimmerman answered.

"Then you going stateside?'"

"Yeah."

"To a stateside pen?"

"Yeah."

"How much time you gotta do?"

"No less than two years, no more than five," Zimmerman said.

Chi-Chi blew out some air. "Wow, that's beaucoup time. I can understand why you wanna bust out."

"But he ain't goin' nowhere," Dawson said.

Zimmerman frowned. "Dawson, there's no hope for you. You just don't have no faith in nuthin'."

"I got faith. Just that my faith weakens when you tell me you plan to bust out. There's nobody ever busted outta this trap."

"There's always a first time."

Chi-Chi broke in again. "Lissen, I don't wanna discourage you or nuthin', but there's searchlights, and starlight scopes, and guards, and radar detection devices . . . I mean, how do you plan to get past all that?"

Zimmerman smiled smugly. "All those technical devices you've just mentioned are man-made. Being man-made devices, they are subject to man-made defects."

"I don't get it?"

"Simple. Searchlights can't see everything, radar can't detect everything, guards can't protect everything."

"That's cool," Chi-Chi said, "but how do you plan to get by them?"

"Don't worry, I'll find a way," Zimmerman said.

"Okay, suppose you do slide out. That's gookland out there. How you gonna get to Saigon once you leave the base? You could wind up in the hands of Charlie, and then you'd really be fucked."

"So? Big deal if I get caught by Charlie. Hell, I figure it'd be no worse than being in the Brig, maybe even better. Fact, if I could convince them to give me a good shake I'd fight for them, become their boy, I got the experience."

"Man, you're crazy."

"Not crazy, my dear friend, Hernandez," Zimmerman said patronisingly, somewhat irked at this youth who could not appreciate the finer workings of his mind. "I am realistic. Reality for me is the fact that I am not going to serve five long years in a State pen, not for the crotch or the country or nobody. To that end I am willing to do anything."

"Your ideas are beautiful, Zim," Dawson conceded, "but face it, you got no money, you don't speak Veetmese, all you got is them jungle utilities. I doubt you know anyone outside the base—so how you gonna do it?"

"Faith, son," Zimmerman said. "Faith and good planning. I'm not ready for my pull yet. But after I figure out the whole setup in this Brig—guards, shifts, everything—you'll see my smoke. No gate can hold me in, electric wire fence or not."

"You better come down to reality, friend," Chi-Chi drawled. "Dawson's right. The chances of you bustin' out are a million to one, shit, a trillion to one. I'd think twice before I try anythin'."

"There's nothing to think over. I'm getting outta here—one way or the other."

He had to. There was no other way for Zimmerman. If he remained in the Brig it would destroy him; the same way it would destroy them all, for the Brig, like the Corps, did not give you a say. As simple as that. No matter how asinine the action, you had to comply. No matter who wound up dead, you had to comply. He had discovered that in his last patrol, just before he deserted.

Zimmerman reflected constantly on how stupid that whole mission had been. He and his platoon couldn't say shit about it, either. He wouldn't have minded so much if it had been like a regular operation. It wasn't even that. The general got a hair up his ass, and Zimmerman had to comply. His platoon had to trek back to Khe Sanh just so the general could show the newspaper people he still owned the place, as if he ever did. It's one thing when a grunt has to get shot trying to take some hill, it's another when he has to impress some newsmen. If that's all they were fighting for then it just wasn't worth it. After all, they did get the living daylights kicked out of them in the operation that had preceded the general's harebrained scheme. That was no picnic. How many men had they lost?—He couldn't even begin to count. Despite what the brass said, when you went out in the bush with a full company and lost half, those weren't light casualties.

That was about the worst mission ever. It started lousy. When his squad had dwindled to one fireteam after two days of fighting, Zimmerman knew they were behind the eight ball. The only thing to be said for it was that almost everybody in the platoon received a Purple Heart. The only two who didn't get wounded were Zimmerman and Dawson. On top of it they lost the company CO. To say the least, they were understrength when they came back.

Truly, they had nothing left. Those men who didn't get wounded got sick on a cache of gook rice they found. Those who didn't get sick on the rice got dehydrated from the lack of water. That was the bad part. It got sogged-in over the landing area and they couldn't get resupplied for four days. They were eating the bark from banana trees.

The men finally had to drink the bomb crater water, which was not the best. It was all black and oily, and there were rats swimming in it. They put loads of purification tablets in the holes. But Zimmerman couldn't take the halizone tablets. Everytime he had swallowed one he had gotten diarrhea. The corpsman advised them to either drink the water or dry up. Zimmerman figured that he'd rather die from the shits than by drying up. Not that it made any difference, given the conditions they had to endure. They couldn't go back and they couldn't go forward. The best idea was to stay put. Those who could still walk or wield an E-tool were ordered to dig trenches. The plan being that, if the NVA attacked again, they would have cover from which to give suppressive fire. At least those men who weren't sick with the shits could still be counted on to fire their weapons, or so the CO surmised.

When the trenches had been completed, both the wounded and able-bodied were consigned to share cramped foxholes covered with excrement and vomit. The men suffered from suppurating wounds whose dressings began to rot on the skin. For four harrowing days the men ate, slept and lived in this environment. Those too sick to move simply relieved themselves where they lay since the dysentery had totally wasted whatever strength they had. The water that had accumulated in the craters converted the ground into a quagmire of mud, excrement and blood so that in the trenches the men found themselves entangled in a substance that defied description. It was just *there*; this strange mix that covered their boots, jungle fatigues, seeped into their packs and plastic canteens and jammed their weapons. The only saving grace was that the North Vietnamese did not attack as expected, not that the men could have put up much of a resistance.

Like most, Zimmerman couldn't keep anything down. He subsisted on Hershey's candy bars he had squirreled away back at the base camp. Anytime he tried eating the contaminated rice, he'd retch. And nothing would gush out, just white-greenish slime that would intermix with the mud, caked blood and feces in the foxhole. The strange thing about it was that he didn't get the shits, and he never knew why.

He wasn't lucky after that. When the cloud cover lifted, big Chinook helicopters were able to initiate a supply drop. But they couldn't land in the area since the landscape had been rendered as impassable as a cratered valley on the moon due to the constant bombing runs that had preceded the mission. And, even if the choppers had accessed a landing site, it was still considered too dangerous a ploy since it was assumed the NVA were skulking about with rockers and antiaircraft weaponry.

So, after the supply drop, they were ordered to move out, carrying their dead and wounded. They humped through the scarred wasteland for a mile or two until they reached what had been their objective all along, an abandoned bunker. They were attacked one more time by North Vietnamese regulars. That's when Zimmerman lost most of his squad. The only ones left after that were him, Dawson and most of the second fireteam. To make matters worse, they couldn't get medevacked out. The marines again had to wait for a break in the clouds so the choppers could evacuate them and they couldn't stay where they were.

They had to march with their dead and wounded for two more days. The only thing that kept them functioning was sheer courage. They had started out with a complement of four rifle companies, roughly a battalion size unit, seven hundred and five men. Less than half made it back in one piece. Even so, when they reached the nearest firebase they were the last unit to be helicoptered out. On their return, Zimmerman discovered he had lost fifteen pounds. The fun started after that.

Two days after their rescue the company was ordered to move out again. None of them had recovered from the last mission, but the I Corps commander wanted to make some good news for the service. Someone at HQ had picked up a newspaper and found out the North Vietnamese were crawling all over Khe Sanh. There was a lot of bad publicity in this. The general decided to show the world the Marines still had the territory. The bigwigs got together and it was decided to send in two companies and have an appropriate ceremony at the old base site. *Stars and Stripes* called it the "Great Return to Khe Sanh." The mission even had an official name: "Continuing Activities in the Cedar 111 Area."

None of the men who had been in the Khe Sanh siege wanted to go back there. Zimmerman had been there during his first tour. He dreaded the idea. He still couldn't decipher why the military wanted the base in the first place. The base was a dump surrounded by hills, just perfect for incoming every day. But it was orders and he had to comply.

They went in and nothing happened. The companies were choppered to a firebase that had been set up about half a mile from the Khe Sanh airstrip—what was left of the airstrip. When they arrived it was like coming back to a ghost town. All the old bunkers had been destroyed and the holes filled up. Nothing was left. Apparently the NVA hadn't used the terrain very much.

The Marines made a sweep from the firebase to the strip where they set up a 360 perimeter, and waited for the bigwigs to come. All the while, artillery and jets worked over the surrounding hills. Every ridgeline facing the strip was blasted by bombs and rockets. The only exciting part of the operation was the fireworks. When it was over, all the *dignitaries* arrived. And this was the one part Zimmerman couldn't believe. The brass brought with them the Third Marine Division Band. They flew in the whole damn ensemble like it was a stand-up parade. To Zimmerman it was the most ludicrous sight in the world. All those men stepping out of a helicopter, carrying their M16s in one hand and drums and bugles in the other. They were dressed like grunts too—flak jackets, ammo bags . . . Zimmerman realized one thing that day. When the Corps went for a stupid idea, it went all the way.

Following the band came the honchos. The general was there, and Zimmerman recognized just about every battalion commander in the area. They also had squads of newsmen with microphones and recorders.

Back home his family got to see Zimmerman on television. His wife wrote to him about how she saw the whole extravaganza on the six o'clock news.

Anybody who was there had their picture taken that day. The cameramen swarmed everywhere, talking to the men, eliciting their opinion. They couldn't say boo. Their CO had warned them that if they spoke out of line they would get the trash detail for the remainder of their stay in the rear.

All the leathernecks did was smile and nod their heads to everything that was asked of them.

The big news was the memorial service. The thing was so patently a fraud Zimmerman almost retched. The Division band played the Marine Corps Hymn, then the chaplain stepped forward and said something about how their comrades-in-arms who had fallen in Khe Sanh would never be forgotten, though Zimmerman couldn't remember who was with him at Khe Sanh. After the chaplain's spiel, the band played up again. Zimmerman recognized a John Phillip Sousa tune and for some reason he thought of the *Music Man*.

The general spoke next and he stood between two flagpoles the engineers had set up. Zimmerman recalled how happy the general looked, right there in the middle of the deserted airstrip, yapping into the microphone while the cameramen worked away. He lectured as to how the Khe Sanh fortress was still his and he could come to it anytime he wanted. Zimmerman snorted then, thinking that if he had two battalions of grunts and the air wing to back him he would go anywhere he wanted, too. He could go to Moscow and say it was his.

The old man was lucky that day. They were all lucky. With so many commanders standing on the airstrip all that was needed was one mortar round to screw up the works. If there had been one NVA in the hills he could've picked them all off with a thirty-thirty.

Nothing happened—not till the end of the ceremony. As soon as the bigwigs finished their speeches and all the film was taken, the infantrymen packed and headed for the choppers. That's when one of the men stepped on a mine. Chester, Zimmerman's second fireteam leader, was the last to leave the position. As he was coming down from the basin around the strip he kicked off a 105 millimeter round. He was alone and no one else was injured. Poor Chester lost both legs, most of his rear end, and his genitals.

The company captain ordered a search of the area to see if there were any more mines. Nine more were found. The objects were butterfly mines that had been put there during the siege—by U.S. Marines.

Sergeant Zimmerman had four men left out of a squad of fourteen. He couldn't fathom any of it. When the company returned to LZ Stud, their main base, the colonel decided to give Zimmerman a commendation. Zimmerman concluded that since he had lost the most men he needed an award for that. He received the Silver Star. Not bad in exchange for the lives of ten men.

Whenever he thought of escape from the Brig, Zimmerman would think ruefully that the medal and a dime could buy him a cup of coffee anywhere in the world.

JULY 17TH

Just after reveille the first Intelligence reports came in. At Admin Sec they were analyzed and digested. There was an 80% probability of enemy attack on the base areas. Furthermore, it was estimated that anywhere from one to twenty enemy projectiles were likely to converge on Da Nang during the next twenty-four hours. Intelligence could not ascertain which areas would be hit. Their paid Vietnamese informers volunteered only a minimum of information.

Brig command was well aware of the accuracy of Intelligence data. If they stated there was an 80% probability of enemy attack, there was an 80% probability of enemy attack—one of these days. Da Nang was shelled by insurgents from time to time to be sure, but never on the days Intelligence specified. The Admin sergeant reviewed the report, shrugged, and handed it to the Brig CO for his perusal. The CO, as required, called for the red alert condition to be maintained in the Brig.

To the men in detention a state of maximum alert offered no significant change. Everything functioned as usual with the normal amount of working parties and tasks assigned to each prisoner. There was no increase in the ratio of guards; nor were any additional arms or emergency measures provided. The only subtle, noticeable stark difference in the lives of the inmates was the advent of the body armor. Two guards came into each detention area, piling a load of flak jackets outside the fenced-in tents.

This was the second time he had been in H&S Casual that Zimmerman had seen the procedure. "We're goin' to get incoming," he whispered out of the side of his mouth.

Dawson, standing next to Zimmerman, watched the two guards count off the men, and dump an appropriate number of flak jackets by the tent gate.

"How can you tell?" he whispered to Zimmerman.

"The only time they give us flak jackets is when they expect incomin'," Zimmerman whispered back.

"We're fucked," Dawson breathed.

The guards finished counting the vests. Miller came inside the tent area, and in a sonorous voice addressed the prisoners. "I guess you turds wonderin' what all the vests are for. I give you three guesses, and any way you figure it's gonna come out one way, *incoming*." He let the word ring in every man. "That's right, *incoming*. Intelligence thinks we might be in for some fireworks today. Charlie just might decide to throw us a few roses. If he does start shellin', you people are not to worry about it."

Dawson felt a shiver. Not to worry about it? Good God, how? he thought.

"I would advise you to keep calm," Miller said. "In case of attack the procedure is for the guards to come get the prisoners and march 'em to the nearest trench." He pointed a finger at the flak jackets. "Them is for your use. Those vests will stay there all day. They'll be removed only when we get the all clear signal. If we do get incoming, the first thing you do is put on a vest. I guess I don't have to tell you that. It's for your protection."

Miller looked at his watch. "Today everything will go as scheduled—workin' parties, everything else. Just 'cause we expect incoming that don't mean you people get a holiday. If you're out on a workin' detail and the rounds start comin' in, you're to follow your guard's instructions. He'll guide you to a place of safety until the attack is over. If you're workin' anywhere on this base you shouldn't worry about gettin' cover. There's holes and bunkers all over the place. No matter where you go you'll find some cover, I guarantee that." He hooked his thumbs in his cartridge belt. "We've had reports like this in the past. They almost never come through. Usually, when Intelligence doesn't tell us a thing, *that's* when we get hit. So if I was you I wouldn't worry too much. If we do get hit, it won't be the last time."

With this tenuous assurance, Miller left the men standing inside the wire. They watched him lock the gate, with their hearts hanging on their ears. There wasn't one prisoner whose thoughts did not follow the same theme: What happens if we get incoming and the guard don't come to let us out? What happens if we get a direct hit on the hooch? The sensation was two stages below panic. They tossed wayward glances at the pile of flak vests. A constant reminder that was unnerving. For the rest of the day no one was at ease.

Dawson gazed beyond the wire, his hand fingering the mesh. "We're fucked," he said.

Zimmerman stood with his back to the fence, leaning on it. "Maybe. Though I'd say your opinion is premature. I was here before when they had one of these alerts. Nothin' happened. It was the same thing as now, the guards came in with the flak jackets, told us about the expected attack, and then, nothin'. Everybody in the hooch was on pins and needles just waitin' for those rockets to come in. The whole thing was a false alarm."

"There's always the first time."

"Maybe," Zimmerman said skeptically. "I'm not worried. I figure if Charlie did hit he'd aim for the airfield or supply depot, not the Brig. There's nothing important in here but me, and I don't think they know I'm here."

"Maybe they might wanna harass us."

"Why?"

Dawson rubbed his nose. "I don't know. Maybe they might wanna shake us up. After all, the greatest concentration of people is in the Brig."

"You're worryin' your ass over nothin', Vic. Think it out logically. If I was a VC with an 80 mortar and I had my choice of targets between a brand new million dollar plane and a couple of jerks in the Brig, who do you think I'd aim for? No right thinkin' gook is going to sacrifice a row of jets on the airfield for a few shacks in the Brig."

"Maybe they might have a short round," Dawson said. "That could land anywhere."

"Victor, you're a worrier. Do you worry this much when you out in the bush?"

Dawson grabbed a handful of mesh, pulled on it. "It's different in the bush. At least I can always fight back. You can't fight back with incoming. You just gotta stay there and take it. I like to be prepared if it does come."

"Yeah, I know," Zimmerman said. "I feel the same way. But if you're going to worry about it all the time, that's bad. It's like the bush, if you go out on an op thinkin' you're gonna get hit, you *will* get hit. Power of suggestion. You expect the worse, you get the worse. Me, I don't want any incoming, and if it comes, fuckit, I've been under attack before."

"I wish I could share your optimism."

"It's not optimism, it's being realistic. Takin' things the way they are."

"Is it being realistic trying to bust outta here?"

"My friend, that's the truest realism of all."

"You're crazy, Zim."

"That's what they keep tellin' me," Zimmerman declared.

After midday chow they were sent to the road detail. This function lasted until late afternoon and went off without incident. Miller and his friend, Gault, were overseers for this duty, but following some unexplained whim, Miller did not ride any of the men like he was usually prone to. This was the more amazing since one of the new men was a quiet black youth who seemed totally unconcerned. Not once during the afternoon was one poisonous remark uttered by Miller the Mole.

Dawson and Zimmerman eyed him nervously, expecting some flare-up. With Miller, one got used to such things. Instead, the guard walked up and down the roadway from one side to another, periodically looking down at the rock quarry where they were working. He would drop some spittle into their midst and that was it, then he would hitch up his cartridge belt and go back to the other side of the road.

The black youth worked along with Dawson and Zimmerman on the left side of the road cleft. His task was to shovel dirt into the sandbags but he was totally alone. Dawson and Zimmerman would throw a few lines to each other. The black man paid no mind to any of it. At one time Dawson approached the man and inquired as to how hot the fuckin' sun was in this goddamn road detail. The man grunted, said nothing. Dawson looked at Zimmerman, shrugged. The brother wanted no part of them. Fuck him, Dawson thought, it's alright with me.

The detail ended at 1600 hours. The prisoners assembled on top of the road; then Miller marched them back to the tents.

They found out about it from Chi-Chi, who came over to their corner and told them of the latest rumor that had become fact.

The black man in full solitary was dead.

"How did it happen?" Dawson asked Chi-Chi.

"Rodriguez thinks he was beaten to death. He says the dude was worked over again this mornin' by Miller and two other guards, then they brought him back to the cell. When the P brought his chow at lunchtime, the dude was dying. He was taken to the hospital but it was no good. He died about an hour after he got in sick bay."

"What they say at the hospital," Zimmerman queried.

Chi-Chi smirked. "Something about 'internal injuries'—accidental, of course."

"That poor, poor brother," Zimmerman lamented.

"Didn't they give any reason for the cause of death?" Dawson asked.

Chi-Chi shrugged. "Dunno. Rodriguez says they'll pro'bly come out with a statement, maybe tomorrow. They gotta say somethin' when a cat dies in the Brig."

"It'll probably come out in the accident report," Zimmerman predicted.

"How do you figure?" Dawson questioned. "If they bring in a dude all busted up inside it sure as hell ain't from an accident."

"I know that, and you know that," Zimmerman explained, "but do you honestly think they're gonna let this thing out? I bet you anything they're gonna put a lid on the whole case. Nobody's gonna know shit about this."

"What about the doctors who examined the guy?"

"What about 'em? They'll probably back up the accident report.

Man, this is the crotch, those people out there stick together. They're not gonna risk a stink over some dead brother. It's happened before."

"It stinks," Dawson muttered. "The whole thing stinks."

"I know, but there's nothin' we can do about it."

"Maybe not us," Chi-Chi said, "but the brothers might. This afternoon when we got the word from Rodriguez there was three brothers with me on the shitter detail. I tell ya, them dudes was pissed. By now every brother in this hole knows about that stud in the cell block. They is pissed, man. They is *pissed*."

Dawson ticked a small cut on his upper lip. "I don't blame 'em. I'd be pissed too if one of my people was murdered."

"The tragedy of the thing is that it's not going to make any difference whatsoever," Zimmerman said.

Chi-Chi could not believe that. Some sort of retribution had to be forthcoming for the black man's death. It just couldn't be left like that . . . "You could be wrong," he told Zimmerman. "I saw them brothers today—and they ain't gonna stand by and let this pass."

"What the fuck can they do?" Zimmerman countered. "The brothers may be pissed now but if they fuck with the Ps they come out losin'. I know those guards are just achin' for a chance to blow away some brothers."

Chi-Chi couldn't argue with Zimmerman's statement. Yet, he still felt the urgency. He couldn't forget how enraged the black men had been that afternoon. "It's a bad scene," he murmured.

At 1935 it began. In the past Intelligence had gambled on a shot in the dark, and had been wrong. That night the Intelligence reports turned out to be all too accurate.

The first rocket scored a direct hit on one of the fuel dumps near the main airstrip, half a mile from the compound. This created a primary explosion whose shock wave was heard all the way to the other side of the base. A series of secondary explosions rocked the storage area next to where the petrol depot was situated. The second rocket came later. The projectile landed on the helicopter pad next to the compound.

Dawson didn't know what to make of it at first. He heard the explosion, of course, but it seemed distant, with the same familiar sound of arty buffeting on a remote hill. The second explosion was much closer, and startling, like a shotgun blast from a few feet away. He sprang up quickly. "We getting hit!"

Zimmerman was sitting beside Dawson on the latter's cot. He followed suit, scrambling to his feet. "That's incoming," he cried.

Chi-Chi was lying on his cot. The second blast had made him jump up with a start. "Wha' happen?"

"We getting hit," Zimmerman told him.

Chi-Chi's face went numb. "Holy shit."

The other men in the tent were stirring. All random talk ceased. They looked at each other questioningly.

"Incoming, man . . ."

"Sounded like mortars . . ."

"No, man, that's a rocket!"

"We gotta get outta here," Zimmerman realized.

They ran out of the tent, stopping at the fence, grasping the steel mesh. Outside the fence, the compound had suddenly come alive like a movie set that minutes before had been dead. Pliant oval searchlights traced freely from one end of the sector to the other. An alarm wailed from every crevice of detention. Guards were running at a frantic pace in all directions. Behind the wire, the prisoners watched helplessly like oxen in a burning cattle car, shouting out for their keepers.

Some guards had already come for their charges, opening the gates and leading the inmates to safety. Files of prisoners rushed by Dawson's tent, running at double time, herded by one guard in front and another bringing up the rear.

Dawson plopped his hands on the fence. "Where the fuck is Miller?"

"He better come get us soon," Zimmerman warned. "This hooch don't offer much protection against incoming."

"We could try climbin' over the fence," Chi-Chi suggested.

"And get shot?" Zimmerman sneered.

Chi-Chi looked out beyond the wire with the greatest of longing. "Anythin's better than being trapped in here."

"Miller will be here pretty soon," Zimmerman forced himself to say. "He can't leave us in here." There was a clipped anxiety in his voice.

Dawson saw two or three guards run by. He thought he saw Rodriguez. "Hey, Rodriguez," he shouted. "Rodriguez, Rodriguez!"

The guard either did not hear him or else refused to stop. He disappeared in the shadow of a nearby tent.

"Goddamn."

"C'mon, Miller, *c'mon*," Chi-Chi repeated to himself.

The beam of a searchlight caught their position. They were engulfed by the solid glare.

Zimmerman covered his eyes with the back of his hands. "Fuck! what they trying to do—blind us?"

"Hey, man, knock that off!" Chi-Chi yelled at the globe that was twenty feet too distant on top of the Admin building for the operators of the floodlight to hear Chi-Chi or anybody else.

The light bounced over their heads, jumped to another fence beyond their tent.

Dawson banged his fists on the wire. "Where the fuck is Miller?!"

Zimmerman wet his lips. His tongue was raw on the soft dry surface. "He better come quick. We ain't got much time."

On the outground, conical shapes from three searchlights crisscrossed paths, illuminating the welter of guards and prisoners heading for the trenches. The loud commands of the guards contributed to the verbal pandemonium.

A group of about six men jogged past the fence; one of the men bolted the line and ran in the opposite direction. The guard that held up the rear gave chase to the prisoner. Dawson watched them disappear around the corner of the next tent.

"He'll never make it," Zimmerman said definitely. "When they catch up with him they'll give him full solitary 'till he rots."

Dawson pressed his face to the steel mesh. "I hope he makes it."

The other prisoners in the tent had gathered at the gate. "Hey, let us outta here!" one of them shouted.

"Open up this place, man . . ."

"Hey. Hey!"

"Come on, Miller, *come on*," Chi-Chi kept repeating to himself.

Zimmerman pulled back and forth on the steel mesh. "Let us out, Zimmerman's in here."

Miller ran out of the darkness and stepped into the dazzle of floodlight. He headed toward the gate.

"Damn, never thought I'd be happy to see Miller," Chi-Chi said.

The men pushed on the gate. Miller fumbled with the chain lock and pulled back the gate. They saw he was carrying a rifle. He unslung the weapon, aimed it at the men, forcing them back. "Take it easy, you turds. We all gonna leave this place, but we gonna do it in orderly fashion. I want you to keep calm and follow my orders."

Another armed guard came running up to him. The man was breathing heavily. "Hey, Miller, Top says to take 'em to supply. Forget the trenches."

"Supply? How come?"

The guard caught his breath, trying to speak normally. "Top says too late to go for the trenches . . . Might get hit before we get there . . . Safest place now is supply depot."

"Okay, okay," Miller acquiesced. He leveled his rifle at the prisoners. "You heard the man, we goin' to the supply shed. I want you to form out here in two rows. Quick!"

The men scrambled outside and assembled in two files of three men apiece. Miller got at the head of the detail. "We gonna double time over there. I want no stragglers." He slung his rifle. "Let's go."

Miller led them at a quick trot toward the supply depot. None of them looked back to note they had left behind the heap of flak jackets piled to the side of the gate.

Before they reached the shed, another explosion erupted close to the compound. They didn't see the direct hit on the helo pad, but the noise was deafening.

The prisoners trotted faster, almost at a run.

"Keep together," Miller yelled over his shoulder. "'Keep together."

They came to the yard outside the supply depot which was congested with prisoners and guards from other sections. They all converged on the doorway to the supply room, standing before the entrance like commuters awaiting the northbound express.

An MP came out of the doorway. He gave a signal to another guard standing outside. The guard motioned to his subordinates. "Okay, let 'em in."

The prisoners were allowed inside the depot, a file at a time. The guards strove to encourage a faster procession. Many of them jabbed their rifles into prisoners' backs and ribs. "C'mon, speedit up . . . Hurry, hurry . . ."

The inmates wedged into the doorway. The shuffling, pushing, cursing was rampant. In back of the mass were about twenty guards, all armed, urging them onward.

Dawson and Chi-Chi were shoved inside. They came to the same storage room where they had worked during their brief tenure in supply. The countertop had been opened, letting in two men at a time. A frantic rush ensued with the prisoners being pushed back toward the storage bins as more of their numbers jammed through the doorway. Over a hundred inmates were packed into a room that at most was designed to accommodate half that capacity.

Dawson found himself surrounded by four walls of people. The continuous inflow pulled him back against Zimmerman, who stood behind him.

"This is worse than the goddamn rush hour on the Long Island Railroad," Zimmerman complained.

"There's more comin' in," Dawson said.

Chi-Chi stood shoulder to shoulder with Dawson. A brawny black man pressed on his back. He looked over his shoulder, "Hey, bro, keep cool, man."

The black man shrugged helplessly. "Can't help it, Jim, they's pushin' on me too."

"Sardines," Chi-Chi grunted. "Sardines."

Dawson had a harrowing thought. "God, all they need is just one round to land in this place and we'll all go up."

Zimmerman looked up at the wooden beams on the ceiling estimating their resistance, if any, against a 122mm rocket. "We're sitting ducks," he concluded.

Dawson felt the heat of many bodies propelling him further toward the wall. "I hope we don't get hit," he mumbled.

Zimmerman kept eyeing the ceiling. "We in a hum."

Five guards entered the supply room, closing the large door behind them. Miller stood in front of the group, his rifle cradled in his left arm. Apparently he was the ranking man. He gazed at the assembly of prisoners separated from him by the countertop. In his thoughts he was measuring their capacity to obey. The fear was visible on his face. He knew they saw it. Miller was as adverse to incoming as they were, and he couldn't hide it. He turned to one of the guards and said something in a low, hollow voice. The guard laughed nervously.

Miller turned his face to the prisoners, showing his crooked grin. The inmates stared at him without emotion. He ceased smiling, frowned instead.

A whooshing sound sliced the air outside the supply room. A second later, another explosion was heard. This one was very close. After a few seconds of absolute silence, the men began to move about in the cramped space, whispering among themselves. Unknown to them, the rocket had scored a direct hit on the cell block row.

There was another whoosh, another explosion. The shockwave seemed to make the walls tremble. Zimmerman observed flakes of dust falling from the wooden beams in the ceiling. He wasn't alone; scores of eyes watched the fragile inner roof begin to shake.

"We gotta get outta here!" one of the prisoners yelled.

The entreaty bounced to the back of the room. Many voices took up the cry. "Hey, man, we gonna get hit."

"Let's get outta here."

"It's rockets! They gonna land on us."

A few prisoners toward the front began to surge forward.

Miller unslung his rifle. "Get back! Get back! Nobody goin' nowhere. Take it easy."

The prisoners squeezed to the countertop, facing the armed guards six feet away. "It ain't safe here," one of them cried. "We got no cover. We gonna get hit!"

Miller held the rifle at his hip. "Nobody gonna get hit. It's only incomin'. It'll be over in a minute."

"We gotta get to the trenches!" a prisoner shouted.

"Nobody goin' nowhere. Get back!"

Another rocket swished over the depot. Miller looked up at the ceiling, listening for the impact. An awesome quiet fell in the room. The men crowded together, waiting for the thunder.

The projectile landed in the backyard of the depot with a loud blast that vibrated the air inside the supply room. It left their ears ringing.

The men were frenzied. They surged forward. "Stop," Miller yelled. "'Stop!"

They charged at him, forcing open the countertop. Miller opened fire on the first man to cross the boundary—a slim black youth who clutched his stomach and doubled over. He fell bleeding to the floor.

The prisoners halted, and for a long moment there was no reaction. And then they rushed at the guards. In their haste they trampled over the wounded inmate. Some ran under the countertop, others jumped over it. Miller squeezed off one more shot before he was overwhelmed by the rabble. A hand wrenched away his rifle. Fists and boots struck his body. He was driven to the ground, the men ran over him. The tip of a boot rammed into his left temple. A black prisoner picked up the rifle and jammed the butt plate into the back of his head. A thread of blood creased over his left eye.

The rest of the guards were similarly overwhelmed and beaten by the flux of prisoners. Their rifles were seized by frenzied prisoners. One of the guards had tried the hopeless maneuver of swinging his rifle at the oncoming men. He was soon overcome by a flurry of fists and kicks. Two of the guards attempted to escape. They didn't even make it to the door before dozens of vengeful hands were tearing at them. The five guards were either shoved aside or thrown to the ground, engulfed by the sheer numbers of the mob.

The men pounded on the door. One prisoner, brandishing a newly liberated rifle, shouted, "Get the keys. Who's got them?"

Mongrel hands roamed over Miller's body. The keys were extracted from one of his trouser pockets. Miller stirred, tried to get up. Someone kicked him in the face. He fell back, blood spilling from his mouth.

The keys were inserted into the square lock, the mechanism turned, the lock was removed. The men rushed out. They yelled and screamed like children on a spree. Their newly found liberty was exhilerating. They ran out in the yard, some taking separate routes and heading for the safety of the trenches, others followed their doomed impulse and headed for the main gate. Every man running with no destination in mind.

Dawson and Zimmerman crossed the threshold to the outside. Some prisoners were already surging beyond the yard. Dawson noted a few guards giving chase to scattered groups of inmates. The siren was shrieking again, and he heard rifle fire.

Zimmerman clapped his shoulder. "C'mon, let's sky."

Inside the doorway, Chi-Chi stared at Miller's body. The guard was lying on his back with his hands spread out on an imaginary cross.

Chi-Chi squatted on his haunches, and observed the body with an almost childish interest. Miller coughed some blood unto his lips and chin. He turned his face slightly to the side, looking up at Chi-Chi, his eyes wide and baleful. Chi-Chi couldn't recognize the former arrogance in the craggy face that was becoming more swollen by the minute.

Chi-Chi could remember the former arrogance. He could remember it very well. He got up slowly, raised his foot over the guard's face, and stomped down with all his force. Miller shrilled a weak "No!"—that was lost under the weight of the boot.

Chi-Chi stomped on the head in rapid succession. He kept at it until there was no movement under his foot.

He stopped, leaned against the wall, breathing feverishly. The sweat fell from his eyebrows, formed in droplets at the tip of his nose.

Miller lay at his feet. The face was canvassed in broken cartilage and bone.

Chi-Chi took a deep breath, exhaled sparingly. When he was sure he wasn't trembling anymore, he ran out the doorway.

Dawson and Zimmerman went across the yard, following no particular path. Next to the depot, one of the smaller supply shacks, annexes they were called, was burning. The front had been caved in by a direct hit, and the inside was a box of yellowish flame. Beams and walls fell to the side like so much discarded cardboard. One man was trying to crawl away from the inferno. Two armed men, who Dawson took for guards, came running to the victim and dragged him away from the fire. The victim's trousers were burning; he was screaming. The guards rolled him on the ground, trying to smother the flames.

They heard the swoosh of another projectile overhead. The rocket hit the area beyond the Medium tents. The ground shook. Zimmerman hesitated, looking from side to side, not really knowing which way to go. Dawson tapped him on the shoulder, leading him in a different direction.

They came to a small trench, jumped inside. Another rocket landed not too far from their hole. The noise sent them into the programmed cover position. They huddled in the trench with their hands covering their heads.

Zimmerman stood up, looked out the trench. The shack in front of the supply depot was still burning. Running figures darted between searchlights that had flooded the area. He heard rifle shots to his right. He looked in the direction and saw nothing.

"They must've found out about the escape," he said.

Dawson stood up beside him. "You think they might be lookin' for us?"

Zimmerman rubbed his chin. "I don't know. I've heard quite a few shots already. Could be gooks tryin' to get in the compound or else guards having target practice on us."

"Either way we're fucked," Dawson said dismally.

Zimmerman traced the paths of the floodlights, taking in their radius. He noticed they moved in an arc pattern from one side of the grounds to the other, converging only at certain spots. The irrepressible idea took hold.

"Maybe we're not fucked after all," he said thoughtfully. "At least not yet."

The alarm blared again, a long uninterrupted cant.

Dawson cupped his ears. "What is that thing?"

"Maybe the all clear signal," Zimmerman guessed.

"For who—Charlie or us?"

"I don't know and I don't intend to find out." Zimmerman looked at Dawson. "I'm gonna bust out."

"You what?"

"I'm gonna bust out," Zimmerman repeated. "I'm gonna do it right now. You comin' with me?"

Dawson felt the old malaise. Zimmerman was proposing what they knew was an irrational plan at best, hopeless at the extreme. He was aware a chance like this would never come again. But he was afraid to go with Zimmerman, and this shamed him. At that moment he hated Zimmerman for placing him in such a fix. He didn't want to go, and yet . . .

"Alright," he blurted, feeling a new pang.

They left the hole and crawled about ten yards, avoiding the searchlights. Zimmerman got up on his knees, looked around. He gestured at Dawson to get down. The beam of searchlight passed over them. They lay prone, very still. Soon the oval lifted, Zimmerman got to his feet. "Let's run for it," he said.

They set out at a quick jog, passing other fleeing prisoners. They made good time, and when they reached the area in front of the Admin shack, they were halted by two guards.

The MPs were coming from the opposite direction. In the darkness they almost bumped into the prisoners. "Hey, you two, hold it!" they yelled. Dawson and Zimmerman halted. The guards came up to them, rifles at the ready. One of the guards had a flashlight which he shone on the prisoners. "Put your hands on your head."

They looked at each other, shrugged, put their hands on their heads.

"What section you prisoners from?"

They said nothing.

The other MP came closer and pointed the muzzle of his rifle at Dawson's chest. "My buddy asked you a question, prisoner."

Dawson looked at the flashlight, then he saw the rifle barrel inches from his chest, and he was ready to say anything, admit anything to get the guard to lower the rifle.

He didn't have a chance to say a word.

Two shots rang out of nowhere. The fast cracks of M14s. The guard with the rifle went down, a bullet hole in his neck.

Dawson and Zimmerman dove to the ground.

The guard with the flashlight fell by Dawson. The MP had been shot in the shoulder. He tried to rise on one knee; another bullet drove into his stomach, flinging him on his back.

Dawson raised his head cautiously. He saw the legs of the MP twitch two times, then no movement. Suddenly the corpse seemed unreal, abstract. He forced his head down and swallowed but it choked in his throat.

"Okay, you can get up now," the voice commanded.

Dawson looked up to find himself surrounded by a group of black prisoners, all carrying rifles or billies. The man who spoke was standing in front of him. "Them Ps is dead, you don't have to worry about 'em."

He looked over at Zimmerman who was rising slowly.

"Who are you?" Dawson asked.

The black man stepped over to the corpse and, with his boot, turned it over face up. "We just busted outta the cell block," he said. "Me and my buddies here, we all from Maximum." He displayed the rifle in his hand. "We takin' over the place. We gonna wreck the joint."

Dawson glanced at Zimmerman. The shudder shared by both.

The black man gazed at the barracks-like construction of the Admin shack. Somehow the chain-mesh windows had lost their oppression. The shack looked very lonely and vulnerable.

"We gonna get rid of this mother," the black man said, pointing at the Administrative shack. There was a clatter of applause from the others gathered around him.

Dawson and Zimmerman felt out of place among the blacks, and very uncertain as to how the events were shaping.

The black man, who was obviously the leader of the group, turned to them and asked, "You with us, whitey?"

Dawson didn't know how to reply. Zimmerman managed a weak smile. "We ain't nowhere, man, we just want to get out of this compound."

The black leader looked straight at Zimmerman. "You wanna bust out?"

"That's right."

The black leader gazed at his friends, smiled cordially. "If you wanna make your bird there's nobody stoppin' you, except I don't think you'll get far. They prob'ly got the whole place blocked by now."

Zimmerman forced himself to gaze into the black man's skeptical eyes. "We'll take our chances."

"You crazy, but if you wanna sky, go ahead."

"What about you?" Zimmerman asked. "Why don't you cut out?"

The black man looked at his rifle. "No, man, we don't wanna slide, we gonna stay here and see this place burn." He spun around and faced the other men. "Ain't that right?" he shouted. "We gonna see this place burn."

The other prisoners hollered their approval.

They're crazy, Dawson thought, all of them. Then he realized that he and Zimmerman had decided to escape from the Brig—in the middle of an attack, an insurrection. We're crazy too, he thought.

"Get some firewood," the black leader ordered. "Who got the fuel?"

One of the men appeared with a jerrycan of gasoline.

"Where'd you get that?" the leader asked.

"There's beaucoup over by the supply hooch," the prisoner said. The leader hefted the can in his arms. "Good," he smiled. "We gonna have us a heavy fire tonight, Jim."

A chorus of shouts and whistles went up from the group.

The leader pointed to the heavy door of the Administrative shack. "Let's open up that door, and get goin'," he commanded. "This is just the beginning, homes, *the beginning!*"

The crowd of prisoners went up to the door and began to pound on it with rifle butts and billies. Two other men appeared with jerrycans; they doused the outside of the shack with gasoline.

"You really gonna burn this place down?" Zimmerman asked one of the prisoners.

"That's right, we gonna burn it down," the prisoner grinned. "We gonna burn it *all* down."

Zimmerman looked at the black man's grin. "Why don't you try to escape? This is the only chance you got."

The prisoner stared at the white man for a few seconds as if trying to determine an inscrutable fact the white man could not understand. "We don't wanna escape," he said. "We can't, not even if we try. There's a million Ps and the whole MarDiv waitin' out there beyond the gate. We couldn't get away. But we can burn this place—burn it down till it's dust." The prisoner looked away, his voice trailing off. "That's the only thing we can do, man. That's all we got."

He's crazy. Dawson was convinced. They're all crazy, even *me*.

The prisoners broke open the heavy door and rushed inside the Admin office, tearing and ripping apart every item that could be disposed of. The files were overturned, chairs broken on top of desks, assorted forms and paperwork scattered on the floor. One man grabbed a jerrycan and began to splatter gasoline in the main room; he continued down the long corridor that housed Admin Sec Detention. All the cells in that part of the building were empty, the prisoners having been transported to other areas once the full alert had been called.

The black leader came out of the building, holding in his hand the wooden desk sign with the CO's name on it. "Here it is," he shouted. "The Man. The one who put the hurtin' on us." He lifted the sign high up for all to see. "See this? It says, Warrant Officer Randazzo. This is what we think of Warrant Officer Randazzo—" he threw down the rectangular sign, spat on it, broke it into pieces with the heel of his boot.

The men roared.

The black leader turned to Zimmerman. "You better sky while you can, whitey, 'cause there's gonna be a big fire here pretty soon. It might get a little hot for you."

A spate of coarse laughter rose from the black prisoners.

Dawson grabbed Zimmerman's arm. "C'mon, let's get outta here."

"Yeah," Zimmerman said.

Someone tossed a match inside the main Admin office, the gasoline burst into flames, and the conflagration began to eat the wood and paper scattered about the shack.

Dawson and Zimmerman headed for the gate in quick strides. They could hear the euphoric outbursts in back of them. The shouts seemed out of place within the compound, like remote cries of victory on a football field.

Dawson stopped for an instant, and looked back. The Admin structure was burning. Flames licked out of the barred windows; fire began to obscure the walls. Sheets of flame crackled with the chaos of falling lumber.

Zimmerman tugged Dawson's arm. "Let's go. We haven't much time."

Dawson was mesmerized by the glare of the fire. The building was about to fall. His mind carried him back to the cell block, to Miller, and Gunny Yeager. What were they really trying to destroy? he asked himself.

He was plagued by a sudden weariness. His thoughts were febrile; he didn't know where he was going or where he had been. Not knowing why, he didn't care.

Zimmerman jabbed him again. "Vic, let's go." He nodded weakly. Zimmerman led the way, and he followed.

They reached a point about twenty feet from the gate.

"Oh, no," Dawson moaned.

Behind the gate, standing in a threatening row, were scores of armed guards with flak jackets, helmets and rifles. Dawson saw two jeeps with mounted fifty caliber machine guns. The vehicles were spaced about twenty yards apart. Overhead and behind the marines the beam of a floodlight showered into the compound. The white cone danced about the ground, jumped back over the fence. It lowered on one of the jeeps, showing three men huddled over a radio unit. The command jeep, Dawson thought.

"Must be a company out there," Zimmerman estimated.

The searchlight aimed in their direction. They stepped back a few feet, dropped to the ground. The light passed them by.

"They don't look like Ps," Dawson said. "Those guys out there are grunts! Look, they even got bloopers."

Zimmerman also noticed the half dozen men or more carrying the dread single-shot grenade launchers. He bit the supple flesh on the back of his hand. "They must've called up reinforcements."

"That means they know about the breakout."

"There ain't no breakout," Zimmerman said. "The brothers may have taken over the Brig but they can't get out." He gestured toward the troops. "Those fuckers have us trapped."

Dawson heard the familiar click of bolts when rifles are locked and loaded. Only it was a hundred and eighty rifle bolts that jammed forward. Staggered sounds that lasted for perhaps ten seconds. A deadening ache was plumbed in his belly.

"They're comin' in," Zimmerman said.

"We're fucked," Dawson mumbled.

Two guards opened the gate. Dawson watched four men—one fire team, enter the compound. His head was spinning. Somewhat distantly he heard Zimmerman say, "I'm going to make a run for it."

"Where you gonna go?" Dawson asked. "They got the fence surrounded."

"But not all of it. I figure back toward the sallyport there's no guards. I'll jump the fence over there."

"But you don't know for sure."

"We'll have to chance it, Corporal Dawson." Zimmerman got up on one knee with the other leg extended and the foot poised behind him. He was in the position of a runner waiting for the pistol shot to start the race. "You coming?" he asked Dawson.

"Yeah," Dawson mumbled.

They took off, running away from the gate.

After the first four men had entered the compound, another fireteam followed. This was when the resistance began. A volley of rifle fire smothered the darkness behind Dawson and Zimmerman. Three guards fell immediately, the rest dropped to the ground and began to fire back at the prisoners. Dawson and Zimmerman halted, stood dazed for a second or two, then fell prostrate and covered their heads while the firefight raged around them and above them.

Dawson forced his face into the dirt, trying to lose himself inside the blurring circles in the back of his eyes. The sound of rifle fire was deafening. His body shook uncontrollably.

The guard detachment lugged M60 machine guns as well as 40mm grenade launchers, and they began to rake and bombard the area in sustained bursts. Their superior firepower was enough to scatter the few prisoners that had initiated the action. The prisoners had fired on the gate from behind the cover of the large squad tent that served as the barbershop. A lack of secure cover had forced the dozen or so inmates to retreat to the inner safety of Medium Detention.

The firing stopped. Dawson kept his head glued to the ground. The pulse in his head began to wane. He heard a faint hum.

Zimmerman lifted his head, looked about slowly. He glanced over his shoulder, saw the guards approaching. They were closer than he had imagined—almost upon him! Without a word he got to his feet and cut out.

One moment Zimmerman was lying next to him, the next instant he was running. Dawson wondered why. He saw Zimmerman dash at top speed toward the darkened hull of the tent where the sniper fire had come from. Dawson stood up and ran after Zimmerman. Behind him a rifle shot went off. It was followed by another discharge. He didn't stop, his legs pumping automatically while his lungs gasped for air. Common sense told him he should drop to the ground, cover his head once more. Perhaps had he yielded they would stop shooting at him, but he kept on, his chest rising and falling and expanding, trying to burst out of its cage. Somewhere far off he still heard the faint hum.

Two shots hit the ground just to his right; puffs of dust swirled next to his foot. Another shot, and then another. He was beyond it. He was so afraid that the mere thought of stopping fed his fear, encouraged it.

He couldn't keep it up forever, that much he knew. His mind sought escape, but his body ached. He cornered the side of the tent where Zimmerman had disappeared, found no exit, and sped away from Medium Detention. But he was about to drop. He could feel it coming; his chest was inching its way up his throat.

Then he looked back and saw no one behind him. Mysteriously, the MPs who minutes before had been firing at him had disappeared as well. He slowed down his pace, and began to cough hard. The phlegm stuck in his gullet.

Not ten yards away he saw the bare outline of a trench. He could tell it was a trench even in the dark; the ground seemed to slope down at the spot like a small cliff; a deep rectangular hole blacker than the nonlight surrounding it. He headed for the trench and jumped in.

"What the fuck—"

He had landed on top of someone. "Get off me, you bitch," the voice cried. "What'd you think I am—a cushion? Get off!"

Dawson felt the body squirming and jousting beneath him. He rolled away from atop the man and hugged the trench wall.

"What's wrong with you, man, you got the hots or somethin'—"

Dawson couldn't hear him, or he did but didn't want to. He was tired, so tired. He closed his eyes and forgot.

Although the voice did seem familiar.

"Chi-Chi, be cool," Dawson said slowly, as if the effort of talking threatened to speed up the pumping in his heart.

"Dawson!" Chi-Chi dragged himself to the trench wall, clasped him on the shoulder. "Dawson, is it you?"

"Who the hell did you think it was—your mother?" Dawson panted.

Chi-Chi lay back on the trench floor. "Man, this is a goof." He covered his eyes with the back of his right hand. "If we get outta this nothin' will ever shake me up again."

"What you doin' here, Cheech?" Dawson asked between gasps.

"Tryin' to get away from the Ps."

Dawson rolled over to Chi-Chi, lay beside him. In the trench the air smelt dank and moist like the inside of a locker room. Dawson felt the earth grinding under his back. "We lost you after the break-out. I was gettin' the feeling you'd been caught."

"Everybody got lost after the breakout," Chi-Chi said. "This joint is a madhouse. Ps everywhere, shootin' us down . . . I wouldn't be surprised if they call in arty."

"I didn't wanna break out," Dawson admitted, speaking with less effort now.

Chi-Chi removed the hand from his eyes. It was the same as if he had kept his eyes covered. All he could do was peer at nothing. "I wanted to break out. But not like this. Now we'll all prob'ly get greased."

Any other time Chi-Chi's prophesy would have unnerved Dawson. But now, he was too fatigued to care. It was amazing how fatalistic he had become in the Brig. He was even prepared to accept his own demise without a qualm; perhaps not wholeheartedly accept it, but he knew he was beaten. They had even stripped him of his instinct for survival. He had lost it. He had lost it completely.

"I don't give a fuck anymore," he said, at last affirming it out loud.

They heard some grenade blasts in the distance, then another explosion, but closer. All of it interspersed with machine gunfire. Dawson felt the ground shake. Loose rocks and pebbles rolled down the trench wall, the dust settling on the two men.

Chi-Chi sat up slowly. "The Ps sure puttin' a hurt on us."

Dawson knew the answer to it already, but nevertheless he asked once more. "Do you think we stand a chance of gettin' out of here?"

"Not a snowman's chance in hell," Chi-Chi replied with equanimity.

"What we gonna do?"

"I don't know," Chi-Chi shrugged, "but I wish I had me a gun."

"You wanna fight it out?"

"That's the only thing we can do now."

"You said yourself we don't stand a chance."

Chi-Chi nodded. "Un-huh. But we can put a hurtin' on them too. I don't plan to lay here and have them blow me away without first giving them a battle."

"What battle, Chi-Chi?" Dawson said cruelly. "We ain't got shit."

Chi-Chi lowered his head very close to Dawson, their faces almost touching. "We got dignity, man," he said quietly. "We got dignity."

Dawson sat up, didn't say anything in reply. He didn't know how.

Chi-Chi took a deep breath. "If we stay here they gonna come for us sooner or later. I suggest we sky outta here."

"Where can we go?"

"Anywhere. But not in a trench—we're sittin' ducks."

Dawson gazed about the trench. It was of the usual depth, about five feet, the trench walls inclining at a slight angle as they touched the trench floor. It could provide great safety against a tank maybe, but not roving foot troops. One frag was all that was needed to demolish a squad inside a trench. He wiped the sweat from his forehead.

"We can't head for the gate," he said. "That's already been blocked by the grunts. The cell block has been blown away, and I bet by now they got the whole compound surrounded. It don't seem we have too much of a chance, does it?"

"I'm gonna take a look-see," Chi-Chi decided suddenly. He stood up in the trench, scanning the dark around him. A few searchlights traced the grounds, hitting the far tents of Medium Detention, and sometimes touching the rubble of what had been the cell block. He knew they were still in the outgrounds of the Administrative Sector. To his right, about fifty yards out, he discerned the outline of the hooches in Medium. No lights were shining inside those tents tonight, but he reasoned correctly there must be some armed prisoners in them, waiting for the guards to charge. Curiously, the firing had stopped, and he didn't see anyone, prisoner on guard, stomping about the grounds. An unspoken, unexplained truce had momentarily settled in the yard.

He squatted in the trench. "It's quiet out there, slick. *Too* quiet. Somethin's going on, somebody's plannin' somethin'." He looked up at the trench wall. "Like I said, I wouldn't be surprised if the Ps called a firemission on us."

Dawson frowned. "That would be somethin'."

Chi-Chi smiled affectedly. "Y'know, every time in the bush when I use to call in arty on the gooks I always wondered how they felt. Maybe this time I'll find out myself."

"Man, don't even joke about it," Dawson said seriously. "I've been under attack by our own arty. It happened when our gunny fucked up on his coordinates, and I tell you, it's not a pretty sight. It's somethin' I wouldn't wish even on the gooks."

Chi-Chi could see it. "Things sure look different when you're on the receivin' end."

"Yeah." Dawson leaned back on the trench wall. After a moment's silence, he said, "We're still here, and that's just as bad."

"You're right," Chi-Chi reiterated. "We gotta get away."

"What would you suggest?"

Chi-Chi scratched his chin again. "I think we should try gettin' to Medium Detention."

"Medium Detention? That's where the Ps are headin' for now."

"Maybe, but I don't think they've taken it yet. When I peeked out just now it was very quiet out there. I think our people still have it under control. Most of the brothers with the guns are up there. They're just waitin' for the Ps to rush them."

"What's the sense of tryin' for Medium? If we make it we'll probably have to fight off the Ps along with the rest of those turds."

Chi-Chi stared at Dawson for a long moment. "And what's wrong with that? Haven't you ever made a stand in your life, Dawson? Are all you fuckin' farmers the same? If you're gonna stay here and get killed then you deserve to die."

Dawson felt pain, and then anxiety, and then pain again. Twice in his captivity he had felt the shame: once at the sandpile when the other black prisoner had stood up to Miller and he hadn't, and again now. Had he lost his nerve as well as his instinct for survival? The pill stuck in his throat.

He got to his feet and motioned to Chi-Chi. "C'mon, let's go."

They climbed out of the trench, huddling close to the ground. "I just hope we don't get greased by our own people out there," he said in a low voice.

"Yeah, well, I hope so too," Chi-Chi seconded. "It's a chance we'll have to take. Let's pray they take us for prisoners and not guards."

"We can yell at them to hold fire as we get closer to the hooches."

"That's not a bad idea."

Dawson rose slowly, got up on one knee. "You ready?" he asked Chi-Chi.

"As ready as I'll ever be."

"Okay. Now!" Dawson called.

And they ran off, heading for the circle of tents enclosed within a smaller fence on the other side of the grounds. They appeared as two shadows crossing various paths of light; they jumped over trenches and foxholes, zigzagged at every juncture in order to avoid the searchlights.

They hadn't run more than twenty yards, less than ten seconds, when the MP sharpshooter hiding behind one of the unoccupied guard tents opened up on them. He fired a short burst, a really short burst from an M16 on full automatic. The sharpshooter was a pimply faced kid, not even eighteen yet, who had joined the Marines because basically he had nothing else to do, and there wasn't much doing in Jacksonville, North Carolina, and he had fired a short burst because from the beginning of his tour he had been assigned tedious guard duty in a Brig when he really wanted to be out in the bush where all the action and shooting was, and in H&S Casual up to now the only weapon they had been allowed to handle was that old M14 and he'd never used a 16 before and so when he saw these two prisoners running toward their buddies in Medium he fired a short burst . . . which nailed Dawson's right palm and tore through his left kneecap, then grazed Chi-Chi behind the right ear, while another ricochet bounced off the sole of Chi-Chi's right foot so that he screamed when he felt the hot pin driving through the leather of the boot and pricking the sensitive area next to a callous he had nursed since he came in-country.

They both fell to the ground at the same time. The M16 gave another burst but this one was above their heads so that they forgot their Basic Infantryman's Manual and began to stir on the ground instead of playing possum like they should have done.

Dawson rolled on his back, his knee stinging like an open cut that had been splattered with alcohol. He noted the searchlights prancing about them, touching them here and there, first their feet and then their heads. A regular dance. The light finally lifted, only to return moments later.

He tried to move his limbs, but his left leg didn't respond, and neither did his right hand, at least not as quickly as the left one. He knew he had been hit, but as of yet he didn't know where—until the pain shot through his hand and the knee at the same time, pinching every nerve ending for all it was worth.

My God, I'm hit, he realized. I'm hit! He didn't scream or yell because he couldn't. Perhaps his vocal cords had been shot out instead of his knee. What is this shit? He moved his left leg painfully—his hand was useless—and when he tried to roll over and stand, the pain was greater. He rolled on his back again, lowering his good hand and touching the knee, feeling the moist essence oozing out of the hole right smack in the middle of the knee cap itself.

I'll be damned, I've been hit.

Chi-Chi stirred. His pain was not as severe, but constant. He felt the blood dribbling behind his ear, settling at the back of his neck. Yet it felt pleasant, like the teasing of a feather. The sting at the sole of his right foot was something else. There was agony there. No one had removed the hot pin. He could feel the sock inside the boot slowly soaking with blood. It was similar to the sensation he had felt whenever he went on patrol around Charlie Ridge and had his foot immersed in a rice paddy. Only this time the shitty smell of the water was missing. He still had to get away.

Chi-Chi glanced to his side and noted Dawson lying on his back, holding his knee cap and moaning. This is a fine mess we got our asses into, he thought to himself, and then he giggled. Shot in the foot. A fine mess.

The searchlight struck his face, and he turned his head to avoid the glare. More shots came by they whizzed above his head. He crouched on the ground again. Repeating in his thoughts . . . a fine mess . . . a fine mess.

The pimply faced kid at the other side of the tent was joined by four more guards. Cautiously, the five of them abandoned the cover of the hooch and approached the two men.

Dawson heard the heavy footsteps circling around him. He had turned on his side holding his knee, but now he tried to rise, propping himself on one arm.

"Want us to finish 'em off, Top?" he heard one of the guards say.

"No," came the response.

Dawson squinted, and peered at the men surrounding him. He had heard right the first time. One of the five guards, the one nearest to him was Master Sergeant Lidel.

"What we gonna do with 'em?" another guard asked.

"Take 'em back," Lidel said, looking down at Dawson. "We'll need 'em to find out how this whole thing started when the riot's over."

"Want me to take 'em back, Top?" the pimply faced youth volunteered, still clutching his rifle.

"Yeah, but not by yourself. Have Clive and Pulaski here give you a hand."

Two guards reached down and grasped Dawson by the arm, trying to force him to his feet. A jolt of pain came from the kneecap again. Dawson cried out. Then he made an effort to push away the MPs.

A guard jammed the barrel of his rifle into Dawson's stomach. He sagged between the two men holding him.

On the ground, Chi-Chi, enraged, forgot the hot pin in his boot and the wetness in the back of his ear. With one effortless movement, which was startling for a man who had been wounded twice in different places, he jumped to his feet, almost hobbling on his good leg, and rushed at the guard who had struck Dawson.

Before Chi-Chi could secure a hold on the guard, Lidel grabbed him, encircling Chi-Chi's smaller body in his huge arms.

While Lidel seized Chi-Chi, Dawson clutched at the two guards to either side of him, trying to take them down with him.

The pimply faced youth gripped his rifle, momentarily stunned, not knowing what to do.

Lidel held Chi-Chi with a massive elbow around the neck, almost choking him. Chi-Chi fought for air. Lidel sought to crush the prisoner.

Chi-Chi managed to get a hand free, and reached behind his back. Feeling for Lidel's crotch, he squeezed with all his might.

Lidel screamed, letting go of the smaller man. He retreated, cupping his groin.

Suddenly free, Chi-Chi flung himself at one of the guards grappling Dawson. The guard tried to parry, swinging his rifle in a horizontal butt stroke, but Chi-Chi saw it in time, grasped the stock of the rifle and tried to pull it from the MP.

The guard was another big man, just like Lidel, and with Chi-Chi's foot still burning from the shot, it wasn't difficult for him to push Chi-Chi away.

Chi-Chi stumbled, falling on his back. Yet he was up again instantly, hopping on one foot, trying to snatch the rifle again.

The pimply faced youth fired his weapon for the third time that night, pumping Chi-Chi's stomach with exactly four well-placed shots, all in rapid-fire automatic.

Chi-Chi hit the ground with a thump. This time he didn't get up.

Dawson was shocked, then enraged. An all-consuming rage that blinded him, excited him. Not even throughout the indignities suffered in the cell block had he felt such hate. If he had had the power to destroy the world he would have done it that night. As it was, he screamed inanely at everything and nothing, striking at the one guard still holding him, not considering the useless kneecap of his left leg, or the trousers soaked through with blood.

Amazingly, he toppled the guard, clinging on top of him somehow. The pimply faced youth aimed the rifle for the fourth time.

Lidel let go of his balls long enough to rush at the youth, grab his rifle and pull it away. "You wanna kill our own men?" he yelled.

Dawson had not let up on the other guard. Despite the injury to his hand he sought to battle the MP with his good arm, clawing at the man's face as they rolled on the ground. The guard who had been battling Chi-Chi, attacked from behind, grasped Dawson by the collar and smashed the butt of his rifle on top of Dawson's head. The treated plastic of the stock almost cracked when it met Dawson's skull. Dawson fell to the ground, a small horizontal gash visible on the bald surface right in the middle of his skull.

The guard who had been wrestling Dawson got up. "Damn," he gasped. "I never seen such dudes with so much fight in 'em."

Lidel removed his helmet and wiped his forehead. "They're assholes." He breathed deeply, panting slightly. "We shoulda kilt 'em when we had the chance." He bent at the waist, holding his helmet in one hand and clutching his knee with the other. "We should kill 'em all."

"Yeah . . . yeah," the pimply faced youth agreed hastily.

Lidel gave him a long, searing look. "You keep quiet, boy, 'cause you ain't no better than they are."

The youth looked at the other men, seeking some sort of approbation, and finding none, he stared at his boots. He trembled visibly.

Lidel straightened up, trying to adjust his shoulders inside the flak jacket. He had not worn a vest since his last tour in-country and he felt leaden inside the unaccustomed weight.

"Take 'em back to the CP," he ordered, motioning to the two prisoners at his feet, one nearly alive, one dead.

"Both of 'em, Top?" one of the guards asked.

"Yeah, both of 'em."

"Why don't we leave the dead one here?" the guard inquired.

"'Cause I don't want you to," Lidel snapped. "We got to identify 'im, along with the other asshole. Now take 'em back to the CP. I ain't gonna tell you again."

The men didn't argue. They glanced at each other, shrugged. Two of them picked up Dawson and, holding him by the armpits, dragged him away.

The other two men took hold of Chi-Chi's legs, and likewise moved him out. His back, arms and head trailed on the dirt like so much meat, leaving small imprints on a small piece of ground.

The insurrection lasted four hours. It was officially tagged as beginning shortly after the first rocket attack at 1930 hours and ending at 2330 hours with the final mop-up of the cell block, the sector that had offered the most resistance.

After the mass breakout of a hundred and ten prisoners from the supply depot, a small number had proceeded to the cell block where they overpowered the detail of twelve guards and liberated the remaining live inmates in Maximum Detention.

Sparked by their sudden freedom, the prisoners tore through the sallyport area, setting fire to the Medium Detention tents while scores more jumped into the trenches behind the sector, overwhelming the few guards that had led their charges to safety during the emergency. Thirty minutes after the mass escape the inner compound was completely under prisoner control. This bred an orgy of rampaging violence, especially on the part of the blacks. The men encouraged a mania of fire and destruction. They set ablaze Admin Sec, almost all of Medium Detention, the supply depot, the Brig barbershop, and the overhanging camouflage netting that served as the roof to the cell-block row. It was estimated that the prisoners burned down a third of the Brig.

Charlie and Delta Company of the 8th Military Police Battalion were called in to quell the disturbance. At the time the revolt began, Delta Company had been guarding the nearby Da Nang Bridge a few miles from base against nighttime sabotage attempts. They were ordered to leave the bridge and head for the compound. For the duration of the night the bridge waterway, a vital link in the Da Nang sector, was left unguarded.

Provided with superior numbers and weaponry, the reinforcements were able to suppress the insurrection in a matter of hours. Nevertheless, the final recapture of the Brig was at a high cost and not only in casualties. Over eighty percent of the personnel in the Eighth Military Police Battalion had at one time or another served in the compound either as guards or regular MPs. As such they could not help but be tainted with an unsavory attitude toward all prisoners. When they charged inside the compound, three of their number had already been killed, and rumors abounded as to how many more had been tortured, mutilated or otherwise rendered manless by the crazed inmates.

In fact, except for the death of Miller, all the other MPs captured at the time of the revolt were placed under prisoner guard inside the various bunkers in the Medium Detention sector. The leaders of the revolt surmised they could get away with burning down the Brig— that couldn't be helped, and anyway it was impossible to stop a disorganized group once the fever got under way. Yet they reasoned that the guards could be used as bargaining pawns with the Brig officials. Even at this late date it was assumed, and hoped, that the Brig honchos would not storm the compound and put their own personnel in jeopardy without first having some sort of parley.

It didn't work out that way. Even as their captured comrades were being liberated from the two or three bunkers housing them, the rescuers were knee deep in their bloodlust. After months of purposelessness and boredom and stored up animosity, the opportunity to strike at the inmates was like a gift to the guards. At last they were fighting something real, not a nebulous enemy or incoming. It was thrilling, a holiday.

They moved through Medium Detention with their rifles and machine guns blazing. Those prisoners who offered any resistance they shot on principle; and those who didn't offer any resistance they shot just the same. When the few prisoners who put up a fight had scattered and gone, those who were left behind or who had been fortunate enough to find weapons, simply put up their hands and came out of their shelters. A sign of surrender or the prospect of it offered no safety at all. Those who stepped forward with their hands on their heads were simply blown away right then and there. The MPs scoured every trench and bunker, occasionally lobbing grenades at the men who were either huddled inside the embankments or else clamoring to get out.

But usually the MPs came up to the trenches and, without a word, sprayed the holes with rifle and machine gunfire two or three times until no movement was discernible inside. There were variations to this. Sometimes after a grenade had been exploded inside the trench, instead of firing into the ditch, the guards would pour gasoline in it and then set fire to the trench, burning alive whatever inmates were left who had survived the initial grenade blast. The more conventional guards would even take prisoners and, not seeing much fun in burning them alive, would smash legs and elbows with rifle butts and billies. But it was in the cell block that true expertise was manifested. Most of the solid construction had been demolished by RPGs, and what remained was a crumpled mess of concrete blocks and iron pilings since the canvas-covered roof had been caved in by a direct hit. Moans and groans echoed from underneath the rubble. The guards roamed over the concrete slum, in most cases disregarding the cries of help from those inmates who had not been able to escape the attack. The MPs had other ideas. They sought those prisoners who had survived the rockets. And they found a few who had been lucky enough to avoid being crushed in the cell block. And these turned out to be not so lucky. Those who were half-alive were dragged out of the rubble, only to have their heads bashed in by rifle butts. Others were kicked to death. Some guards were even more enterprising. One fireteam of four MPs was able to find a black prisoner who had escaped almost unscathed. The guards grabbed his arms and legs and pinned him to the ground, then they spread his legs apart and shot him point-blank in the groin.

When the confrontation ended, the score was forty-eight prisoners dead, twenty-two wounded; six guards slain, none wounded.

Dawson was taken back to the large squad tent that served as the command post for the MP Battalion. He was fortunate in that before any vengeful guards got to him, regular Marine infantry units arrived on the scene with certified corpsmen to administer aid to all wounded and bring things under control.

He was given preliminary medical treatment and then sent to the base hospital along with the other seriously wounded. There, in sick bay, during those quiet moments when he felt safe, he entertained a wholly preposterous thought. What had happened to Zimmerman? Had he made it to the outside? He fervently hoped so.

Zimmerman was found the next day. Hanging limply from the hooks of barbed wire.

He had survived the night, darting and hiding in abandoned bunkers as the MPs moved on. At daybreak he tried climbing the Brig fence, covering his hands with the rags of discarded fatigues he had found somewhere. The material wasn't sturdy and the barbs ripped the cloth, shredding his skin. Discarding it he climbed up eight feet to the top. Seeing the other side almost within his reach, he doubled his efforts. Just as he was about to fling his right leg over the top slanted portion of the wire, three bullets punched into his back, driving him against the fence. His body went limp, the upper torso bent over the wire while his legs balanced the lower part on the inside of the compound.

Three guards emerged from the shade of the tent about ten feet away. They walked up to the body dangling on the fence. One of the guards removed the magazine from his rifle, hooked the empty clip on his cartridge belt. He took another magazine from his flak vest pocket and inserted it into the rifle well.

PART THREE - EPILOGUE

U.S. BASE HOSPITAL
DA NANG
AUGUST 21ST

"So we finally leaving the place," the Marine patient said. "It's about time."

He sighed and scanned the rest of the article in the *Stars and Stripes* morning edition. "Dig this," he announced. "Of the four thousand marines that were suppose to be withdrawn, only seven hundred and forty were returned to the States. The rest were kept in Vietnam with other units." He snorted. "What a con. And they call it a *withdrawal*. Shee-it. Leave it to the crotch to pull the wool over yore eye."

He looked to his right and spoke to the other patient in the bed nearby. "Hey, you was in the Sixteenth Marines, wasn't you?"

Dawson was lying on the bed, his head cushioned by the loose fluffiness of the pillow. He turned his head and said yes.

"Yore people left the Nam," the patient proclaimed, looking at the news caption in the paper. "The whole damn regiment." He put down the newspaper. "Well, not actually. Only them dudes with a completed tour. The rest of them assholes was sent someplace else." The patient leaned his head on the pillowed bedrest. "Withdrawal or no

163

withdrawal ya still gotta do a whole tour in Nam. I thought they'd take out everybody at the same time. Guess they're not doing that."

Dawson gestured toward the paper with his head. "Let's see that."

The patient picked up the newspaper and reached over to Dawson, handing the paper to him.

The headline struck him instantly.

FIRST U.S. MARINE TROOPS
RETURN HOME

SAN DIEGO—Lead elements of the 16th Marine Regiment, one of the first American units to be withdrawn from the Vietnam War, arrived at San Diego's Lindbergh Field on Thurday morning.

On hand to greet the members of the 16th were BGen Howard Linder, commanding general Force Troops, FMF Pacific, and MajGen Albert R. Flynn, commanding general, Marine Corps Recruit Depot, San Diego. Col. Thomas N. Ronson, commanding officer of the regiment, was the first Marine off the aircraft. He had assumed command of the unit in May of 1968.

The Leathernecks formed part of the first phased withdrawal plan of American troops from the Vietnam War as outlined by President Nixon and Defense Secretary Melvin Laird earlier this year.

Six commercial jet liners and one Air Force jet transport were used to return the 4,300 Marines to San Diego. Prior to their flight to the U.S. the unit had been transported to Okinawa directly from Da Nang.

It was in August of 1965 that the 16th Marine Regiment was first deployed in

Vietnam, being among the first ground
troops committed to the large scale
buildup in the war effort.

The returning Marines, all veterans of
one tour of duty in southeast Asia, will
be installed at Camp Lejeune, N.C., the
regiment's home base.

So they were going home. All of his old outfit, except for him and
those who had been wasted. When would he be going home? There
must be some happy assholes in my outfit, he thought. The ones who
rotate, that is. Some happy assholes. He sighed, recalling each and
every man in the platoon, in his squad. Most of his squad would not
be making it home. Or, they would, but it'd be in body bags. I won't be
making it home. Yeager won't be making it home. Chi-Chi won't be
making it home. Zimmerman won't be making it home. How many
more?

He lowered the paper and stared at the gray concrete hospital ceiling. "The crotch never gives nothing for free. That's the first thing I
learned in this organization. They never give nothing for free."

The other patient nodded in agreement. "Amen." He was a slim
black youth with very sharp features. "How much time you got left
in-country?" he asked.

"I don't know," Dawson replied.

"Either way you skyin' back to the world sooner or later. Me, I got
five months left." The patient looked at the tubular cast on his right
leg. It covered the entire limb from ankle to thigh. "Who knows?
Maybe if my leg is bad enough they might send me home, too."

Dawson eyed the patient's cast. "What's wrong with your leg?"

"It got messed up by a whole buncha' shrapnel. My squad leader
stepped on a booby trap and me and two other dudes were right
behind him. We all got fucked. The squad leader got blown away,
another dude lost an arm and I got hit in the leg. I din't come out too
bad compared to the other guys. Just got some cuts that's all."

"You were lucky."

"That's what worries me," the patient confided. "The doctor says
my leg don't look so bad, it might heal up in a coupla months or so.
That's bad shit. I might be goin' back."

"To the bush?"

"Un-huh."

"That's flaky," Dawson said. "Any guy who gets hit once should automatically be sent home."

"There it is," the black patient agreed. "Fuckin' crotch, they wait till you're dying 'fore they send ya home."

"Who was you with in the bush?"

"Two-seven."

"I hear you people got into a lotta shit up in the Dodge City area."

"You ain't shittin' we did. That's where I got hit, and I sure as hell don't wanna slide back there."

Dawson gave solace. "I know how it is. I'd feel the same way if I was in your shoes."

"I wish I had a month left," the patient said longingly. "Hell, I wish I had *two* months left. They say if you get hit and have less than ninety days to do in-country they hafta send you home. I figger I missed out by about three months."

"You never know. You just *may* go back to the world." Dawson thought over what he had said, decided there really wasn't much chance for the patient trying to cut short his tour. Of course, he didn't voice this out loud. "If I was you I'd be copping a plea with that doctor so bad . . ."

"I tried it already, man," the patient asserted. "Why, I been eatin' that doctor's mind somethin' fierce." He became glum. "The fucker still don't believe me. Dumb sawbones. All them Navy doctors know is patchin' ya up and sendin' ya back."

"Keep trying, buddy, it don't hurt none."

"Don't worry 'bout me, man, I'm hangin' in there. I'm gonna give 'em some jive before I go back—"

The black patient stopped short, noted the white uniformed corpsman who passed by his bed and called on Dawson. Standing beside the corpsman was an MP with cartridge belt and billy club.

Dawson tried to ignore the MP. "What's up, Doc?" he asked.

"Got good news for you, Dawson," the corpsman said. "You're going to skip sick call this morning. Doctor Winslow wants to see you in his office."

"You mean now?"

"Yeah."

"How come?"

"I don't know," the corpsman said.

Dawson could not ignore the MP forever. He gestured toward the guard and asked, "Does he have to come along?"

The corpsman shrugged his shoulders and said rather apologetically, "Technically you're a Brig inmate. Whenever you leave the ward you need a guard with you. It's the rules."

Dawson looked at the lanky young man with the cartridge belt. "Sure, rules. I guess the honchos in Casual might be worried I'll try escapin' even though I got a bum leg and can hardly walk."

The MP stared back at Dawson and said nothing. He was here to do his job, no more. The young man didn't give a hoot if Dawson tried to escape. His only concern was escorting Dawson to the doctor then getting back to the compound before noon chow. That's the one thing he didn't want to miss.

Dawson pursed his lips, his displeasure very evident.

He sat up slowly. "Let me go see the good doctor then." He grabbed hold of his bad leg and lifted it over to the bedside. "Hey, Doc, could you hand me that, please." He pointed to the cane hooked to the bedpost at the foot of the bed. The corpsman handed Dawson the cane and helped him get up, then assisted him in donning his patient's robe.

"How's the hand?" the corpsman asked.

Dawson held up his bandaged right hand. "It's better, I guess. I can't feel nothing in it."

"It doesn't hurt anymore?"

"No."

"Maybe that's a good sign."

Dawson dismissed it. "Who knows." He waved to the black patient. "Catch you later."

The patient nodded.

Dawson grasped his cane and turned to the MP. "You ready, fuzz?"

The MP didn't reply.

"Can you make it to the office?" the corpsman inquired.

"Yeah, Doc, I can make it." Dawson tapped the cane on the concrete floor. "I'm gettin' pretty good at walkin' around with this."

He walked into the starboard aisle of the orthopedics ward, followed by the MP. Going up the aisle, banked on each side by rows of beds with patients in casts, arm slings and braces, Dawson did not walk in the ordinary sense. Actually he limped along with the aid of the sturdy wooden cane clutched in his left fist, and dragging his left leg which the physicians had assured him would get better, maybe in the near future.

They walked out of the ward and turned left, heading up the main hallway on the hospital's lower level. So many doors, so many wards. Dawson was caught by the unusual texture of it. The place did not smell like a hospital, not in the way he thought it would. The odor of ether and camphor was missing. About the only section permeated with an antiseptic smell was the Intensive Care Unit, and that was an isolated ward way at the other end of the hallway. It gave one pause. Air conditioning but no hospital smell. Sometimes, in the mornings, he could get a whiff of it, during sick call, when the nurses came around following the inspecting doctor with a wheeled cart full of bottles, pans and bandages. This was a short-lived experience. By ten o'clock sick call would be over and every trace of medicine was gone. The patients would then settle down to prolonged games of checkers or chess or parcheesi, or compare notes on which nurses had the cutest behinds, or perhaps wait for the freshly scrubbed nurses to come by and offer them books and help them write letters. And naturally the men would flirt harmlessly with the nurses and dream of home.

Sometimes the smell would come back when the staff brought in a new patient just injured in combat, or an amputee who was then kept on the port side of the ward in a special bed with metal railings all around it. The smell would be there, at the stumps of the legs that had been cut off or the arms that had been sawed and then wrapped in loads of bandages saturated in some foul-smelling liquid that faintly resembled chlorine.

The smell could get to you, and so could the kids carrying it. Like the youngster who came in just four days after Dawson had arrived on the ward. The kid had lost both legs just above the knee. He screamed the whole first night after his operation. They gave him morphine, sedatives, you name it. The kid still complained about the pain. On the third night the kid suddenly became quiet, and nobody paid any attention. What the hell, everyone had his own pain to contend with. Like everyone else, Dawson was given a couple of

Darvons so he could sleep. It was during this chemically-induced slumber, when everybody in the ward was counting Zs, that the amputee decided to kill himself by rolling his trunk off the bed and jumping to the floor—on the stumps of his bandaged sawed off legs.

The kid tried, alright. All Dawson recalled were the lights being turned on, doctors and nurses rushing up the aisles, and the kid's trunk lying on the floor in a pool of blood. A lot of men in the ward, patients and attendants both, puked their guts out that night. Dawson couldn't eat for two days afterwards.

That's why every time an amputee came in and the chlorine smell got to him, Dawson would rise from his bed and approach the nearby window, force it open and stick out his head to breathe in the vibrant air redolent of pine trees and stale beer from the alleys half a mile away where the hustlers and young prostitutes strutted their wares, and waited for the hospital personnel like carrion birds. With his head out the window, he would take in as much air as possible. Except that, in the end, it was self-defeating. Before long, all the patients in the ward emulated Dawson's antic and this did not sit well with the chief medical officer who issued a memo prohibiting the patients from opening the windows on the pretext that it was dangerous to their health. Even here the rules of the Corps reigned, especially for a wounded jailbird who was not allowed to leave his ward without the escort of a stone-faced MP. This grated on Dawson. At least the other guys could saunter about the hospital premises.

Ward 6A, Ward 7A, 10A. He counted them as he went past. He had been thirty-five days in this hospital and he knew it like the palm—his good palm, the one that wasn't shot. Ward 11A, just a few more doors and he would be at the doctor's office.

Up and down the hall, patients were sauntering idly, almost all of them wounded Marines, and each in the standard uniform: light blue pajamas topped by navy blue robe with a cord around the middle. Some patients carried urine samples in their hands, others toted the large manila folders with their X-rays. A few of the men used crutches and others were pushed in wheelchairs. Some of the more daring walked about without robes, flaunting their defiance of the rules by showing off their pajamas while the doctors and nurses tried not to notice. Every place had its ten percenters.

A goodly portion of the patients were black. Even here, their pound of flesh. C'mon, Dawson, he chastised, stow it. This place is getting you paranoid—whatever the fuck that means.

He passed a group of brothers coming out of the hospital mess hall and they gave him the usual blank stares.

He continued walking up the hallway.

Everywhere he looked the brothers were showing their newest "Nam fist-shake." When they didn't know each other personally they gave the celebrated salute, and when they did know each other they stopped in the middle of the hallway and went through a new variation of the old fist-shake. They tapped each other on top of the fist, then the bottom, and then they followed it up by tapping the sides of the fist, and lastly, hitting the front knuckle portion twice. It was a far more complicated procedure than the old salutation back at Quang Tri. Dawson looked at his hand. Had he been black it would have been difficult trying to do it with a half open fist. Shoot, no fist at all, he thought. The black handshake *had* spread. Wonder what kind of salute the brothers are using back home. Interesting thought. It can't be the old slap five shake. That was outta style even before I got to the Nam. He grinned to himself. Symbols. All of it symbols. Symbols that don't mean shit.

One black patient with a large yellow cone sticking out of his wooly hair nodded to another brother as they passed. Both men gave the salute. Dawson watched the Negroes walk on. They all had that peculiar bee-bop gait that no matter how hard a white man tried to copy he could never get pat.

Dawson touched his lame leg. There was some feeling in it. He had a peculiar gait too, just like the brothers, but all his own. Everytime he tried to walk right the leg hurt like the dickens. So he limped like a goddamn frog. I must look ridiculous, he told himself.

He looked over his shoulder. His shadow was still there. The MP never said anything, he just followed along, like a dog. Dawson frowned.

The door to the doctor's office was open. Lieutenant Commander Winslow, USN, was sitting behind his cluttered desk, spouting some medical gibberish into the dictaphone. Dawson couldn't understand a word of it. He knocked on the open doorway and stuck his head inside the office. "Sir, you wanted to see me?"

The doctor put down the microphone. "Corporal Dawson. Yes, I do want to see you. Please come in."

Doctor Winslow was a heavy bespectacled man with very bushy eyebrows. Whenever he saw him, Dawson felt ill at ease.

He entered the sanctuary and stood about uncomfortably, waiting to be asked to sit down. All was very formal with Navy doctors.

Conveniently, the MP did not follow Dawson into the doctor's office but stayed outside in the hall. There was no worry here. Where could Dawson go? There were no windows in the office and only one door. The MP leaned against the wall, and lit a cigarette.

While he rummaged through his desk file, the doctor asked Dawson to sit down. He took out the correct patient card, looked at it and mumbled something about "Partial reflex on left index digit."

Dawson gathered the doctor was talking to himself at the moment.

Lieutenant Commander Winslow put down the index card. "Well, Dawson, how does your knee feel?"

"It's getting better, sir. I can move my leg some and the knee doesn't hurt as much."

The doctor approved. "Good. I can safely say that progress on your knee is coming along just as we predicted. In about another month or so your leg should be in perfect condition."

"That mean I'll be completely alright, sir?"

The doctor arched his bushy eyebrows. "Yes, I've just said it, perfect condition. You should walk, run, do anything you like."

Dawson leaned back in his chair, played with the head of the cane in his hand. "That's the best news I've had in a long time. For a while there I was scared. When I first came here they told me that a fractured kneecap was a serious condition."

Winslow leaned his elbows on the table. "In your case it wasn't that serious. When the bullet hit your knee it didn't shatter it, it just split the kneecap cover in two, the part we call the patella. See, all we did was take out the shell fragment in the wound and fuse the two broken parts together. That's why you wore the cast for three weeks, remember?" Winslow rubbed his eyebrows. "In a short while the bones should be set enough so that you can move about naturally. Of course, in the meantime we'll keep you on a lot of PT so your leg muscles won't go to pot."

The doctor pushed his glasses back up his nose with a forefinger. Did all medical personnel have that irritating quirk? Dawson fidgeted in his chair.

"Actually, Dawson, what I wanted to talk to you about was not your bad knee so much as your hand." Winslow joined his fingertips, chose his words carefully. "There hasn't been much improvement in it, has there?"

"No," Dawson murmured. "I still can't feel a thing. Fuckin' hand—sorry, sir—the hand is numb most of the time, y'know, like when they give you a shot of that sleeping stuff and the muscle feels heavy. That's how it is."

The Doctor fingered his eyebrow again. "I know. I've checked your PT progress report and it seems they can't do anymore for it." He motioned to Dawson to extend his right hand forward. "Let's see." He inspected the ligature. "When did they put this bandage on?"

"Yesterday," Dawson said.

Doctor Winslow picked up a scissors from his desk and began cutting the tape. "When you go back to the ward you tell the corpsman not to bandage your hand again. The scar is just about healed so there's no need for the covering." He removed the bandage and peered at the wound. An indented cicatrix curved around the fatty portion of the thumb and up to the part of the flesh that separated the thumb and first finger. The wound had healed with the skin curling inward, making the scar appear like a reddish line. The Doctor removed a pin from his coat lapel and pricked gently on each of Dawson's fingers. With the pinky and next to the last finger there was no response at all. When Winslow pinned the middle finger, it flicked up lightly. The same with the first finger except the response was less. With the thumb there was no movement.

Doctor Winslow put down the pin. "Same as before. You get a small measure of reflex action with that middle finger but that's about it."

Dawson had to say it. "I guess that's bad, huh, Doc?"

The Doctor wouldn't commit himself that quickly. "Well, let's just say it's not good." He pointed to the scar tissue. "When you got hit the bullet ripped one of the nerves inside the hand. It's located right here—" he touched the spot on the palm. "We can't tie that nerve back together again so that subsequently you're left without any sense of feeling. This doesn't incapacitate you completely but you'll have to watch where you put your hand. It could be a hot stove, burning, and you wouldn't know it. There's always the possibility that you could harm yourself unintentionally." Winslow looked down at his desk pad. "It's going to be a tricky situation, you'll have to be careful."

Dawson had heard it before, and to an extent he had come to accept this new handicap. Yet, medical science being what it was there had to be something. "Sir, isn't there anything that can be done? I mean, maybe an operation or somethin'."

Doctor Winslow leaned back in his chair. "We can't operate on the nerve. The only thing we can do is try to revive the motor function in your hand, allowing you to close it." He leaned forward, folded his arms on the desk. "Right now you can't make a fist but perhaps in the future we might be able to get you to close your hand enough to hold a ball or a pencil. It'll just take time and effort."

Dawson stared at the scar on his palm. "In other words, Doc, I got a crippled hand." There was a certain distaste, and even more, disgust in the way he said it. The self-pity was barely noticeable.

"No, I wouldn't say you have a crippled hand. It's just injured, that's all. The hand can still function to a certain extent like any other limb. Basically you've lost a tactile nerve sense but you can still use that hand in any other way. You can lift weights if you want. You won't be able to slug somebody with it but that in itself doesn't make you a cripple. You'll just have to be more aware of what you do. It doesn't make you any less of a man."

"I didn't mean it that way, Doctor . . ."

"I know, but that's what you're thinking," Winslow said. "Forget it. You're just afflicted with an ailment like any other, and it can be overcome."

Dawson kept staring at his palm. He was wondering if he would ever hold a pool cue again. Some of the thoughts burned. He wasn't a lefty but now he would have to master the technique of writing with his left hand; trying to shave would be a pisser; there would be no more games of softball or handball. But then in H&S Casual when would he ever get a chance to do such things?

He sensed a severe loss.

The doctor knew it also. "You're right handed, aren't you?"

"Yes," Dawson mumbled.

"Before your time is up we'll make sure you're proficient enough with your left hand so that you can do everything with it—write a letter, handle a weapon, paint a house if you want."

Sure, Doc, Dawson thought. Anything you say. Now the self-pity was alive. *Write a letter, paint a house if you want.* A cripple—in the Brig. I'll never come out alive, he decided. He could not think of anything that did not involve the use of his right hand, but he could not define any of these things. He only knew it would be very difficult trying to adjust to a left-handed existence. How could he indulge in any love play with a useless right hand? For some reason the thought seemed humorous and he almost laughed out loud. My goddamn hand is like a piece of ice. I can't feel a thing.

"There isn't much more we can do for you, Corporal, so we've decided to send you out of country. You'll spend the rest of your sick time at Yokosuka Naval Hospital in Japan."

"And what happens after that?" Dawson asked.

"What do you mean?"

"I'm from the Brig, remember?"

Doctor Winslow scrubbed his chin with the back of his hand. He had tried to avoid the subject. "What can I say," he answered. "You'll probably go back to the Brig, that's all. Finish out your time." He paused for a second or two, and then added, "There's nothing we can do about that."

Dawson smirked. "Yeah." He continued staring at his hand. "A cripple, in the Brig."

"You're not a cripple, Dawson," Winslow said sternly. "And as far as the Brig is concerned . . . well, that's your own affair. You're in it and there's nothing you can do about it."

"When will I'll be going stateside?" Dawson asked.

"I really don't know, that's up to Administration to decide. I don't think they'll keep you forever in Japan. You'll be there for postoperative treatment only. Shouldn't be too long."

"And then to a stateside pen," Dawson added bitterly.

"Look, if it makes you feel any better, I'm recommending you for a medical discharge on the basis of your hand. It's a service induced injury and that may have a bearing on your case. I'm not promising anything but I'll do whatever I can with Administration to have your sentence reduced or at least have you placed in a convalescent hospital instead of a Brig. I don't believe in incarcerating men who have been wounded in any kind of combat—even if it's a jailbreak."

Well, some of them do have a heart, Dawson thought, surprised. "I'd appreciate anything you can do, sir," he said, forcing a smile. "Believe me, nobody wants to go back to the Brig. Not even in the world."

"We'll see, Dawson, okay?" Winslow seemed sincere. But how could Dawson be sure? "We'll see."

Dawson wondered how many Brig inmates had passed through the hospital ward, through Winslow's office, and heard the same story. How many had made it back to a hospital instead of a cell? They ain't gonna cut me no slack. He *knew* it. No slack at all. I'm going back to a cell crippled hand or not. The crotch never forgot nor forgave. To be back in the world, but in a cell, not even on the fuckin' street. I'd be better off staying in the bush. At least there I'd be my own man. And how could he face his family? A fuckin' jailbird. He had accepted that, too. Will the folks visit me? A fuckin' jailbird.

"I'm going to have your travel orders made up right away," Winslow promised. "You should leave in about a day or so, maybe tomorrow if we can get those goldbricks at Admin to hurry up on it."

"Yes, sir," Dawson muttered.

"Don't worry about your hand too much. You'll see as you go along that you'll transfer all your motor ability to your left. It really isn't that difficult."

Really, Doc. How would *you* know?

The Doctor grinned slightly, affectatiously. "You're going to become a southpaw, Dawson." He looked at his own hand. "I'm a lefty myself."

"Yes, sir." Dawson stood up. "Thank you for your time, Doctor." He limped out of the office, and went down the hall, ignoring the MP, who ground his cigarette under his boot and dutifully tailed the prisoner.

When he passed a few doors, Dawson decided he did not want to go back to his own ward. He looked again at the scar on his hand. Going back to his sickbed would be intolerable. He turned, limped to the main stairway, then a hand grasped his elbow. He turned to face the MP.

"We suppose to go back to the ward," the MP said.

Dawson jerked his elbow from the MP's grip. "Look, can't I get some air? I ain't gonna escape. I just wanna be alone for a few minutes. Okay?"

The MP glanced at his watch. Chow wouldn't be for another hour or so. He shrugged. "If you go topside I gotta stay with you all the time."

"I wouldn't think of going without you," Dawson gibed sarcastically. "Every boy should have his own shadow." He turned and hobbled up the stairway one step at a time, using the power of his right leg to drag his other leg supported by the walking stick. When he reached the top of the stairs he was very tired and sweat furrowed his forehead. He glanced sideways at the MP still standing a foot or two behind him, and showing no sign of exertion whatsoever. Don't these mothers ever get tired? He wiped off the sweat with the back of his injured hand, and walked ahead to the terrace at the rear of the building.

The terrace was a large open balcony shaded by a huge striped awning and enclosed by a metal balustrade. The place was accommodated with game tables, camp chairs and lounge seats, but at the moment there was nobody on the terrace except for two patients having a card game on a table in the left corner of the balcony. They gave Dawson and his escort a casual glance and then went back to their game.

Dawson walked up to the balustrade and gazed down on the concrete yard of the hospital. From the second story he could see as far as the hospital gate and beyond the base road to a small brownish hill that obscured Da Nang City from his vision. He had never gone beyond the base compound and he really wasn't interested in exploring the famed Alley outside the gate where all the soldiers and marines were fleeced out of their money. He just wanted to go home.

Yeah. Home. And then . . . a disabled veteran. A disabled veteran dishonorably discharged. He couldn't go back to school. The GI Bill was closed to him and with it the possibility of finishing college. It would have been nice going back to State U, or any other college for that matter, just so long as it got him away from what he knew. What was it the shrink told him when he first got to the hospital? To forget all that had happened? Easier said than done. Especially now. The struggle was just beginning. Back home, that's where it was. How many men thought of it that way? How many men *white or black* thought of it that way? A dress rehearsal for what was to come. Perhaps. He did know something: he had learned how to kill; the breaking down of a weapon, the setting up of a booby trap. It could count for something someday. One box mine can disable an entire police station. Somebody would have to pay some dues. So many men destroyed for nothing. Somebody would have to pay some dues. Their faces swirled before him and he could barely recall them—the grunts, the prisoners, the guards, the squads.

Somebody would have to pay some dues. In a month's time perhaps he would be back in America. Serving time. And after—who knows? But it couldn't end like this. He wouldn't let it end like this. Somebody would have to pay.

"Hey, mac, we can't stay here all day." The voice came from behind.

He turned to face his shadow. It always struck him how in the hospital area even the MPs wore pressed and starched fatigues, every crease in place. Just like garrison duty back in the States. The MP even had a name tag above the right breast pocket, Dawson noticed. The name plate had "Suggs" written on it. Dawson frowned. *Suggs.* It figures.

"C'mon, leave me alone," he said. "I just wanna be by myself for a few minutes. Do you mind?"

"You're suppose t' be back in the ward," the MP reminded him. "We're breaking the rules being up here as it is."

Dawson stared deliberately at the name tag. "We ain't breaking no rules, *Suggs*." He spat out the name contemptuously.

The MP recognized his animosity. "Look, buddy, I don't like this any more than you do. If I had my way I'd be in the chow hall right now. But I'm not, I'm here, so don't give me no trouble and let's make the most of it."

"I don't want no trouble," Dawson maintained. "I just wanna be left alone, by myself. For a few minutes. Even a shadow like you realizes a man sometimes wants to be alone."

The MP looked at Dawson warily.

Dawson took in the whole terrace with a wave of the hand. "Where the fuck am I gonna go?"

The MP folded his arms over his chest and deliberated a few moments. Why were these wounded prisoners so difficult? They were worse than the regular jailbirds. The fuckers got an idea into their heads and that was it. He grimaced. Dopes. All of 'em, dopes. He looked at his watch again. Maybe if I give this dope a coupla minutes to himself we might get back by chowtime.

The MP walked over to one of the recreation tables, sat down on a folding chair, leaned back, placed his boots atop the table, and pulled the brim of his cap down over his eyes.

Dawson leaned on the balustrade. Behind him, in the hospital yard, a large van had just come to a stop before the rear entrance. Dawson turned and looked down. New customers, he told himself. That ice box must be full. An attendant dressed in white jumped out of the driver's compartment and walked to the back of the van. Presently, he was joined by two corpsmen. They opened the rear of the van and began to take out the bodies, or remains of the bodies closed in green plastic bags. The men went about their work with a monotonous formality, lugging the bags to the hospital ramp where three other men placed the wrapped cadavers on a wheeled dolly and pushed them inside to the hospital morgue.

Somebody musta hit the shit real bad, Dawson figured. He counted over twenty bags before he became bored. Out of habit he reached with his left hand inside his front robe pocket to extract a pack of cigarettes. The pack was empty. He frowned, and was about to throw it away when he had a sudden impulse. He raised his right hand and stared at the wound. The sun warmed the scar tissue, made the curved line in the palm seem deeper and redder than it was. With his left hand he pressed the cigarette pack into his right palm. He sought to close the fingers around the pack. His index finger flinched and that was it. Motherfucker! He grasped his hand and tightened the inert fingers around the paper, trying to crumple the pack in a useless fist. He grasped harder and his hand began to tremble. There was no pain, but the fingers refused to close. The hand was like a fixed object.

He gave up on it. Nothing more could be done, and he accepted the truth almost with pleasure. The cards had been cut against him. A bum deal for a bum hand. A lefty. Lefty Hernandez, Lefty Gomez. Lefty Dawson. He could make it up with his other hand, and his leg would get better. Only . . . Only there was something humiliating in it. He felt he had lost something and not only in terms of his wound or the Brig. There was much more, and he could not explain, even to himself. In the bush and the Brig it had been fire and rain. And what had he gained? He was left with defiance. That sense of absolute failure had to be rejected if he was to survive. He would never again accept such a defeat. There was a score to be paid back in the world. He had some dues coming.

Dawson raised his injured hand with the cigarette pack in it, turned his hand palm down, letting the pack fall into the yard below.

One of the attendants kicked the empty pack aside, and lifted another body bag onto the hospital ramp.

GLOSSARY OF TERMS

ADMIN SEC: Administrative Section

AIR WINGER: a Marine assigned to the air support wing of the Corps.

AK47: standard assault rifle utilized by NVA and Viet Cong forces.

ARTY: artillery

ARVN: (or "ARVIN") Army of the Republic of Vietnam. A Vietnamese soldier; allies of the American forces in Vietnam.

A6: Navy and Marine attack jet, military designation: Skyhawk. Used for ground support missions.

BLOOPER: grunt slang for a single-shot, 40mm breech-loaded grenade launcher; it also fired buckshot as well as grenade cartridges.

BOX MINE: heavy cased land mine, either circular or square shaped, and concealed just above the ground, containing a high explosive (usually TNT). This mine was mainly intended for use against heavy tanks and vehicles.

THE BUSH: the jungle; a combat area.

BUTTERFLY MINE: antipersonnel mine, usually dropped via aircraft. Its configuration was similar to that of a butterfly with two wing-like appendages filled with shrapnel and blasting powder.

CELL BLOCK: Maximum Detention area in the Da Nang Brig.

181

C4: white, putty-like odorless plastic explosive; during the Vietnam conflict, it came packed in 2½-pound blocks.

CHARLIE MED: a field medical hospital

CHARLIE RIDGE: a furrowed ridgeline in a mountain chain in the northern sector of South Vietnam that came under constant enemy attack.

CHICOM: Chinese-made hand grenade (manufactured in the People's Republic of China).

CHOPPER: helicopter

CID: Criminal Investigations Division; investigative arm of the military police.

CLAYMORE MINE: portable, antipersonnel fragmentation mine carried by troops in the field. It could be used as a controlled weapon as well as a booby trap, and contained 1½ pounds of plastic explosive (C4).

COIC: commanding officer-in-charge

CORPSMAN: naval personnel assigned as medical orderlies to Marine units.

CP: command post

C-RATS: military issued food rations

THE CROTCH: the Marine Corps; derogatory in-country slang.

DEE-DEE: from DIDI MAU; to run or move fast.

DI: drill instructor

DODGE CITY: area in the central highlands, so named due to its constant combat activity.

E-TOOL: portable, folding entrenching tool that resembles a small shovel.

81 MORTAR: heavy mortar firing 81mm shells.

FIREBASE: artillery outpost in an outlying area.

FIRETEAM: basic fighting unit of the Marine Corps. During the Vietnam War, this consisted of a fireteam leader (corporal), an automatic rifleman, an assistant automatic rifleman, and a rifleman.

FLAK VEST: body armor in form of a vest worn by infantrymen to protect from shrapnel. At the time, it could not protect against a direct bullet hit.

FO: forward observer

45s: seven-shot .45 caliber automatic pistol.

FRAGGING: (or "To Frag") the killing, usually of an officer or higher authority, via the surreptitious use of a fragmentation grenade.

GOOK: synonymous with the enemy. An Oriental person. The word is from the Korean War; some claim that its derivative is "MEE GOOK," or a "foreign person." The phrase was first used by Koreans to describe American troops in Asia. It could be said that the Americans were, in reality, the "Gooks" in Vietnam.

GREASED: to be killed; also, to waste or be wasted.

GRUNT: infantryman

GUNSHIP: Huey helicopter armed with machine guns and rocket pods, and used to provide support for ground troops.

HANOI HANNAH: silken-voiced females (there were more than one) who broadcasted anti-war propaganda to the American troops in-country. In between the proselytizing, their programs were filled with country & western music and rock n' roll.

HALF-TRACK: armored vehicle for transporting troops.

H&E: (or HE) high explosive; usually attributed to mortar and artillery shells.

HEAT TAB: small, flammable tab used for heating canned C-rations.

HELO-PAD: helicopter landing strip or site.

HOOCH: a hut, or tent; also, an enclosure in the field or in a Vietnamese village.

H&S: acronym for headquarters and service division.

INCOMING: enemy attack by artillery, mortar or rocket projectile.

IN-COUNTRY: serving within the combat zone of South Vietnam.

KHE SANH: Marine base in the northernmost part of South Vietnam that withstood a prolonged siege by NVA forces. The base was later abandoned by U.S. troops.

KIA: killed in action

KIT CARSON SCOUT: Vietnamese personnel, mainly VC defectors, used as scouts by American forces.

K-RATS: (or "Long-rats") a modified and, supposedly, more nutritious and tasteful version of C-rats.

LAAW: light assault antitank weapon. A 66mm rocket, packaged, sealed and issued inside its own launcher. Portable and shoulder fired. Because of its light weight (approx. 3 pounds), more than one could be carried by a Marine in battle.

LIFER: a career military man.

LOOEY: short, for lieutenant; used disparagingly to describe a new fresh-faced 2nd lieutenant assigned to a unit.

LZ: helicopter landing zone

MARDIV: Marine division

MEDEVAC: medical rescue helicopter

M14: precursor to the M16 rifle; heavier than the M16, it was issued and equipped to fire semiautomatically only, although it could be converted to fire automatically.

MONTAGNARD: Vietnamese hill people residing in the highland areas of both South and North Vietnam.

MP: military policeman

M16: the standard assault rifle used by American troops in Vietnam.

M60: belt-fed, air-cooled machine gun.

NCO: noncommissioned officer or noncom

NVA: North Vietnamese Army

155s: heavy artillery piece firing 155mm shells.

105s: light artillery howitzer firing 105mm shells.

AN OP: a military operation; not to be confused with OP, or observation post.

PERIMETER: (as in "base perimeter") the protective border or boundary encircling a position such as a base or bivouac area.

PFC: Private first class

POGEY-BAIT: junk food

POGUE: (or Office Pogue) a rear echelon clerical type; the antithesis of a rifleman in the field.

POINT MAN: lead soldier in the lead element of a military sweep or operation.

PURPLE HEART: the first medal awarded by the American Republic; it is bestowed on military personnel wounded in action.

RECON UNIT: reconnaissance team usually deployed to scout an area before a military operation.

RED LINED BRIG: a detention area for Marine and naval personnel known for its painted red lines on various areas inside. Supposedly, if an inmate crossed or walked over any of these red zones, he was beaten or otherwise punished.

THE ROCKPILE: a firebase and LZ in Quang Tri Province, in the nothern part of South Vietnam.

RPG: rocket propelled grenade, fired from a shoulder held launcher.

R&R: rest and recreation, or rest and recuperation; given usually at mid-tour to all American military personnel in Vietnam.

RUBBER BITCH: inflatable, rubber air bag used for sleeping in the bush.

SALLYPORT: Medium security detention area in the Da Nang Brig.

782 GEAR: the full complement of combat equipment that a rifleman carries

during a military operation (includes ammunition, backpack, canteens, rations, etc.).

SHORT ROUND: artillery shell or mortar round that, through a misfire or other error, falls short of its target, frequently landing on friendly troops.

SHORT-TIMER: military person in-country whose tour of duty (365 days) was about to end before transfer back to the States.

SILVER STAR: medal awarded for acts of bravery in combat.

SIX-BY: 2½-ton medium truck used for transporting troops and supplies.

SKATE: (skatin' duty) to be assigned an easy duty or light work detail. During the Second World War this was known as "goldbricking."

SKY UP: to leave the Vietnam combat zone, alive, via airplane transport; also, SKY OUT.

SKS: semiautomatic rifle of Russian design utilized by enemy forces; eventually it was replaced by the far more effective AK47.

SQUAD LEADER: sergeant who leads a squad, which is made up of three fireteams.

S2: battalion intelligence unit

STARLIGHT SCOPE: infrared field scope, used at night.

38s: six-shot .38 caliber revolver. Commonly known in the U.S. as a policeman's special.

TIGER PISS BEER: South Vietnamese brew; so called, since to most American servicemen, it was akin to drinking urine.

TWIN 40s: light armored vehicle mounted with to 40mm cannons.

UA: unauthorized absence; replaced the World War II AWOL (Away Without Leave).

UD: undesirable discharge from military service.

VC: (Victor Charlie) military arm of the National Liberation Front. Commonly known as the Viet Cong.

WATER BO: (water buffalo) a water trough, mainly in rear areas, used by infantrymen for washing and shaving.

WIA: wounded in action

WILLY PETER: (white phosporous) poisonous, flammable chemical carried in a hand grenade version, and also delivered to its target via artillery shells.

THE WORLD: civilization; the United States of America.

XO: executive officer

THE Z: the DMZ, or demilitarized zone separating South from North Vietnam.